The Engineer

RICHARD C P SCOTT

Book Cover by Solway Print Ltd

Edition 1 2023

Prologue

I woke in a hospital bed. Images flashed through my mind like a movie trailer.

A beach, a sinking boat, men in the dark with knives.

And James.

What about James?

I tried to sit up as if that would help me think but it brought stabbing pains to my head, shoulder and ribs. Through the pain came the vision of a funeral in the rain.

James's funeral.

I lay back with a groan as I heard a door open.

A pretty young nurse came in and asked in an adorable French accent, "Can you tell me your name and where you are?"

I knew my name and I knew I was still in Morocco, but I didn't answer as the memories were flooding back now and with them came a deepening sense of dread.

Was another woman dead because of me? I couldn't bear to ask as I knew I couldn't live with any more guilt.

But I had to know. "Jessica? Is she…"

Chapter 1

The coming gale was the reason we'd cut the dive trip short, the ever increasing wind was rocking my old Land Rover as it rattled along, dragging the orange RIB on its trailer through the rugged landscape of Sutherland in the northwest Highlands of Scotland.

Usually, I linked my phone to the stereo for music to drown out the noise of the old 4x4. But after my last call to James, I'd laid it down and another diver promptly dropped his weight belt on it. I foresaw an expensive purchase in my future.

The SIM card now sat in my wallet. Mainly because the phone kept beeping with incoming messages, mostly from James, I could tell by the ringtone I'd assigned him, but I couldn't read them.

The dog was curled up nose to tail on the passenger seat, snoring quietly. The bright red collar given to him by my goddaughters, James's daughters, standing out against his black fur.

Every hour or so the news came on the radio. War, inflation, global shortages of this and that. Everyone unsure and therefore scared. I recalled my recent conversation with James, my oldest friend, a solicitor in London specialising in property law. He always lectured me on my lack of interest in current affairs. And I'd point out that the island we live on had survived ice ages, volcanoes and collisions with other continents, so it'd probably survive the current events. Besides, humans are just a fleeting presence on this planet, in the grand scheme of things we won't be here much longer anyway. But he didn't share my long-term view.

"You live in a different world to the rest of us," he'd told me.

"I try," I replied flippantly.

"You still stopping in next week?"

"Of course, will you be working?"

"Of course. I have a proper job. But I'll be there in the evenings."

"Sucks to have a proper job." I'd be driving from Scotland to Morocco soon and would stop off and see him, his wife Claire and my goddaughters near Cambridge.

"You've no idea," he said with deep meaning.

"Lacking job satisfaction?"

No reply.

"James?"

A pause. "I'm glad you're back to your old self," he said. "I'll send you some information."

I was about to say 'please don't' as he had a habit of sending me emails, links and documents about things I didn't care about like politics, property, finance. But he was gone. Unlike the polite, happy man I'd known all these years, but we all had bad days, so I didn't think anything of it.

Entering Ullapool, I parked at the side of the road a little way down from the pier and unfolded myself from the seat, donned a waterproof jacket and took the dog for a walk on the beach to do his thing before the next leg of the drive.

Loch Broom is a large sea loch running north-west to south-east and a mile wide at most. Ullapool is nestled in a shallow natural harbour just inside and to the north of the seaward end, protected from the Atlantic swells and westerly winds.

The area relied more on tourism than fishing now so there were only two full-size trawlers tied up to the pier. The remainder were a mix of small pleasure craft and hobby boats for lobster or crabs.

As we walked the stoney beach in the darkening afternoon a lovely old ship of a design not built for at least fifty years swooped majestically into the brooding loch. Sixty metres long with a rich blue hull and teak decks shining with varnish even in the gathering gloom. A final shard of sunlight before the arrival of the incoming gale glinted off highly polished brass work. The brilliant white superstructure practically luminescent in the late afternoon.

She was probably one of the small luxury cruise ships that plied the west coast of Scotland and the Hebrides. Carrying ten or fifteen passengers in great, if compact, comfort. Her relatively small size meant she could thoroughly explore the craggy West Highland coast.

She was a beautiful sight. But she was going fast. No doubt seeking a sheltered harbour to sit out the imminent gale. But the speed she was doing would make the sweeping one hundred and eighty degree turn in to the pier uncomfortable, to say the least.

Even at this distance I could see several figures on deck, but they weren't leaning casually against the gleaming brass railings as passengers on a cruise often do when coming into port. They were dressed in white from head to foot, which suggested they were crew, and they were running.

Maybe they were just late for whatever duty they had to perform when coming alongside.

More people appeared on deck, definitely not sailors. I could see they were smartly dressed. Lots of deep black, crisp white and stockinged legs.

Only then did I faintly hear the klaxon. The strong wind carrying it away from me down the loch, I just caught faint wisps of it in the lulls.

She started her turn to port at speed and keeled over sharply, too sharply. She went too far over, wobbled unnaturally, came upright, then keeled far over to her starboard again and stayed there. Then she went dark, every light blinking out. The black smoke from the funnels ceasing. The bow wave dropped away, and she lay on her side, slowing to a stop as she shed her momentum, maybe half a mile from shore.

Silent and dark, listing away from me with her deep blue hull I wouldn't even see her in the darkness out on the loch if I didn't know she was there.

After a few seconds a dim yellow glow emanated around the vessel. The battery-powered emergency lights coming on.

I closed my eyes and shook my head in case I was seeing things. Opening an eye slightly I squinted down the loch.

No, it was definitely there.

And then, being Scotland, it started raining. Proper ice-cold drops of rain the size of golf balls. "Bloody typical." I grumbled.

I instinctively went for my phone forgetting it was broken.

Hard to believe that I was the only one seeing this, but there were no alarmed shouts, no sudden activity, and not a soul in sight.

The stricken vessel was too small to carry lifeboats, but she must by law have at least life-rafts which they should be launching now. This would all be taking place out of my sight on the far side of the vessel. They'd still need a boat to drag the rafts in to the pier otherwise they'd just be blown down the loch, so I had to raise the alarm.

I ran along the waterfront and didn't see a single person to borrow a mobile phone from, nor a phone box. A nearby bar attached to a hotel looked like the best bet.

I crashed in the door.

"Call the police. There's a boat sinking."

A busty landlady with bottle blonde hair stared at me from behind the bar.

"Call the police."

Still no movement.

"OK, I'll do it," I mumbled, striding over to the bar, vaulting it and dialling the number everyone knows on the phone beside the till.

A polite female voice answered, I explained the situation.

"Your full name, please." The voice asked.

One of the locals shuffled to the door and looked out. "Aye, he's right enough."

The voice on the phone asked for my name again, so I passed the phone over to the landlady. "Here, give her a name, please."

"Do you know the local lifeboat crew?" I asked the room in general and got a few nods. "Call them."

"No point," an old boy said. "Lifeboat's away for repairs."

I realised I hadn't seen a bright orange lifeboat in the harbour.

"No, it's not a hoax," the landlady was saying into the phone. "No, I don't think he's drunk."

I went back to the door. No sign of life-rafts in the water.

"Any of you have a boat out there?" I asked. No nods.

"Know anyone that does?" Several nods.

"Call them. We need to get boats out there."

The landlady was still on the phone as I left.

I ran to the end of the pier and stared into the gloom. The emergency lights were still on, she still floated in the same position, but no life-rafts were in the water. They'd had enough time to launch one by now, which probably meant they couldn't. With no way of knowing what caused her to roll, there was no way of knowing if she would roll over completely, sink like a stone, or just float like that indefinitely. Someone had to get out there, and at the moment it looked, sadly, like it would have to be me.

I glanced at the vessels tied up to the pier, but the two large trawlers were entirely too much boat for me to mess around with, and they wouldn't start with just the turn of a key.

The small boats out on the swinging moorings would probably be simple enough to hot-wire, but I couldn't guarantee it. I figured the fastest way to get a boat out to them would be to launch mine. I started running.

Chapter 2

I reversed my Land Rover and trailer back along the waterfront, then down the slipway. Pausing only to release the cargo straps holding the boat to the trailer I backed it ungracefully into the water until the RIB was floating.

I jumped out of the 4x4 and into the boat completely ignoring the first rule of powerboating - never cast off before starting your engines. I gave a small prayer as I pressed the starter buttons. One of the two outboards grumbled into life, good enough.

I came wide around the listing vessel from the north, off her bow.

There were maybe thirty people clinging to the steeply slanting decks. The reason for the lack of life-rafts in the water became apparent. One had been mounted in a cradle on either side of the bridge. The starboard canister, which was on the low side of the ship as she listed over, was floating in the water but had failed to inflate, a crewman was still tugging furiously on the inflation line.

The port life raft on the high side had come out of its cradle and smashed through a bridge window, inflating inside the bridge itself.

I nosed the RIB in under the starboard rail level with the bridge, very conscious that if she rolled further she could take my little boat under very easily.

I glanced around the crowd on the deck. Maybe half were crew judging by the uniforms. The remaining fifteen or so were passengers, older, smartly dressed. Men in black tie or kilts and the ladies in cocktail dresses. I reckoned the amassed jewellery on display would buy my humble cottage many times over and still leave enough for a new Land Rover.

Luckily the vessel was listed away from the wind and horizontal rain, sheltering them somewhat, but I realised the wind would be having other effects. I was directly downwind of her so turned one hundred and eighty degrees and saw a rocky, jagged section of shore behind us. It was a fair distance away, time enough to ferry everyone to shore, even with having to do several runs, before she was blown on to it.

I had a GPS unit bolted to the console of the RIB. I pressed a couple of buttons to record our position as a waypoint as I called up to the people gathered at the rail.

"Over you come. One at a time." The crew lowered the first lady over the rails, I grabbed her and seated her on the tubes.

"Are you all there is?" the captain called down.

"Yup," I huffed, as the next lady landed none to gracefully in my arms. The thigh-high split in her skirt showing remarkably good legs for a woman of her age.

"Heels off, ladies!" I called out after realising most of them were wearing fearsome-looking spikes.

"Where's the lifeboat?" said the captain.

"Being repaired. Is everyone accounted for?"

He took a quick head count. A little belatedly.

"Two missing, I think."

"You think!"

He bridled as one of the lesser officers, young and sharp looking, spoke up. "The Mackays aren't here."

"Find them," he barked; the young officer disappeared from view.

"What happened?" He looked at me as if I wasn't worthy of his explanation.

"Bilge alarms went off, then the engine room flood alarms, we lost power on the turn," he said begrudgingly.

"What caused the flooding? You hit something?"

"Don't know."

"You came in fast."

He just glared.

He'd buggered up.

It's called 'free surface effect', defined as the change in stability of a vessel caused by liquids moving about freely, an important thing for operators of large vessels to know about. It means his boat had been filling up with water which was free to slosh around as water does. When he turned at speed all the water moved to the outside of the turn, obeying the laws of physics, then back to the inside, back to the outside, and so on. If he'd reduced speed he'd have probably made it OK.

She was an old boat, unlike the commercial vessels I had some experience with. I asked the crew if and how she was compartmentalised but didn't receive a definitive answer.

With eight women in my RIB, its limit in these conditions, we headed for shore to offload.

Coming out from the lee of the vessel the wind hit us full force, my cargo shivered as we pitched in the short, steep waves. The storm was picking up as forecast.

The water calmed to nearly flat as I ran the boat gently up the concrete ramp beside the pier and started unloading the cold, wet, women.

A small crowd had gathered. "A little help."

Some youngsters broke into a trot down the slipway and helped my damp cargo out of the RIB.

"Take them to the pub. Dry clothes. Hot drinks."

I tipped the last lady, a large one, into the arms of a small blonde girl who gamely staggered up the slipway under the weight.

Back at the listing boats railing I checked the GPS, she'd drifted appreciably since I first checked. Glancing behind at the jagged shore there was still enough time to get the remaining passengers off with maybe three more trips.

"Have you got the last two passengers?" I called up to the captain.

"The companion way is flooded, there's no way to get to them," he said gravely.

I don't know why I assumed I could do something when they couldn't, but I did, and hauled myself up on to the slanting deck to look for myself.

"Eight people, no more," I said to the crewmen.

"Where are they?" I asked the captain.

"I told you, it's flooded..." he said haughtily.

"I heard you. Where are they?"

"Sir," the young officer said.

"Sir," he said again. I didn't realise he was talking to me.

"I'll show you," he said and disappeared inside the bridge.

I followed, to be faced with a wall of white PVC material - the life raft that had smashed through the bridge window and inflated. The young officer shimmied past it and disappeared down a narrow set of stairs. The emergency lighting cast a dim, orange glow. Getting around was awkward with everything canted over at forty-five degrees and rocking. Two decks down from the bridge we stopped at the flooded companion way.

"What's the layout?" I asked.

"That companion way is the main guest accommodation. Five staterooms along each side. The MacKays are third along, starboard side. Deck below is staff accommodation and utilities, eight cabins along each side, the hatch at the far end leads into the engine room," he said concisely.

"Can you swim?" I asked inclining my head towards the water, it looked cold and black. He looked a little horrified at the idea of taking a swim in a sinking ship. I couldn't blame him and let him off the hook.

"If I'm not back in two minutes, come and rescue me," I told him. The poor lad's eyes were the size of saucers.

Stripping off I plunged in, taking a second to recover from that momentary paralysis you get when hitting cold water.

She must be down at the stern as the forward end of the companionway was almost flooded to the roof, but the water level dropped as I went aft. I half swam, half pushed myself along.

The stateroom doors were actually old-fashioned watertight hatches. Four feet tall by two wide with a brass wheel in the centre. I turned the wheel. Stuck fast. I heaved with all I had but it didn't move a millimetre. I assumed the corresponding wheel on the inside of the door was also jammed otherwise they'd just let themselves out.

I knocked on the door, but my knuckles made practically no noise on the steel plate. Grabbing a nearby fire extinguisher I banged on the hatch and received a tapping in reply.

They were alive, or at least one of them was.

I tried to knock the polished brass wheel around with the extinguisher but got nowhere as there were no edges to get a purchase on.

Already shivering uncontrollably, I could do nothing to help them without some equipment, which was in my Land Rover. I hated to leave, but there was nothing I could do if I didn't, and it would be time to take the next load of passengers to shore anyway.

I gave a chirpy tap on the door and swam back to a relieved-looking young officer, who, although I'd been away more than two minutes, didn't look like he was on the verge of diving in to save me.

I didn't waste time explaining and indicated up, he needed no encouragement to get out of the bowels of a sinking ship. The RIB was full, I noted our drift on the GPS, and took us back to the slipway.

I poked the button for my second outboard motor, nothing. All I needed now was for my lone working outboard to die on me.

Sixteen down, two more trips for the rest.

"Any of you driven one of these before?" I asked the group of youngsters that came down the slipway to help again as we nudged up to the concrete.

Lots of headshakes and 'noes' but the small blonde girl raised her hand.

"You're hired."

The crowd started helping passengers up the slipway as I put out a hand to help the young girl which she ignored and jumped nimbly into the boat.

"Make yourself at home, don't leave without me."

My Land Rover was rocking on its springs with the dog jumping around inside, desperate to be let out as things were happening and he was cooped up.

The empty boat trailer was in the way, I unhooked it and shoved it to the side. Swinging open the rear door the dog shot past me, darting this way and that.

I hauled my diving gear, cylinder, BCD or Buoyancy Compensation Device, which is basically a chunky vest that the cylinder is strapped too which you can inflate and deflate to float up or down, regulators, fins and mask into the RIB.

The dog streaked past me, leaping into the RIB towards the girl, determined not to be left behind again. The muscular black dog flying towards you would look fearsome if you didn't know him.

"It's alright, he's..." I was going to say harmless. But she'd worked that out for herself.

My fearsome hound was licking the poor girl to death as she vigorously rubbed his flanks.

I shrugged and left them to it, stripping off my wet clothes and pulling on a thermal under suit then a neoprene drysuit as a vaguely official looking man turned up with a patch saying 'Harbour Master' on his oilskin jacket.

"Do you know what you are doing?" he asked.

"Depends. There's two people stuck behind a jammed hatch in a flooded companion way," I said, pointing at the half-sunk boat.

"Is there anyone here who can do anything?"

"The emergency services are on their way."

"How long?" I asked.

"At least an hour."

"Then I know what I'm doing," I said, and hoped I was right.

Rummaging around in the back of my Land Rover I tossed a crowbar, hammer and duct tape in the RIB - just some of the tools I carry in the back of my old vehicle just to keep it running. The crow bar and hammer were to open the MacKays' jammed door. The drysuit was to keep me warm and functioning whilst doing so. The duct tape was just habit, you can fix anything with duct tape, and the diving kit was in case the boat actually sank.

I cast a glance at the girl and grabbed spare jackets for her and jumped back in the RIB.

She backed away from the pier and span my boat with confidence.

"Why are you running on one motor?" she asked.

She had a nice voice, but wasn't as young as I first thought, late twenties, maybe thirty? I took a closer look.

"Your engine," she prompted.

"Oh, yeah, sorry, the left-hand red button would normally start it."

She glanced down, poked it, and the second outboard coughed instantly to life.

Bloody typical, I thought as she grinned and pushed the throttles forward with enthusiasm.

I handed her the spare jackets and held the wheel as she slipped them on, they dwarfed her, but they'd keep her warm and people functioned better that way. I dumped a woolly hat on top of her mane of blonde hair.

She smiled broadly in thanks, the corners of her eyes crinkling, early thirties I decided.

The rain was horizontal now, stinging exposed skin. My little RIB pitched violently, and we were in sheltered waters, the stricken vessel was lucky she made it into the loch, she wouldn't have had a chance on the open sea.

"Take eight at a time and keep going," I said. "But don't forget me."

"What's his name?" She indicated the dog.

"Beetle. Take us in level with the bridge."

Back at the MacKays' cabin door I jammed the crowbar through the spokes of the wheel and heaved. Nothing. I added the hammer to the equation but there was something very wrong with this door. I'm a biggish man and I had a couple of feet of leverage, but it wouldn't budge.

The door was lying at an angle away from me, maybe I wasn't bringing my full weight to bear on it.

I contorted myself until I was standing on the end of the crowbar with my shoulders wedged against the ceiling, bringing my full weight and the force of my legs to bear on the end of the crowbar.

I heaved, heard a metallic snap, and landed in a heap in the water. With a searing pain in my leg I splashed around, gurgling and clutching my thigh before plucking up the courage to look. Standing on my good leg I raised my other clear of the water.

The end of the crowbar was imbedded in my thigh, but the crowbar hadn't snapped.

The wheel had snapped off the door.

I had just condemned the couple inside the cabin.

Chapter 3

I took a deep breath, wrenched the crowbar from my thigh in a convulsive jerk the blood quickly washed away by the sea water.

Staring at where the wheel had been on the door I ran through the options in my head. It didn't take long - there weren't any, it had snapped off flush with the steel plate of the hatch.

Until now I'd envisaged the wheel yielding to sufficient force and we'd simply take the RIB back to shore. Easy.

Now we were in a sinking ship drifting towards a rocky shore of which the MacKays' cabin was on the side that was going to hit first. A vessel of this age wasn't double hulled. The hull, also their cabin wall, would open like a tin can, drowning or crushing them.

I tried the next cabin door along, the wheel spun freely. The cabin inside was small, luxurious and a third full of water. I checked the far bulkhead in the hopes there was an adjoining door. No such luck.

Back up top I dropped into my RIB and searched a locker for the rags I used when tinkering with the outboards.

"Are you alright?" the girl asked, which people do, even when you're obviously not alright.

"Fine," I replied, as you do, whilst enlarging the hole in my drysuit leg with my dive knife. The rain diluted the blood and made it look worse than it was.

"There should be some duct tape kicking around," I said. The girl found it.

"Thanks, could you lift up the edge for me?" I was about to cover the wound with the oily rags and tape them in place when she spoke up. "That's filthy."

"There's nothing else." I shrugged.

She looked around for a second.

"Hold these," she instructed a passenger, stripping off jackets down to a thermal top and peeling it off to reveal a sports bra.

She had a fit and lightly tanned upper body, just a hint of a six-pack, I focused higher up. There was little left to the imagination in the cold rain. She folded her thermal into a square pad. Squatting down she pushed the pad inside my dry suit, over the wound.

"Hold that," she said. I did.

"It'd be good to stay waterproof," I said.

She nodded and started wrapping the tape around my thigh, starting above the knee being careful to make sure each wrap overlapped the last and stopped at the top of my thigh.

She tore through the tape and smoothed the end down, I didn't meet her eyes as I obviously wasn't suffering from blood loss. I hoped the neoprene dry suit was thick enough.

A smile tugged at the corner of her mouth. Damn.

She stood smoothly, slipping the jackets back on.

With a groan and a glance at the GPS, which didn't show anything good, I assembled my cylinder, BCD and regulators.

"What are you doing?" she asked.

I explained.

"Can you stop the ship sinking?" she asked a little dubiously.

"Don't know, I'll have a look."

"You'll have a look,' she said slowly, as if talking to a slightly backwards toddler. "Under a sinking ship?"

"It seems to be sinking slowly," I said in defence as I opened the valve on the cylinder and looked at my pressure gauge. Seventy bar, I hadn't refilled it after my last dive. You'd normally start a dive with around two hundred and thirty bar. You'd abandon a dive when you got down to a hundred bar to leave a decent safety margin. It would have to do and I wasn't going deep, hopefully.

"Seventy," she said, leaning over my shoulder looking at the gauge. "Is that good?"

She was very close, touching my shoulder. It felt electric, but the image of a tall, dark-haired woman flashed through my mind as the guilt flashed through my gut, still, a year later.

"Do you dive?" I asked.

"No."

"It's good," I said confidently, strapping the dive gear on.

"Bring radios back out with you. Tell the harbour master to find cutting gear, oxyacetylene's probably all he'll find locally but Broco or plasma would work. We need a boat powerful enough to stop this one drifting on to those rocks." I nodded towards the shore behind us as I put the mask on. The girl looked that way and grimaced having not noticed that particular problem yet.

"Thanks for the leg."

"You're welcome," she replied with that broad smile again. Oh God, I thought, and rolled into the water.

I started a grid search at the stern. The hull above me was rolling and heaving constantly, which was disconcerting. I looked straight down but couldn't see the bottom of the loch, just blackness.

A third of the way through the search I felt a tug on my right fin, it was sucked flat to the hull covering a round four-inch hole that was sucking in water, it looked like a sea water inlet or sea cock. I unbuckled the fin and left it sucked flat to the hull as it effectively sealed the leak, at least temporarily. The remainder of the search showed no other holes or leaks.

I surfaced to discover I was alone. The girl ferrying the last group of passengers to the pier.

The handrails were heaving up and down just out of my reach. I shrugged out of the BCD, inflated it and straddled it to give me the height to grab the lowest railing and haul myself on the deck. I scrambled through the bridge on to the high side of the boat. Standing on the superstructure looking towards the shore revealed a large crowd on the pier, and numerous of flashing lights of emergency services. Hopefully, I was done here, and the professionals would take over. I saw my little orange RIB leave the slipway.

I checked the bridge console for anchor controls, but nothing would work without power so I clambered from bow to stern checking deck fittings, winches and equipment to see if there was any way to manually drop an anchor and halt the drifting but found nothing I could use.

"Who's there?" I called out as the girl got close.

"Ambulance, police and fire."

"Radio?"

She threw a handheld VHF up to me, which I fumbled, doing that uncoordinated juggling thing.

"Can you grab my dive gear, should be floating around somewhere." The outboards burbled as she went looking.

I turned up the volume. "This is the sinking ship, anyone in Ullapool listening?"

"This is the harbour master. You are loud and clear."

"Any emergency workers coming out here to take over?"

"No. None of them are allowed on sinking boats apparently. Coast guard team hasn't got here yet."

"Then I need cutting gear, oxyacetylene, Broco or a Plasma cutter. A big grinder would do at a pinch. There's a jammed door with two people behind it. We'll need a big enough boat to tow this one and do you know what the bottom is around here?"

"What's a Broco?" was the reply. I rolled my eyeballs so far it hurt.

"An exothermic cutting tool. Try the big trawlers, they must have something. Ask the firemen if their 'Jaws of life' will work on a watertight steel door. Failing that try the local garages and blacksmiths. Find someone that knows the seabed around here and get a big boat or lots of little ones fired up."

"Uh, OK."

The girl came back with my dive gear in the boat. She waved. Beetles tail wagged. The radio was silent. My leg throbbed, I wanted to lie down and have a nap.

"There's one of the trawler captains here," said the harbour master's voice.

"This is Fergus Mckinlop, captain of the *Heather Dawn*, the larger of the two trawlers tied up here. To whom am I speaking?" The powerful, broad Scots accent burst from the radio. A trawler captain would be a useful man.

I repeated all I had said to the harbour master, adding, "She's drifting on to a nasty shore. She'll hit starboard side, where the people are trapped."

When I finished he just said, "standby". A minute later he was back.

"I've sent lads to the garage and smithy, might not have a Broco or plasma, but they'll all have acetylene. We don't have any on our boats. Bloody health and safety," he grumbled. "The bottom here is shifting sandbanks so the depth varies from nothing to thirty metres or more. Standby."

"The firemen have the 'Jaws of life' but it comes with a large hydraulic power pack that's fixed to their appliance, they won't send men on to a sinking ship and he can't let a civvy use their gear, even if they could unbolt it from their vehicle."

"Can you use your trawler to tow us?"

"We're in for repairs. We've got power but can't go anywhere."

"How many little boats could you get underway?"

"Not enough, quick enough."

"How about your winch?" I asked, clutching at straws, most trawlers I'd seen had a powerful winch on the rear deck for hauling in nets.

"I see where you're going. Standby."

Beetle and his new friend bobbed up and down in the lee of the stricken vessel watching me. The girl had her hood up and Beetle sat there utterly impervious to the wind and rain in his thick fur coat. The girl was holding something in front of her. A phone? She lowered it as she noticed I was watching. I scowled at her to pass the time.

"We've auxiliary power to the main winch, I can pull fifteen tons now, thirty when the mechanic gets here to start the main engines. Two small boats will bring the cable out to you."

"They'll need a heaving line on the end to throw up to me," I replied. "And have them take the weight of the cable ten metres back from the end, I won't be able to manhandle the weight. We'll make fast to the bows to bring her round and reduce the windage."

I could see activity around one of the big trawlers and soon enough two small boats were heading our way, slowly dragging a heavy winch cable between them.

I stared at the rocky shore we were bearing down on, uncomfortably close now, and tried to estimate distance and time. I could ask the girl to check the GPS on the RIBs console for an accurate estimate, but there was no need. We'd either make it or we wouldn't. Either way I wasn't leaving this boat without the couple below.

With nothing to do I sat down to rest my throbbing leg and studied the blonde girl. I figured she couldn't see where I was looking at this distance. I smiled as I thought about earlier. The fact that I was finding someone attractive was a good thing, I guessed, but not without issues. Luckily the radio burst into life before I was drawn down that path.

"I've got the mechanic from the *Glen Nevis* here who says there's acetylene in the engine room," said Fergus.

"Great. Where's the *Glen Nevis*?" I asked.

Fergus's paused. "You're on it," he said slowly.

"Oh," I said dumbly, then sighed as I realised what I was going to have to do.

"The lad says it's on the aft bulkhead behind the starboard engine," Fergus relayed usefully.

I waved the girl in close to get my dive gear from her.

"You're not going to do what I think you are, are you?" she asked as she passed my gear up. I grinned at her, because I couldn't think of anything witty to say.

The two small vessels had arrived, bobbing and corkscrewing awkwardly in the swell as the weight of half a mile of heavy cable worked against their natural motion. A man in oilskins threw up a light line. I caught it, braced myself against the sloping, pitching deck and heaved up the inch-thick winch wire through a hawsehole in the bow and secured it to bollards on the fore deck.

The small boats released the cable from where they'd fastened it to their boats to take the weight of it for me.

"Fergus, secure here, hold her there and we'll see what happens. You have a load indicator?"

"Aye, of course."

"Keep an eye on it."

The boat now tethered at the bow the wind pushed her round till she was heading into it which reduced the surface area for the wind to push against. But it could affect the stability of the vessel with its load of water inside now that she was being pulled down at the bow by the weight of the cable. But she wasn't broadside to the wind and waves so her rolling motion should subside, reducing the likelihood of her tipping over. In theory.

I debated whether to use the winch to pull her in to the pier and away from the rocky shore downwind of us. Her hull could already be just inches away from a sharp point of rock just below the water, an increase in wind and wave action could rent her hull. But if Fergus pulled us towards him we could catch on one of the shifting sandbanks he'd mentioned which could roll us further over, or less, or maybe beach us entirely which would be good, unfortunately there was no way of knowing which of these things would happen.

The couple were still trapped below, if I couldn't get them out then surely the closer the boat was to shore the better their chances of survival. I made a decision.

"Fergus. Take in as gently as you can. Any increase in load, stop."

I limped back to my dive gear, slung it over a shoulder and stumbled along to the bridge. The girl motored in close to the railing and kept pace with me.

"Keep your distance in case she goes over," I said.

"You can't dive inside a sinking ship," she said.

"Course I can," I said confidently.

"That's past brave and in to stupid."

I went to say something, stopped, how could I explain?

"You don't have to do this," she said.

But I did. My conscience was already at breaking point, quite literally waking me up at night. It wouldn't cope with another two lives on it.

"He likes you," I said, nodding at the dog, tail wagging like a metronome.

She thumped his side affectionately and he gave her a happy lick in return.

"He likes long walks in the country, lots of affection, Frosties for breakfast and Lady Gaga," I said. Foster mother organised, just in case. I ducked inside before she could object.

Chapter 4

Through the bridge, down the stairs, leaving the dive gear floating by the stairs and the radio on a dry step above, I swam to the MacKays' door and tapped.

Agonising seconds later came a weak tap in response. Still alive.

I opened the next cabin door and checked the water height, not good.

Donning the dive gear, wincing a little as I checked the air gauge, I dropped into the cold water. Pulling myself down the stairwell with one arm, illuminating the way with my dive torch. At the bottom I was faced with the same layout as the level above. The engine room at the far end. The emergency lights weren't working down here, shorted by the water. Other than the narrow beam of my torch it was pitch black and claustrophobic. Approaching the watertight door to the engine room I mumbled a small prayer. *Please let it open, please let it open.*

If the engine room beyond wasn't flooded I wouldn't be able to open the door against the pressure.

The wheel spun easily. Planting my feet against the bulkhead either side I hauled.

The engine room was totally flooded. The door swung open easily.

The space was the full width of the vessel and twice my height. Big lumps of diesel engine sat either side of a narrow central walkway. Rags, oil and random objects suspended in the water. I pulled myself along between the diesels, turned left and the torch beam picked out two tall cylinders, about five feet high and a coil of hose with a cutting torch on the end. The hose was maybe five metres long, not remotely enough to stretch to the level above. I looked around, there could be more hose somewhere, but maybe not. I decided not to waste time looking.

Opening each cylinder's valve in turn to check the contents I disconnected the hose jamming it under my BCD along with a sparkler that was hanging off one of the cylinders. I hauled each cylinder in turn from its brackets. On dry land I would have struggled with the weight but underwater it was manageable. The extra weight kept my feet on the deck so I removed my one remaining fin as it was just inhibiting • progress now, besides, whichever way the next few minutes went I wouldn't need it again tonight.

I was breathing heavily now but didn't bother to look at my air gauge, it would run out when it ran out, I'd carry on until that point. Grabbing a coil of rope I held the oxygen cylinder by its valve in one hand and the acetylene cylinder the same way in the other and in slow motion, as is inevitable underwater, trudged out of the engine room and along the corridor dragging the cylinders behind me. The rocking motion, water movement, and slanting decks throwing me constantly off balance.

At the stairwell I tied the rope to both cylinders, floated back up the stairs, paying out the rope. Bracing myself at the top I hauled the cylinders up and dragged them to the MacKays' door, lashing them upright to a the handrail next to it. I shrugged out of my BCD. The water was about two feet from the top of the door now. The door and bulkhead on that side of the boat still slanting away from me, halfway between upright and flat, water sloshing against it constantly.

Reattaching the hoses to the cylinders I cracked them open. Unsurprisingly, the sparkler didn't work. I considered using just the oxygen cylinder to dry it out but dismissed the idea. Filling a confined space with oxygen prior to lighting the acetylene of the cutting torch wouldn't be my best idea this year. Pure oxygen is an accelerant, I'd blow myself up.

I pulled my dive gear close, pushed in the large button on the regulator to activate free flow and stuck the round end of the sparkler into the stream of dry air, squeezing the handles as fast as I could in the hopes the friction would help dry it out quicker. The load hiss slowly died away to nothing as the air finally ran out.

So that was that, if the boat rolled or sank I probably wouldn't survive. I could hold my breath for longer than most, but not long enough to fight my way out against the force of water flooding into the boat and the darkness and disorientation of it rolling.

In the relative quiet that followed the hiss of compressed air the only sound was the harsh rasping of me frantically squeezing the handles of the sparkler.

I swore at it, because that always helps.

It obliged by letting out a single pathetic spark. The brass cutting torch spluttered as the gas forced out the sea water before the acetylene caught with a *whoomph*. I fiddled with the mixture until I had a small orange and blue flame burning around three thousand degrees centigrade, hot enough to melt steel.

Putting my dive mask on to protect my eyes I looked at the door. Made of five-millimetre-thick plate, the edges folded back to fit over the coaming on the bulkhead. The wheel I'd snapped off had a corresponding one on the inside with a system of bars that would be pushed out past the edge of the door to lock against sloping lugs on the frame sealing it tight. I'd have to cut through the door and then the bars.

I took a big step left and put the tip of the small orange flame to the adjacent bulkhead instead. Simpler and quicker, I hoped. The cabin next door hadn't been panelled, the flat steel plates had been painted a gleaming white. I hoped the cabins were all the same. I let the flame heat up the metal for a few seconds, the paint blistering and burning giving off a noxious smoke, then boosted the oxygen. The flame jumped up a notch in intensity and burst through the steel plate. Starting high and left, moving the torch slowly in a rectangle. I squinted against the brightness wishing I had protective dark glasses or a helmet, not to mention welder's gauntlets and coveralls. With no gloves on I could feel intense pin pricks of pain and smell burning rubber from my dry suit for the same reason.

Finally, a slab of the bulkhead splashed into the water in the cabin with a hiss.

I poked my head through carefully, the edges still glowing. They were huddled in the corner, up to their necks in water, trying to keep away from the flame and sparks. A tough-looking older man and a scared looking woman, both pale and shivering.

They started towards me when the boat reared upright suddenly. Throwing me off balance, my chest landed heavily on the lower edge of the hole I'd just made as I saw the couple thrown aside by a wave of water moving across the cabin.

I knew what happened, I'd been half expecting it, one of the cons of deciding to pull us in with the trawlers winch. As we were being pulled slowly through the water the keel must have caught on a sandbank. Even if Fergus stopped pulling the second his load indicator flickered, the weight of half a mile of inch-thick winch cable would have kept pulling us as it sagged to the bottom of the loch when the tension was released.

A mass of water surged back and forth in the companion way, knocking me off my feet as the hull rolled alarmingly. When I surfaced, I could see the water pouring in and out of the hole I'd just cut.

"Quick," I barked.

Luckily the water had cooled the edges of the hole so as soon as they were within reach, I hauled them out and pushed them along the corridor. I could feel a deep heat in a strip across my chest where it had contacted the hot edge. I hoped it was just the neoprene of my dry suit that was burnt, but knew it wasn't. But it was way down my list of concerns right now.

With each roll the old boat went a little further over and came a little less upright. We'd soon reach the point of no return.

We were going over.

We all swam, staggered and pulled ourselves down the corridor against the chaotic force of water, I dragged the woman with me as she was pretty much done for.

At the stairwell I abandoned any form of politeness, threw the woman over a shoulder and pushed the old man ruthlessly ahead of me, manhandling him when necessary to get up narrow, dark, pitching stairs.

We passed through the bridge at a clip, the girl in my RIB was just feet away, waiting bravely.

The old boat rolled so far the railings almost touched the bow of my RIB so I unceremoniously tipped the man and woman in.

I launched myself at the RIB and felt an upwards heave as my foot left the deck.

As I landed the girl was already pushing the throttles to the stops, spinning the boat on the spot and roaring away. As I turned back the *Glen Nevis* reared fully upright, trembled, and started rolling towards us.

Fergus was still be winching in, her keel caught on a sand bank she'd been pulled upright, but the keel must have slipped off as now she was rolling down on us with a vengeance. Instinct told me she'd go all the way this time. The outboards screamed and bit deep into the water, but RIBs don't have great acceleration from a standing start, and mine was old and tired to begin with.

We were in line with the bridge, the roof of which was forty feet above sea level, normally. Which meant we were in line with the mast above that, stretching another thirty feet to a platform at the top festooned with aerials and dishes.

We wouldn't outrun it, our only chance was to get out of the way.

"Turn!" I bellowed at the girl.

We were perfectly in line with the mast accelerating down towards us.

Even as I shouted I knew we wouldn't make it as I didn't feel the boat respond immediately, which meant that human nature had won out.

Instead of blindly following my order and spinning the wheel, she'd turned to look back, wasting a valuable second. She'd looked at me, looked at the *Glen Nevis*, come to the same conclusion as me, another couple of seconds. Turning back around, spinning the wheel, another second, a slight lag while the boat responded. Too many seconds.

I tossed the old couple as far from the boat as I could, which wasn't far, but would be enough. Without breaking stride I wrapped an arm around the girl's waist, grabbed the dog by the scruff of its neck and launched us all off the side of the boat as a crashing sound came from the transom behind us.

The bow of the RIB flipped up violently as the top of the mast smashed the outboards under the water. As we hit the water I caught a glimpse of the orange remains violently flipping up and smashing upside down into the water with enough force to have killed us all.

The girl and the dog took the brunt of the impact as I held them in front of me, but both came up spluttering and unhurt.

I could see a head of short silver hair close by but no sign of the woman. I duck dived. It was pitch black, but it had been only seconds since she hit the water next to the man, she couldn't have gone far. I swam down, changing direction every few strokes to cover as large an area as possible until my lungs reached their limit. I stroked for the surface and bumped into her on the way back up.

She was having a rough day, but she was alive.

One of the small work boats, who'd sensibly kept their distance, was on us quickly. We were hauled out, the old couple and the girl were pushed into the tiny wheelhouse, which had a heater, squashing the helmsman against his wheel.

I was warm enough in my drysuit, the duct tape was doing its job and keeping the water out of the hole in the leg, and the deckhand lent me a spare oilskin, so I stayed on the open deck with him and the dog.

As we motored back to the pier I caught the blonde girl and the old man staring at me through a steamed-up wheelhouse window. He was shivering, but perfectly calm, watching me intensely through hooded eyes. The girl was white-faced and wide-eyed. I smiled encouragingly and chatted with the deck hand as I leant against the stern railing to rest my sore leg and watch the upturned hull of the *Glen Nevis* recede into the dark night.

Chapter 5

There'd been not a soul to be seen in Ullapool when I first saw the *Glen Nevis* steam into Loch Broom, now the pier was a bustling mass of spectators and emergency services.

I wanted no part of either, so as the girl and the old couple were helped up the slipway by waiting ambulance crews I returned the oilskin to the deckhand and slipped away to where someone had relocated my Land Rover a hundred yards down the road.

I tried to take off my drysuit to find it stuck to my chest, melted to my skin where I'd hit the hot edge of the hole I'd cut. A painful tug told me it was well adhered. The drysuit was wrecked anyway so I awkwardly, and carefully, started cutting it off with my dive knife.

"Are you running away?" I heard a few minutes later. I turned to see the tough-looking old man, MacKay, with a blanket wrapped around his shoulders but otherwise looking utterly unfazed by the whole incident.

"General Euan Mackay." Sticking out a hand. "You saved our lives life tonight. Thank you."

"Don't mention it," I said.

"Don't like the limelight?" he said, indicating the crowd on the pier.

I just shrugged. "How's your wife?"

"Mildly hypothermic but she'll live, she's a tough old bird. Has to be, been married to me for forty years, this was our ruby wedding anniversary."

"I wouldn't give the cruise line a good review on TripAdvisor if I were you."

"It was her idea, I wanted to go to Vegas," he chuckled. "Hell of a risk you took..."

I shrugged again.

Beetle nuzzled the man's hand who patted him robustly, the dog practically purred.

"What do you feed your dog? Steroids?" he asked.

I smiled, not the first time I'd heard that.

I looked past the general to the pier. I half wanted to see that blonde girl, half not.

"She's interviewing people," he said, chuckling, reading my mind.

"Interviewing?"

"She's a reporter."

"Oh god," I groaned. Last thing I needed.

The general belly laughed at my reaction.

Most people would need therapy after what he'd been through tonight. He was just laughing it off.

He handed me a damp business card. "I am in your debt," he said.

"No, you're not." I glanced at the card. Lots of letters on it on it, MoD was the only one I recognised.

"Here, let me do that, you're making a right arse of it." And with that he took my knife off me and gently cut around the neoprene stuck to my chest. He then applied a dressing from my first aid kit, holding it in place with bandages wrapped expertly around my chest and shoulders, then one on my thigh. He caught my raised eyebrow. "Been a soldier all my life. Dressed plenty of wounds worse than this."

We parted on good terms as Beetle and I rumbled away unnoticed into the night.

I didn't notice the blonde girl running down the waterfront after us, which was probably for the best, I needed neither a woman nor publicity in my life.

Although, I was still thinking about her later lying in the A&E department of Raigmore Hospital in Inverness. My chest was anesthetised as the melted neoprene was peeled and cut off leaving a deep trench across my left pectoral. Apparently nothing short of a skin graft would prevent a substantial scar. Wouldn't be my first, so it was nothing to worry about. My leg required a few stitches and I soon left with a paper bag of drugs, spare dressings, and instructions on taking care of the wounds. So as not to be associated with the events in Ullapool I'd told them it was a DIY accident, which raised a couple of eyebrows.

An hour's drive south saw us home to a remote cottage high on a hillside overlooking a large loch with an island and a ruined castle on it. From the single-track tarmac road at the loch's edge I took a rough track up the hillside to my cottage, crunching to a stop on the gravel between the cottage and a big, weathered shed, half-buried in the woods behind my home.

The only heating was an old solid fuel Raeburn in the kitchen which also heated the water in a back boiler, and a wood-burning stove in the sitting room. I laid a fire in each, lay down on the sofa and fell asleep.

When I woke much later the cottage was warm and the water hot. After showering and eating I took the dog for a walk. A slow walk, in my case, the stitches in my leg pulling a bit. We followed a faint path through the heather to the top of the hillside.

The glen was like a vast, shallow bowl many miles across. A single-track tarmac road ran through the far side, almost out of sight, and a track meandered through the moorland around this side of the loch. The only other dwellings visible from my cottage was the Victorian shooting lodge down on the shore of the loch. Empty for years, slowly falling into disrepair, the last owners went bankrupt and the lawyers were still fighting over it. And of course, the ruined castle on the island, once the lair of the infamous Wolf of Badenoch.

My father had been the deer stalker up here for most of his adult life, back when the laird lived in the lodge below and the area was a thriving sporting estate. This cottage and a couple of acres of woodland around it had belonged to him, and now me. He'd been widowed when I was too young to remember my mother and had brought me up alone in this glen.

He did the only thing a man in his position could do with a young boy, he took me to work with him. As soon as I could walk I was out on the hill with him through scorching summers and bitter highland winters. I learnt to track, trap, snare, stalk, and shoot when most boys were learning to ride a bike. I was running around these hills with shotguns and rifles at an age most parents wouldn't be letting their children loose with a pair of scissors.

When I was not yet ten, not far from where I was resting now on the lip of the glen high above the cottage, more than twenty years ago, my father and I had walked quietly up here before dawn on a September day. The rut was starting, the stags' roars echoing around the misty glen. We'd been on the hill day after day watching for a particular stag, an old friend of my father's. He'd seen this stag born the same time I was, he'd watch it grow into a magnificent beast, effortlessly dominating all the other stags.

But he was old now, had struggled through the last winter, time catching up with him. We'd watched him over the summer and at the time of year when stags are packing on weight and muscle in preparation for battle he was getting thinner and weaker.

In the wild, with no natural predators, their life span is determined by their teeth. When their teeth wore away or fell out they starved to death. It's a long, miserable death, starving in a highland winter. As a deer stalker, my father saw his job to be preventing his animals unnecessary suffering.

After couple of hours lying quietly in the heather the old stag appeared in the distance leading a group of hinds. My father silently passed over his binoculars, telescope, rifle, and knife. The tools of a deer stalker.

"You know what to do," he said quietly and moved off.

Was it a test? A sign of trust? My young brain didn't understand. But I knew what was expected of me.

I lay there watching, assessing the wind, the lay of the ground, the movements of the herd and quietly started crawling to what would be a good vantage point uphill of the herd if they kept grazing in the same direction. They didn't, of course.

I crawled miles around the moor using the natural cover, long heather, peat hags, streams, and gullies. The wind would shift a little and draw them away or the midges would come out and they'd seek higher ground and a breeze. A plane flew low overhead, spooking them so they ran hundreds of yards before settling.

The day wore on and still they kept moving, denying me a shot. As night fell I had a choice, I could give up and go home for a hot bath, a meal and a good night's sleep and accept that in doing so I would fail in this test.

I could sometimes make out the indistinct dark shadows of the deer so I followed them through the night. When I couldn't see them, I tracked their movement by the stags' roaring and the hinds' snickering. In the small hours the first snow of the winter arrived. I'd followed, crawled, and shivered through the long night. As the dawn light arrived the glen was a blanket of white. The herd lying below in sheltered hollows covered in snow, indistinguishable from the surrounding landscape. I couldn't tell one from another until, one by one, they stood and shook off their white blankets. I spotted the old stag as he struggled laboriously to his feet, stiff and weak with age and cold. The once powerful stag wobbled and swayed, took a couple of faltering steps and stopped, his great head drooping.

With a heavy heart I shifted the old .308 slightly, aimed high to allow for the bullet drop at this distance and gently squeezed the trigger.

The thunderous boom rang out, bouncing around the glen. The herd scattered. The old stag suffered no more.

Sometime later my father appeared with our sturdy garron pony to carry the stag off the hill, this bit was usually my job when not at school.

I'd asked him why the test? "It wasn't a test," he replied. "I know what you're made of, just wanted you to know too."

After walking Beetle I went to see my nearest neighbour to let her know I'd be away for a while in Morocco. Old Mrs Leven lived in a cottage five miles away as the crow flies. She'd been a friend of my father's and had lived there forever, alone since her husband died many years ago. We had an arrangement; I was usually away a lot so the local postie left my mail with her to save the ten-mile round trip to my cottage. It gave me an excuse to drop in on the old lady to make sure she was OK and do any odd jobs she could no longer manage. I live a simple life and receive no post that ever requires immediate attention.

Returning late in the afternoon I set about preparing the Land Rover for its road trip. I serviced it, which didn't take long. The long wheelbase Defender was more than twenty years old. Over the years every part has been replaced several times, it was on at least its third engine and God knows how many springs, shocks and bushes, so although the paint had long worn off in places and every panel was dented, mechanically it was perfect.

I started filling it with equipment I'd take to Morocco. This trip, amongst other things, marked my return to normal life. I'd spent too long alone up here. The first six months I'd been recovering physically, which was justifiable. But the last six months over the winter I'd just been hiding. As the snows melted and the land came alive, I forced myself back into the world. I'd spent a year mourning, I was alive, fit and strong again, if I didn't use that life than what was the point?

But my old line of work didn't hold the appeal it used to.

Beetle marched over to the top of the track, growling quietly.

I kept the track rough to discourage tourists who come to see the castle on the island in the loch in the summer months. A rusty, burgundy VW camper van appeared, complete with surfboards strapped to the white roof. Gears crunching and engine howling as it struggled with the track. It was driven by the girl that had been behind the wheel of my RIB in Ullapool the other night. The reporter.

A door creaked open and she dropped athletically to the ground. Snug, low waisted jeans and a tank top left a couple of inches of flat, tanned abdomen on display. She stooped to greet Beetle who was in the throes of ecstasy on recognising her.

"You're a hard man to track down," she said, marching toward me with a hand sticking out. "I'm Holly."

Oh dear, I thought. "Cup of tea?" I said.

She was standing at the door of the shed when I handed her a mug of tea, peering in at a lifetime of both mine and my father's kit. My skis and snowboards propped up in a corner with Dad's walking sticks and fishing rods. All sorts of fleece, neoprene and tweed clothing, colourful climbing wear intermingled with drab camo and khaki hunting clothes. Diving equipment, kayak, climbing ropes, harnesses and karabiners, ice axes and crampons hanging on nails alongside Dad's rusty old traps. A scarred workbench took up one wall.

"So, tell me about yourself," I said.

"Isn't that meant to be my line?"

She'd been an investigative reporter in London. She'd become disgruntled with the sensationalist and amoral nature of her chosen industry. After refusing to disclose some information she'd discovered because she knew it would damage an innocent family, she was fired.

Taking it as a hint that she wasn't cut out for that kind of journalism she sought change and got a job at the paper for the Highlands and Islands, based in Inverness. A long way from London.

"Best thing I ever did," she told me. "I don't do anything of importance, but I don't hurt anyone either. And occasionally, what I do helps."

She'd been heading home from a surf trip when she'd helped me in Ullapool the other night.

"Your turn," she said.

"Promise not to publish my name."

She protested. "Why not?" I wasn't going to tell her, that was a story I didn't want to tell.

"Take it or leave it."

"Take it."

"Start a fire in the pit and I'll tell you over dinner," I said, indicating to a pile of firewood.

A short while later a fire was roaring away in the ring of stones outside the cottage. Dinner sizzling on a griddle in the fire. She had accepted a small glass of white wine and we were sitting against a chunk of old tree trunk as the sun dipped towards the heather on the far side of the loch.

She gave me a brief synopsis of my life. Born and raised right here by a widowed father, local schools followed by a stint at an English boarding school then an engineering degree at Edinburgh University.

"Your name cropped up in all sorts of things: Himalayan expeditions, ski-mountaineering in Iceland, diving, climbing, caving. You've worked all over the world as field engineer: Oman, Qatar, Angola, Nigeria, the list goes on and on. Bridges, oil rigs, dams, marine construction and salvage. Which explains how you knew what to do the other night."

"I was mostly winging it the other night," I confessed. "How did you find all that out?"

"I'm an investigative reporter, it's what I do. And that was a quick search," she stated. "I haven't really started looking yet," she said with a grin.

"How's the food?" I asked, changing the subject.

"I'm guessing the son of a deer stalker didn't buy this in Tesco's?" she said.

"The trout came from the loch and the venison used to live over there." I pointed to a far hillside. Technically, it was poaching, I hoped that wouldn't occur to her.

We chatted amiably on through the evening and ended up sitting shoulder to shoulder, close to the fire for warmth. Beetle's head lying on her thigh. She laid her head on my shoulder.

"I wish all my assignments were like this. Last week I was up to my knees in cowpats investigating cattle rustling," she sighed. "But I must go."

Beetle and I watched her taillights disappear over the dark moor, and I was left, for the first time in a long time, not wanting to be alone. I sat by the fire till it died out, trying, and failing, to reconcile these new feelings with the old ones.

Chapter 6

My plan for the day was to deal with the paperwork, post, messages, and emails I had been ignoring. Clear the decks before leaving for Morocco. I flipped up the lid of my Mac, opened my email account, groaned, scrolled, and deleted eighty percent straight off.

Most of the remaining emails were from James. As promised, he'd inundated my inbox with emails, most of which he knew I wouldn't read, I tried valiantly to skim through some of the more interesting-looking ones. I'd been the best man at his wedding and he would have been at mine, I was godfather to his daughters, Emma and Lizzie, the ones that gave my dog his collar.

A framed photo stood on the desk of us all a few years ago when they last visited Scotland. Claire and James, Emma and Lizzie, Beetle in his new red collar, Rebecca and me, on the deck of a cruiser on Loch Ness. My eyes lingered on the tall, dark-haired Rebecca, as they always did, and I forced the image of the last time I'd seen her out of my mind, as I always did.

I'd come into a bit of money recently and after expressing an interest in investing it somehow James took it upon himself to help me and started sending emails and links about all things financial and property related in London. I made little effort to wade through the dry literature. The latest emails were about how the law to make people register ownership only came into force in the eighties. Before that, if you held the title deed then you held the property. Even I could see a flaw in that, but I didn't see the relevance to me and skimmed through the remaining emails.

I'd be stopping off to see them in Cambridge on my drive out to Morocco, no doubt James would give me a summary then. Soon enough I'd whittled my paperwork down to basically nothing. I live a simple life.

I was idly leaning back in the chair, feet on the desk thinking about the reporter, Holly Shaw. I'd slept soundly last night, no dreams, but I still slept on the sofa downstairs in front of the stove. The bedroom upstairs still too full of memories and the bed too empty.

The phone rang, I let it go to the answer machine.

"Ruraidh, are you there? It's Jessica."

A voice I hadn't heard in a long time. James's sister-in-law, a super-confident, icy London businesswoman.

But today she sounded hesitant.

"Hello Jessica." This would not be a good call, she didn't do social calls with me, my eyes sought out the framed photograph sitting on the desk.

Something had happened to one of them. Or more, I thought, with dread.

"Ruraidh, I have some bad news."

It was not a good phone call.

It was James.

With a cold numbness I asked, "How are they?"

"The girls are so young they don't really understand. Claire is..." She searched for the right words. "Devastated but coping."

"I'll be there by morning." I told her.

Empty, angry, disbelieving, numb. James...*dead*. I set aside my feelings. They were irrelevant. Only Claire and the girls mattered.

I left the cottage ten minutes later after throwing a few last things in a bag, turning off the water, and hiding the door key under a rock behind the shed.

I phoned Old John. Local gamekeeper, friend of my father and breeder of my dog, which he looked after when I was away.

"Aye, drop him off whenever suits. I'll be around and about, just honk your horn," he replied in broad Scots.

Pulling up at Old John's house in the woods, somewhere between the town of Aviemore and village of Carrbridge I honked my horn and John appeared wearing the uniform of a game keeper: tweeds, check shirt, flat cap, and wellies.

"Hello lad, you well?" he said sticking out a gnarly hand.

"Surviving."

"You keeping an eye on old Mrs Leven?"

"Of course. Saw her this morning. Thanks for taking the hound early."

I let the hound out, he landed solidly on all four paws, spread wide, muscles rippling beneath the glossy black coat as he looked around.

"Jesus man, he's even bigger," he exclaimed. "I am sorry," he continued. "I don't know what happened. The rest of the litter is perfectly normal. So, where are you heading this time?"

"Morocco." No point in telling him about James.

"Put his food in the steading for me, you may as well use those muscles for something useful."

I did as I was told. Walking back, John was watching me.

"You're limping," he said simply.

"Old age," I replied. He looked at me from under his heavy-browed eyes.

"Do you remember when you were maybe fifteen and fell off your mate's motorbike, after you were told not to ride it, and broke a couple of ribs?" He didn't wait for me to reply. "You never told your dad, did you?" I shook my head. "Soon after, you were due over here for a couple of days' work. Your old man called me that morning and told me to take it easy on you because you had broken ribs."

I smiled sadly. "Didn't think he ever knew."

"He knew." He put out his hand. "Take care lad."

Chapter 7

After driving through the night I turned off the old diesel and stretched the kinks out of my back as I walked towards the house. Emma and Lizzie burst out of the front door shortly followed by Claire. We had a four-way hug for a minute before Claire ordered the girls to continue getting ready for school, she wanted normal life to continue for them.

When I spoke to Claire on the drive down last night I'd promised to take the girls to school. I'd never done a school run before, I'd happily not do one again.

Turns out there's a lot to organise for a funeral so it was late in the day when Claire and I got a chance to talk.

"How did you cope when Rebecca died?" she'd asked.

I'd been dreading that question, but it was bound to come. I was going to say that it was a different situation, but it wasn't. It was essentially the same. A loved one dead for no good reason. Hers had been found beaten to death in the leafy woods of England, an unfortunate victim of a random mugging gone wrong, apparently.

Mine had died slowly, painfully, unnecessarily, held captive in a cage in the jungle alongside me. Sick, injured, full of fever and utterly helpless. I survived, she didn't. The stuff of nightmares, from which I still suffered.

The official version was that whilst I had been working down there on a civil engineering project, Rebecca had flown out for a holiday. We'd trekked into the jungle to climb one of the many rock towers that jutted spectacularly from the rain forest canopy. We'd become lost, disorientated, and succumbed to one of the many tropical diseases. Far from help we'd sweated it out in the jungle and Rebecca had died. That was the simple, clean, version which I recounted to Claire now. She deserved the truth, and I felt wretched for lying to her at a time like this.

"We didn't see you for a long time, James always told me not to ask," she said.

"I was in a poor state." Which was putting it mildly. Captivity, fever, dysentery, sepsis. I'd lost nearly half my body weight by the time I'd left the jungle. But that was in the past.

James had been dead only a few days now. Claire's pain was new and intense, that was what mattered now.

We talked for some time before she went to rest before her meeting with the police later in the day. I sat alone in the house, staring at the family photos lying around. James smiling out of most of them.

I knew from the papers where James's body had been found so I went to have a look. A seemingly random piece of woodland not far from the train station James used every day.It turned out to be a complete waste of time. So many people had come and gone from the crime scene any tracks were long gone, and anyway, professional crime scene investigators had combed the place, quite literally, so anything to be found had been.

Even so, it wasn't hard to work out where James's body had lain.

I spent some time there, just standing in the woods, alone.

The old anger of helplessness, of failure, washed through me. With Dad and Rebecca long gone James had been the human I was closest to on this earth, I pushed the thought out of my mind as it was selfish. His wife and daughters had exclusive rights to the sorrow here.

I returned to the house and drove Claire to the police station. They wouldn't let me sit with her during the meeting and when they came out the detective inspector would not speak to me, a non-family member. He disappeared deep into the police station where civilians could not follow. My dislike of the authorities was not lessened.

I asked Claire as much as was decent, I dearly wanted information, but felt I could not press her too far. The police had decided it was a mugging gone bad. James had no enemies, no debts, no secrets. There were no witnesses, no physical evidence, no murder weapon. Nothing. James was just in the wrong place at the wrong time, just one of the seven hundred people, give or take, that were murdered in England this year.

We picked up the girls on the way home. Claire was expecting a lot of people this evening, tonight was the wake, prior to the funeral tomorrow. Claire wanted to bury her husband and get the girls in to a new normal routine as quickly as possible. Everyone was to leave straight after the funeral. Back at the house we laid out food and drink. I walked down to the pub to shower and change, I'd booked a room there knowing Claire's house would be full of immediate family. As I passed through the bar I caught sight of a tall man I vaguely recognised.

"Harry Stone," he said, standing up. A friend of James's from London. We'd met briefly at their wedding years ago. I was roaring drunk at the time, my memory of the event a little hazy. He offered me a pint, so I pulled up a stool.

I recalled he was a financier of some sort in the city, which could mean anything, he informed me he was currently between jobs and living in North Devon. Here for the funeral tomorrow, of course. After the pint he came with me back to Claire's house to offer his condolences. He was a tall man, long powerful legs, built like a hill runner. He carried himself ramrod straight.

"Ex-military?" I asked. "A runner?"

He nodded, as we passed my Land Rover he asked, "Yours?"

"Yes, how'd you guess?"

"Fits," he said. "10 Shore Road, Woolacombe. If you find yourself passing Devon on your travels."

The house was full. We waded in, Harry sought out Claire, I sought out the kids but found myself cornered by a tall, burgundy haired woman who looked like she'd stepped out of the pages of Vogue. Claire's younger sister, Jessica.

"Hello Ruraidh," she said with a cut-glass English accent. We had a bit of history, Jessica and I, of nearly-but-not-quite. But that was a long, long time ago now.

"Hi, Jess." She hated the abbreviation of her name.

She smiled, planted one of those polite air kisses either side of my face. "You're looking... rugged," she said.

"You look good too, have you had some work done?" I eyed her suspiciously.

She fixed me with a cold stare, she was stunning and knew it, so I'd long considered it my duty to keep her feet on the ground.

"You'll get bunions wearing heels like that." I motioned to the towering stilettoes that brought her nearly to my height.

"You'll get some kind of fungal infection from those...things." Indicating my somewhat less sophisticated footwear.

Our usual banter faltered, didn't seem right in the circumstances. We spoke of James and I pressed her for more information but she knew no more than Claire, and the police had been no more forthcoming with her than they had with me.

The next morning we were gathered around a damp, dark, six-foot-deep hole. James was skilfully lowered in and Claire cast the first handful of earth. Her tearful little girls clinging to her legs. Another image that would never leave me.

Harry and I walked along to the carpark where he slipped behind the wheel of a powerful looking Porsche and roared away just as Jessica caught up with me.

"So. Morocco?" she said.

"Yes," I said slowly.

"I may have some leave coming up. Maybe I could come out for a few days if..." She left the question unfinished.

A lot went through my mind, but all I said was "sure", and explained my phone's demise and that I'd pick up a cheap pay-as-you-go in Morocco, she could get the number off Claire in due time. I didn't for a minute think she'd go through with it so wondered why she'd bothered asking.

With a last look towards the ancient graveyard I pointed the blunt bonnet of the Land Rover south without ever having noticed the black Range Rover that had been parked up the street from Claire's house for the last couple of days. Never knowing that as James was being lowered into the ground the two men that had killed him were searching Claire's house. Had I been more observant, more suspicious, I may have been able to save a whole lot of pain in the months to come.

Chapter 8

A lot of diesel, a few cat naps, and lots of service station coffee later I was leaning against the railing of the ferry crossing the Strait of Gibraltar. Five hundred and seventy kilometres to Marrakesh. I vowed to never again to drive an old Land Rover non-stop for nearly two days. Apart from anything else it gave one too much time alone to think. I let the bright Mediterranean sun burn away the darkest thoughts, the kind you have at three in the morning on an empty motorway.

Dan and Laura greeted me happily at the riad in Marrakesh and we had a happy dinner on the roof overlooking the famous Jemaa el-Fna. They lived in Aviemore, I'd known them for years, worked for them now and again back in the day. They ran a trekking business and their invitation to lead a few treks in the Atlas Mountains came at just the right time for me. Having decided at the end of the winter to be less of a hermit in my remote cottage.

The next morning I showered, then using the tiny pair of tweezers and scissors on my penknife I removed the stitches from my leg one by one. It had healed up OK and left a round scar the size of a ten pence piece. I could feel a lump in my quadriceps below it as the tissue went about repairing itself, but I could walk on it OK. My chest was going to take a bit longer to heal, being a wide and shallow wound. All I could do was keep it covered and try not to let my rucksack straps rub on it.

I spent the day lost in the famous souks of old Marrakesh and in the evening met the group I was to lead on the trek up the Jebel Toubkal, the highest peak of the Atlas Mountains. Dan and Laura had asked me to lead the treks as I knew the Atlas Mountains well from previous climbing trips out there.

The next day we drove to Imlil in Dan and Laura's aged minibus, the traditional starting point for the treks, a small mountain village at the road end. A night there and in the morning we loaded up the locally hired donkeys and set off. Several days later we returned with a group of tired, dusty, sunburnt and happy trekkers.

I spent the next month in the Atlas Mountains leading one group after another.

Not exactly a Himalayan expedition, but it was a welcome interlude. By the time we waved off the last group my leg and chest had healed well, I was feeling fit. James still dominated my thoughts as I lay in mountain huts and tents at night. I was ready for a change, ready for a little time away from people, but didn't get what I was hoping for.

Instead, I found myself sitting in the hot, sweaty, crowded Marrakesh airport.

Jessica's flight was late. I was getting grumpy.

To my surprise, and dismay, she'd actually got in touch and told me she was coming out - didn't ask me, told me.

A throng of sweaty, harassed travellers flowed out of the arrivals hall. Jessica strode along after the rush looking confident and aloof in light, well-fitting linen.

"I know this is Africa, but you could have made an effort," I said, indicating her clothes.

"We can't all maintain your high standards," she said, taking in my sandals, frayed cargo shorts, and dirty T-shirt.

"Just blending in with the locals."

"You're twice the size of any local here, try harder."

"I'll endeavour to be smaller immediately," I promised.

"You could endeavour your way to a haircut too," she shot back.

I scowled, took her bags and walked out.

"So, where are we going?"

"Two options: stay in Marrakesh with lots of other sweaty tourists in forty-degree heat or drive a couple of hours west to beaches and cool water. Maybe sleep under the stars, cooking over an open fire. Á la Bedouins."

She pulled a thinking face. "Hmmm. Tricky one..."

Several hours later we arrived on the outskirts of Essaouira on the Atlantic coast where the cool sea breeze kept the temperature bearable. Thankfully old Land Rovers are noisy, especially with all the windows down because I didn't have air conditioning, so I didn't have to speak to her much on the way. This wasn't her kind of holiday. She'd be more at home in Monaco or St Tropez. It would have been better if she hadn't come, and I was wondering why she had.

"How about a night of luxury and we'll slum it on a beach tomorrow night?" Jess said.

After a month of tents and mountain huts a shower and a real bed did sound good. She picked a hotel by tapping and scrolling on her phone and calling them on my local mobile.

I noted she reserved two rooms.

"Can I afford it?" I asked as we pulled up to an expensive looking place.

"Of course. You can't possibly be as poor as you look."

After checking in we agreed a time to meet later.

I enjoyed a long soak in the bath, scraped my face, tamed my hair and donned the suit that had been scrunched up in the back of the Land Rover since leaving the UK. Before going down I texted Claire and the girls, as I had been doing a lot recently.

In the opulent lobby the lights had been dimmed for the evening and there was a low murmur coming from the bar. It could have been any expensive cocktail bar in London, Paris or New York. Not really what I had envisaged when coming to Morocco, but you roll with the punches.

There were several small groups seated around low tables illuminated by candles and a group of men at the far end of the bar. I didn't see her until two of the men at the bar parted slightly and I got a glimpse of a long, figure-hugging dress and a tastefully small sliver of endless leg. Hair piled up on her head gave her extra height and a delicate pearl choker pulled one's attention to her neckline. Tall, poised, and elegant.

Ordering a gin, I leant on the bar. There wasn't a chance in hell I was going to join her throng of admirers, I was tempted to walk out. Instead, I pictured Holly Shaw, the reporter, in a black cocktail dress. I'd spent a lot of time thinking about her recently. Nearly as much time as I'd spent thinking about James and the conversations we'd had in the months leading up to his death.

Jessica broke my train of thought as she sashayed along the length of the bar leaving the group of men looking after her wistfully.

"Where do women learn to walk like that?" I asked her absently.

"Like what?" she asked innocently.

We moved to the dining room and after ordering food and ridiculously expensive wine I was working my way through the basket of miniature bread rolls.

"You know there are several courses coming, the bread isn't the entire meal. You're not in some mountain hut now."

"Just hedging my bets," I told her. "You never know what kind of minuscule portions they serve in a posh place like this."

"I know for a fact your father sent you to a boarding school to make a gentleman out of you, I just can't see any evidence of it."

I pocketed a couple of rolls, just to annoy her.

"You were going to tell me about your job," I said. I'd asked earlier but as usual she'd adroitly avoided answering.

"I'm a forensic accountant."

"Why so secretive about it?"

"I'm not secretive. I just don't advertise."

"Why?"

"Our clients are often wealthy, and usually in trouble. If your appearance is…memorable, and people know what you do then a client will not want to be seen with you. People will assume they are in financial difficulties, or worse, and appearances are everything in the city."

Interesting, perfectly plausible, I wondered what she wasn't telling me.

"When did you last hear from James?" she asked.

"Shortly before he died, we spoke often, you know that."

"Did he seem normal to you?"

"He was maybe a little preoccupied," I said. "But nothing dramatic."

"Who are your usual clients?" I asked, hoping to catch her out.

"Looks like the locals want to go home," she said, avoiding my question. The dining room was empty save for the waiting staff loitering in the shadows.

We retired to the bar for a night cap and some unremarkable small talk.

"Which way are you?" I asked at the top of the sweeping staircase.

She indicated to her left and we walked in silence along the corridor.

She opened her door a little, paused, and turned to me.

I smiled at the situation, not her.

"Breakfast by the pool at eight?" I asked.

She nodded, a slightly questioning expression on her face.

"Sleep well," I said politely, turned and walked to my own room where I slept like the dead in a proper bed.

In the morning I found Jessica already seated at a table by the pool.

"Good morning, sleep well?" she asked.

"Marvellously," I replied happily. "You?"

"Could have been better," she said pointedly, eyeing me coolly.

I managed to stop myself asking the obvious question.

"Well, hopefully you'll have a better night tonight," I said encouragingly.

She just looked at me.

After checking out and buying a few supplies, we were wending our way down the coast south of Essaouira. Dan and Laura were keen to run more climbing and trekking trips in Morocco and I'd promised I'd check out the area if I came this way.

We spent the rest of the day exploring isolated bays, cliffs and beaches with plenty of potential. I had climbed several easy routes with Jessica belaying me, somewhat absentmindedly, this wasn't her sort of thing. I wondered again why she was here.

The end of the day found us in secluded sandy bay, many miles off the nearest road, ringed with cliffs about twenty-five metres in height. After a bit of climbing about we went for a swim to cool off. Afterwards Jessica lay flat out on the sand, her long, slim limbs stretched out. I couldn't help but study her, but my imagination saw the blonde reporter lying in the sand.

"I can feel you watching me," she called out.

"Yeah, surprised to find a beached whale in Morocco," I called back.

She raised a hand in a very unladylike gesture.

"Let's camp here for the night," I said.

She didn't object but didn't look overjoyed either. I shrugged.

Before dark I walked up the steep, loose path to where my Land Rover sat a hundred yards back from the cliff edge and gathered what we'd need for the night, including firewood and hauled it all down to the beach.

Soon enough a fire was going, a lamb tagine and rice were bubbling away and we were well in to a very warm bottle of red wine under the stars.

"Well, it's not my usual sort of habitat but I have to admit it's not bad," she said.

"It is my usual habitat and I agree."

She laughed at me. "Your usual habitat is having dinner with women by firelight?" she mocked me.

I shrugged. "Happens more often than you'd think."

"Your usual habitat is some remote country covered in oil and grease," she said. "Are you going back to work soon?"

"Technically, I'm at work."

"Proper work, I meant."

"I am reconnoitring potential venues. So, it is work...at least, as far as the taxman is concerned."

"So, I'm a tax-deductible expense?" She tried to look offended.

"My accountant is used to me claiming beautiful women as expenses. I think he files them under corporate entertainment."

"I'd be interested in knowing how you file me," she said carefully.

"I've been thinking about that myself," I said. Which was totally true, but probably not how she thought. "I'd have to file you under CS," I told her.

"Elaborate."

"Claire's sister."

We didn't speak for several minutes.

"You're a good man," she said after a while.

"No, I'm not, and I can give you some examples if you like." And with that we returned to small talk.

Sometime later we were lying on our sleeping bags either side of the fire, few words passed between us, and I started to doze off to the background crackle of the fire and soft crash of the waves.

Time passed in that comfortable place between sleep and wakefulness. I heard rustling and felt a coolness as something passed between me and the fire. I didn't open my eyes, didn't move.

A delicate hand gently took mine and moved my arm. The long, slim form lay down next to me. She laid her head on my chest and pulled my arm back round her shoulders.

OK, maybe she was cold.

A long leg moved over mine.

Maybe not.

I lay still. I'd meant what I'd said earlier. But I was still flesh and blood. I didn't understand why she was here, and I still couldn't shake the feeling it wasn't just for me.

After a few minutes I felt her tilt her head a little upwards to look up at my face, as she did so the rest of her body moved infinitesimally against mine, a softness against my rib cage, breath on my neck.

She uttered the slightest sigh. "You are a good man, Ruraidh Maclean."

I didn't move, just lay there staring up at the stars until I felt her breathing deeply and evenly.

I, however, was wide awake and considering going for a swim as a substitute for a cold shower when I heard the slightest clatter from the cliff behind us.

At least I thought I did.

The remains of the fire were still crackling and the sea a constant murmur.

I lay there listening. But all I heard were the waves. I rolled my left wrist to look at my watch, but it caused Jess to move in her sleep, her arm and leg unconsciously wrapping tighter around me.

God help me, I thought.

I don't know why, but I craned my neck around to look towards the cliffs. There was no reason to - I was well used to sleeping outdoors and all the little, inexplicable, noises that came with it.

I nearly missed them in the dark, just the tiniest glint of the dying fire reflecting off a metallic surface made me look hard at the shadows, until I saw it again, a brief glint off a steel blade.

Jess must sensed something change and stirred.

I felt nothing other than an absolute and all-consuming certainty that this time I would not hesitate, would not stop, and would not fail.

Chapter 9

"When it starts, you run," I told her. "Don't look back. Don't stop."

There were three of them, walking slowly, silently, through the sand.

Maybe fifteen metres from us. Without taking my eyes off them I pushed Jessica behind me as she rose to her feet.

The starlight was enough to see the evil-looking curved knives glinting in their hands. They'd been going to cut our throats in our sleep, or worse.

I scanned the area. Not much to work with. Within reach were our sleeping bags, the fire, an empty bottle of wine, the pots I had used for cooking, a couple of mugs, two plastic sporks and the remains of the firewood stacked off to the side.

The three typically Moroccan-looking men swapped a few quiet words in a language I didn't understand. They seemed uneasy that I was on my feet. They'd obviously been hoping to catch us off guard.

I ran through scenarios in my head. Best case was they'd rush me as they were, three abreast, I could at least slow them down enough to let Jessica run to the sea which would give her a chance. Worst case was they'd spread out, circle around and come at us from different directions at once.

They started forward, slowly. Nine metres away, eight, seven. Still three abreast.

I pushed Jess further behind me. "Get ready." Wearing just swimming shorts I widened my stance, lowered my head, flexed my shoulders and grinned at them. I was hoping the sight of a big, scarred man in the firelight, grinning instead of cowering, would give them pause for thought. It would me.

Left, middle, right. That was the order they would go down in.

Five metres. Four. They sprang forward.

I pushed Jess away.

"Run."

Rotating back round I swung low, grabbing the two pots beside the fire, scraping them through the embers of the fire and flinging them at the three men in one fluid movement.

My left hand grabbed a sleeping bag and my right the empty bottle of wine as I launched myself through the cloud of burning ash towards the left-hand man, simultaneously body slamming him and ramming my forehead in to the centre of his face as I wrapped the sleeping bag around his upper body in a bear hug, arms pinned, knife neutralised.

I threw him in to the second man who had his hands to his face, still holding the knife whilst swiping at burning ash in his eyes. He went down on his back with the first man lying face down on top of him, still wrapped in the sleeping bag. I used him as a springboard, stamping hard on his spine between his shoulder blades to launch myself at the last man.

The last man knew I was coming even through streaming eyes, flailing his knife wildly in my general direction. I was committed to the move, seeing as I was temporarily airborne, so brought the wine bottle down on the crown of his head and fended off his knife with my left hand. I held the bottle by the neck and the body of it smashed on contact, jagged ends tearing down his forehead and face.

My momentum took us both to the ground. His right hand still held the knife. The wine bottle had neither knocked him out or killed him so I rammed the jagged end into his neck as I felt a blow to the back of my shoulder, I twisted the bottle neck through ninety degrees with a gristly tearing, bubbling noise.

Without pause I started back to the first two men.

"NO JESS," I bellowed.

She had guts. I'll give her that.

Instead of running, she'd stayed to help.

I wished she'd ran. She'd picked up a branch from the remains of the pile near the fire and was swinging it towards the heads of the two men lying in the sand.

The one on top appeared paralysed from the point I had stamped on him downwards, which was gratifying, I'd hoped his dead weight would pin the other one down for the few seconds I needed to dispose of the last man. The man below was struggling to free himself as Jessica swung the branch.

The sand slowed me down, like one of those nightmares where you feel like you're running through treacle. I could see it happening but couldn't get there fast enough to stop it.

The branch was light, baked dry by the harsh Moroccan sun and Jess was not a strong woman. The man's hand flicked out, a dull flicker in the night, she fell back screaming, clutching her side.

The man underneath was almost free by now, so in one of those cruel twists of fate, if she hadn't tried to help but had run we'd have both escaped this attack unharmed, mostly. He saw me coming and slashed at me with the knife. But he was in a weak position. I spread my arms wide just outside the range of his knife, left hand empty, the broken bottle, slippery with blood in my right. He took another wild swipe, I grabbed his wrist, and rammed the broken bottle home.

Jessica was in a bad way.

"Why didn't you run?" I groaned. All the nightmares I'd spent the last year dealing with being replayed as I held another dying woman in my arms.

"I'm sorry, I've got to look." I gently moved her hands and she cried out.

It looked horrific, a gaping black wound. The knife had just caught the lowest rib on her right-hand side, halfway round towards her back. The rib must have taken the force of it as I could see a sliver of white through the flowing blood, the blade had rolled off the rib towards her abdomen and cut through the softer flesh leaving a long gaping laceration from her side around to near her sternum following the bottom of the rib cage.

I couldn't see any pulsing arterial bleeding. She could breathe, her rib cage rising and falling so her diaphragm was intact. She had actually been lucky. A half-inch higher and the full force of the slice would have landed between two ribs, cut through the intercostal muscle and into the lung, possibly the heart too. A half-inch lower and the rib wouldn't have deflected the worst of the blow, she'd have been completely disembowelled.

It was still bad.

I scrabbled around for my T-shirt, folded it up and held it to her side. As I held it there I realised the backs of all my fingers were blistering and stiff.

"Ruraidh," she said weakly.

"Quiet, don't talk," I said, as I made ready to gather her up in my arms.

She raised a hand to me. I thought she wanted me to hold it, so I did, but she shook it off, pointing to my own ribs.

I looked down.

"Oh bollocks," I said with feeling, and then it started to hurt.

But I'd been luckier than her. It must have been the man on the right. I'd thought I'd swatted his knife away, but apparently not. He'd caught me in the same place as Jessica but had sliced upwards, perpendicular to my ribs, not penetrated, just sliced open the relatively thin, tight skin over my rib cage.

I could see slivers of white bone, my own ribs. But it wasn't life-threatening, so I ignored it as best I could.

"I'm going to carry you up to the Landy." I wrapped her in the remaining sleeping bag and picked her up.

"I'm glad you're skinny," I told her with a smile.

I started towards the path up the cliff. After a few paces I caught up with the man I had paralysed. He was trying to pull himself through the sand with his arms, not getting anywhere fast. He still held his knife. I stood on his wrist and plucked it out of his hand.

He was gabbling away in what I guessed was Berber, as it didn't sound French to me. He turned towards me and spat words with hate.

"Who are you?" I growled.

More gibberish.

"Who sent you?" I asked.

I was wasting time. He wasn't going anywhere. I'd come back once Jessica had the medical care she needed and question him, if he was still alive.

The rocky path cut painfully into my feet as I hadn't stopped to look around for my flip-flops, I ignored this pain too as it was nothing compared to her wound. The back of my shoulder was beginning to hurt abominably as I carried Jessica, I figured I had another wound I was only feeling as the adrenalin faded.

Jessica was conscious and groaning quietly. I tried to be as gentle as I could.

At the top of the path I made straight to where we'd left the vehicle. Hoping it was still there. It was, no mistaking the boxy shape of it. There were no other vehicles parked there. I wondered how the three men got here. They couldn't have walked; it was a long way from the main road.

I concluded they must have driven in a normal car as far as they could and left it when the track became too rough for anything but a 4x4. Or maybe motorbikes - off-road scramblers were common in Morocco, being cheap and easy to maintain.

As we approached the Land Rover my heart sank. She was sitting too low. As we got nearer I circled the vehicle, all the tyres were flat.

This wasn't the complete disaster it would appear. There was an old bush trick where you could fill the tyres with straw, grass or anything you could find and you could make some progress as long as the tyres hadn't been completely slashed to ribbons, and it was hard to slash thick off-road tyres. It's what they were built to withstand.

The complete disaster was that they'd done a thorough job on the engine. Handfuls of wires had been yanked out. The diesel injection lines had been smashed with a rock, the oil filler cap was off and they'd poured handfuls of sand into the engine block.

Simple, but effective.

My Land Rover wasn't going anywhere.

Chapter 10

I laid Jessica down and opened the trashed 4x4's back door. It looked like all my kit was still there so I fished out a head torch and first aid kit, using its contents to fix Jessica up as best I could. Having used everything in the first aid kit on Jessica I folded up a T-shirt and duck taped around my rib cage.

Using a wing mirror, I looked at the back of my shoulder and sure enough there was another deep cut. I couldn't reach it, let alone dress it, so I ignored it.

The harsh light of my head torch illuminated the damage to the back of my fingers as I worked. As I'd scooped up burning embers from the fire I'd held the pans with my fingers on the inside and thumb on the outside. The backs of all my fingers had been burnt, already blistering and stiffening, bending my fingers was excruciating but there was nothing I could do about them either so added them to the list of things to try and ignore.

I considered the distance to the main road and had to admit to myself I couldn't carry Jessica that far, and leaving her to go and get help was not an option.

I rummaged through the toolbox and set to work removing the bonnet. A Land Rover's bonnet is more or less flat with downturned edges, vaguely triangular in shape with a blunt front end. I placed it on the ground upside down, and punched holes through it with a sturdy screwdriver.

With ropes, slings and karabiners from my climbing kit I fashioned a rudimentary harness with two lengths of rope tied to the holes punched through the front of the bonnet.

I piled up all the soft clothing and padding I could find and laid Jess gently on top of them on the bonnet. Then punched more holes through the upturned edges all around her and lashed her securely in place in the foetal position to keep the wound closed.

I had long ago hollowed out a bit of foam from the underside of one of the back seats where I stashed valuables when I was going diving or doing something where I didn't want to take them with me. I fished around and pulled out passports, a wallet, Jessica's purse, a wad of cash I kept there for emergencies and our phones - neither of which had a signal since shortly after leaving Essaouira.

At the back door of the Land Rover I threw them all in a small rucksack with the remains of the first aid kit, food and water. Just as I pulled the drawstring on the top of the rucksack closed the rear door slammed into my back.

My upper body was inside the back of the vehicle, facing forward. The bottom edge of the door grinding into my hamstrings, crushing the front of my thighs against the back of the Land Rover as someone pinned me there. I strained maniacally. Trapped like that, if they had a knife like the others it would be child's play to take a swipe at the ligaments at the back of my knees, exposed and immobile beneath the lower edge of the back door. I'd be flapping around on the ground like a beached fish, my legs as useless as the man I'd paralysed on the beach.

And I'd just lashed Jessica to the bonnet on the ground. She was utterly helpless.

I thrashed uselessly for a second. There was nothing I could get any purchase on. I couldn't pull my legs into the vehicle and I couldn't push back hard enough from the position I was in.

As I'd thrashed, my hand painfully hit the corner of the toolbox I'd been rummaging in. It was an old-fashioned metal cantilever type, and heavy. I threw it back over my shoulder with the strength that blind panic gives you. The weight of it punched out the back window on to whoever was pushing against the door. The pressure on the door lessened and I scraped out to the side and threw myself at the man without pausing to take stock. I drove him back, throwing wild punches and had a hold of his clothes just as he lost his footing and we both went over the side of a small, steep ravine. I kept a hold of him, throwing punches as we rolled and bounced. My head contacted something sharp and hard, I saw stars as the darkness closed in, I fought it and staggered to my feet.

The man was a blur, I lurched at him anyway swinging wildly, my fist connected with something. But the blow lacked any real force as I couldn't focus properly. My feet, still bare, felt like they were being sliced up by sharp rocks. I heard him scramble away down the ravine. I didn't want to lose him, but I couldn't chase him so groped my way unsteadily back up to Jessica. She seemed untouched.

I clipped the rucksack I had been filling to the makeshift sledge and tugging on socks and walking boots shrugged myself into the makeshift harness and started walking.

I hoped that last assailant had been alone. He must have been. If there'd been more why would only one attack? Was he their leader?Had he been watching from the top of the cliff, sending his men down to do the dirty work? Hiding when I made my way back up with Jessica until he saw his opportunity?

The first mile or two were hard going. The sledge scraped and banged over the rocky ground, frequently catching on bigger rocks and holes. Several times I untied Jessica to carry her as the going was too rough for her on the sledge.

My balance and coordination were returning slowly, but I was still stumbling regularly, and my head was pounding to the point it was affecting my vision. But the upside was that it took my mind off the cuts on my ribs, shoulder and increasingly painful fingers.

It seemed to take an eternity to reach the track where the going was easier and I could leave Jessica in the sledge. When I lashed her in that last time I checked on her again carefully with the head torch. Breathing, but non-responsive. Pale and clammy even in the heat. I hated to think what internal bleeding might be happening. All I could do was get her to proper medical care as quickly as I could.

I hauled on through the night, bent almost double most of the time staring down at the track in the moonlight. It said much for my state of mind that it took me a while to take in the fact that I was staring down at tyre tracks as I walked.

My own tyre tracks were obvious in the sandy sections of the track. My big, all-terrain tyres had a distinctive tread and were about eight inches wide. Less obvious were the thinner tracks left by tyres with barely any tread on them that had been laid down after my vehicle had passed.

So, they had come in an ordinary car. Stopped when it got too rough and then walked. Which meant the man that ran away from me came back to the car and drove off.

I tried to think clearly, subjectively. But my thoughts were scrambled, the side of my head ached appallingly, the darkness round the edges of my vision threatened to close in constantly. I wanted to lie down and let it.

Would he come back with others?

I reckoned I had been walking for a couple of hours. Time enough to drive to Essaouira and be returning with more men or maybe he wouldn't be coming back. I had to work off the worst-case scenario - that he'd driven straight back to Essaouira, picked up more of his mates and would be coming straight back to finish the job. Which means they'd return down this track soon. We'd meet them head on.

If they drove with headlights on I'd see them coming miles away and have time to hide. But it was a gamble as to whether there'd be sufficient cover. And on this terrain, dragging an unconscious woman, they would run me to ground in no time if they saw me.

I could hide now, wait till they passed me, backtrack to where they parked their car and steal it, driving to the hospital in Essaouira. I liked that idea. But I might wait all night for them not to turn up and still have to drag Jessica to a hospital having wasted a lot of time she might not have. If they came without headlights I wouldn't hear them until it was too late as the metal bonnet made a lot of noise on the gravel track.

I hung my pounding head, thoughts swirling aimlessly, then struck off from the track at forty-five degrees to my left. Heading roughly north-east. I'd parallel the track a hundred metres to the north, on the Essaouira side. Far enough away not to be seen from the track, hopefully, but close enough to see the lights of any vehicle going down the track.

The cross-country route was harder going than the track, but safer. There were large flat fields where I'd run as best I could. Ditches to go around, rocky ground to manhandle the sledge over.

I stopped every hour or so to check on Jessica, pouring a little water on to her lips. The night wore on and after a while I started talking to Jessica. Maybe it would help her to hear a voice. I doubted it, but I talked to her over my shoulder anyway.

I babbled whatever came into my mind; I told her about my cottage, all the ridiculous stories I could think of about Beetle. I wished my hound was here. At times I saw him ahead of me, tail wagging, body language chivvying me along. It was at this point I realised my head injury might have affected things a bit more than I first thought, seeing as I appeared to be hallucinating.

It was frustrating, normally Jessica's weight would have barely slowed me down on the flat. I'd been dragging red deer off the hills with my father since I was a kid, Jessica's slim frame was half the weight of a decent stag but still I was struggling.

As I panted and heaved I told her about the events in Ullapool, the sinking Glen Nevis. For no particular reason, other than something to say, I described the reporter in great detail.

We chatted about James for a while. It was a very one-sided conversation. I commented on the similarities of James's apparently random killing in the UK and our random encounter tonight. What are the chances we'd both be in the wrong place at the wrong time, a month and a continent apart?

That sent me thinking about another continent, another wrong place and time.

So, I told her about the jungle.

I told her how I'd left Rebecca in our camp at the foot of the cliff we were planning to climb, too ill to move. How, a day later, I burst back into the clearing with a rucksack of medication and a rescue team hours behind me. I told her of the small dark men in tattered, quasi-military clothing, rusty AK-47s slung across their shoulders. They'd been standing over Rebecca, talking animatedly in a language I didn't understand when I burst out of the jungle and we all stared at each other. In my naivety I assumed they would help. Why wouldn't they? Why wouldn't you help someone you came across in that condition?

I was just an engineer, an adventurous one, but just an engineer with little experience of the nastier side of human nature. By the time I realised they weren't going to help it was too late and from that second to this day I have cursed my stupidity, my naivety. I could have, should have, done something before they swung their guns forward. But I didn't, it simply hadn't occurred to me what these men could be capable of, and Rebecca died because I was an idiot. Because I didn't act, because I hesitated.

More small dark men arrived. I was tied up and made to carry Rebecca as we trekked through the jungle at gunpoint. When I stumbled or fell I was beaten and whipped. I was soon exhausted, barely able to move. Rebecca's groans when I fell had fallen silent by the time we reached their wretched camp deep in the jungle, by then I too was in the grip of a fever. We lay inert on the mud floor of the wooden cage we were thrown in. When my fever cleared, I didn't need to be a doctor to know Rebecca had died days ago. I held her until they dragged her body out of the cage.

When it became clear I was going to live they started giving me a bowl of some nasty looking food and a cup of dirty water each day. As the days turned into weeks I lost a phenomenal amount of weight, but my body had reached some kind of equilibrium where it could survive on the meagre rations I was being given. As I recovered, in a manner of speaking, I started to take in my surroundings. I began to study my quarry.

The ground steepened suddenly, I went down on my knees, cracking them painfully off the baked dry earth bringing me back to the present. I cursed till the old anger burnt through the pain.

Digging my toes and fingers into the dirt I dragged us both up. Panting and doubled over I reached the top where the going was blessedly hard and smooth, the bonnet screeching loudly. I carried on and within a few steps was tumbling down a slope every bit as steep as the one I'd just ascended, the sledge sliding of its own accord.

I lay on the ground at the bottom with the sledge half over me, staring up at the sky. I felt like staying there.

I forced myself up and put one foot in front of the other.

Then stopped dead.

I focused on my scrambled thought process, there was something I'd missed. My unconscious was screaming at me, I just couldn't work out why.

I dragged the sledge around one hundred and eighty degrees and started back up the slope I'd just tumbled down.

At the top, I stood on the smooth tarmac of the Essaouira to Agadir road. No mistaking it, the only main road in the area, it was raised up on a banking. I'd just scrambled up one side, crossed the road and tumbled down the other side without recognising it for what it was.

It took me a full minute to work out which way to go. Concussion, maybe blood loss too, taking its toll. I concentrated. I'd been heading east, crossed over the road, turned around and come back on to the road.

I turned right, towards Essaouira.

The going was better on the hard asphalt of the road. I broke into a shambling run.

Time passed. My legs burnt and it felt like I was being stabbed with every breath as the movement stretched the wound over my ribs. I focused on the old anger until I felt nothing else, it had served me well in the past.

A truck roared past with its horn blaring, taking me by surprise but not stopping, I kept an eye out behind us after that.

When I heard the next one coming in the distance I slipped the rope harness off. Pushed the sledge safely off the road and stood in the trucks path waving my arms frantically.

God knows why he stopped. I was covered with blood, sweat and dirt. Still wearing just shorts and walking boots with duct tape wrapped around my ribs.

But the small flatbed truck squealed to a stop. Only when he stopped did it occur to me the man that who escaped me earlier could be on the road looking for us. I wouldn't be hard to spot. A man dragging a car bonnet down the main road. I peered through the cab's window to see a wizened old man on his own. Safe enough.

"Hospital," I croaked. He nodded and indicated to the flatbed with a thumb. He didn't get out to help.

With a monumental effort I hauled the sledge and Jessica together up on to the flatbed, which had no sides. I banged on the back of the truck cab signalling the driver to go.

The last thing I remember is lying on the sledge next to Jessica, face down with an arm stretched to either side gripping the edges of the truck's flat bed, pinning her in place and finally letting the darkness win.

I was told much later it had taken several people to pry me off when we got to the hospital.

Chapter 11

I woke in a hospital bed. Images flashed through my mind like a movie trailer.

A beach, a sinking boat, men in the dark with knives.

And James.

What about James?

I tried to sit up as if that would help me think but it brought stabbing pains to my head, shoulder and ribs. Through the pain came the vision of a funeral in the rain.

James's funeral.

I lay back with a groan as I heard a door open.

A pretty young nurse came in and asked in an adorable French accent, "Can you tell me your name and where you are?"

I knew my name and I thought I was in Morocco, but I didn't answer as the memories were flooding back now, and with them came a deepening sense of dread.

Was another woman dead because of me? I couldn't bear to ask as I knew I couldn't live with any more guilt.

But I had to know. "Jessica? Is she…"

"Your name first," she stated.

"This will go much better if you tell me how Jessica is," I growled.

She looked at me a little startled. "Mrs Aitken is doing well. We operated on her days ago."

"She's alive?" I said.

"Oui," she replied. "Of course. Get back into bed, I will get the doctor." She left and reappeared seconds later with a doctor who spoke very good English.

"Mrs Aitken is recovering nicely. Now I need to check you."

I relaxed back with a sigh.

"Can you tell me your name and where you are?"

"Ruraidh Maclean. I was trying to get Jessica to the hospital in Essaouira, but you said she was stabilised and 'sent here' to be operated on, so we aren't in Essaouira, but we're still in Morocco?" I paused. "The nurse said she was operated on 'days ago' so maybe you can tell me where we are and what day is it?"

"You are in the Clinique Internationale in Marrakesh," he said. "You turned up at the hospital in Essaouira at five o'clock in the morning three days ago. Do you remember what happened?"

"I hit my head; things are a bit fuzzy in places." I recalled babbling a lot, I hoped Jessica hadn't heard it.

"You're very lucky and have a very thick skull."

"Thank you," I said automatically.

"Mrs Aitken was stabilised easily enough in Essaouira, she lost a lot of blood but otherwise it looked worse than it was. But you had a combination of blood loss, dehydration and exhaustion but mainly your brain was swelling due to the blow you took. They didn't have the ability to carry out neurosurgery had it been necessary to relieve the pressure on your brain, so you were sent here, but luckily you responded to the medication." He paused and looked at me.

"I should tell you that as of forty-eight hours ago you are wanted for the murder of three Moroccan men. This is a secure ward. There are guards from the British embassy outside the door and once you are deemed fit you will be released to the Moroccan authorities."

I took a second or two to digest this. "How long until I'm declared fit?"

"As long as I can manage," he said very quietly. "I have been told what happened. But I do not think the two of you decided to attack three men on a beach in the middle of the night for fun while on holiday."

"No, not my kind of a holiday," I agreed.

"Can I see Mrs Aitken?" I asked.

"I have been told you are not to, but the embassy attaché in charge is not here. I'll tell the guards that you seem to be suffering memory loss from your brain damage and someone who knows you will help me ascertain the extent of it," he told me. "But just in case, try and look like a bit of a vegetable."

They wheeled me out of the room while I lolled my head to one side vacantly and dribbled a bit. I noted the two guards outside my room, one either side of the door. Big men in suits. They followed us down the corridor and stood either side of a door as I was wheeled through.

"Oh my God," Jessica shrieked as I was wheeled in still doing my vegetable impression. "What happened to him? What's wrong? What..."

"I'm OK," I said as soon as the door closed, walking over to her carefully, the soles of my feet felt like they were on fire.

Jess reached out. The sophisticated, aloof woman I was used to was entirely absent. Tears coursed down her cheeks as she tried to speak, words tumbling over themselves.

"You mustn't move Mrs Aitken," the doctor said.

"I'm sorry. I'm so sorry. I didn't know..."

"Nothing's your fault. You were brave trying to..."

"No, not that. It is my fault," she insisted, almost speaking in tongues she was talking that fast.

"I lied. It's my fault they were there. They were there for us, for you. They knew we were there. Someone told them..." She took a deep shuddering breath. "They told me what you did.

Your injuries. They said you shouldn't have been able to do it. I've been lying here for days, waiting for you. They said your brain...your cuts." She stopped, took a deep breath. "Doctor, could you give us a few minutes?"

"I can't leave you two alone. The guards won't allow it," he said.

"What haven't you told me?" I asked her very quietly.

"So much. But you knew that, didn't you? That's why...on the beach..." she tailed off.

"We may not have a lot of time. Tell me everything," I said. "Now."

"I am so sorry," she said again.

"We've covered that," I said.

"No. I'm sorry for what's coming next," she whispered. "You need to run. Run now, while you can."

This wasn't going to be good. "Explain."

"As soon as you are fit you will be arrested and go to jail to await trial. You will die there. You cannot survive a Moroccan jail. They want you dead. They tried and failed once. In jail they know where you are. They'll kill you in there, you will have no chance. None. You can't fight an entire prison on your own."

"Why do they want me dead?"

"James's death wasn't random. I think that they think you know something."

"Why do they think that?" I said slowly staring hard at her.

"Because I came here."

"Claire and the kids?"

"They are in no danger," she said.

"You're sure?"

"They're being watched now."

"Watched by whom? Who are you?"

"Rurai..." she started as the door slammed open and a man stormed in.

"You were supposed to inform me when he woke up," he said to the doctor.

"I wanted to ensure his memory and brain functions were OK before you spoke to him. The best way to do that was to..."

"Bullshit," the man broke in. "How stupid do you think I am?"

The doctor sensibly stayed quiet.

"Who are you?" I asked.

"Go back to your room," he said.

I studied him for a moment. Five-foot-ten and maybe twelve stone in weight, roughly my age, dark hair neatly combed, pale face. An average suit hung on an average physique. His hands looked soft.

"Who are you?" I repeated.

"I told you to go back to your room." He said this adamantly with a finger waving in my face.

"John Edwards. British embassy attaché. He's been tasked with looking after us," Jessica said.

"You have arranged to get her home?" I asked.

"Go bac..." he started.

"This will go much better if you talk to me in a civilised fashion," I cut him off. "And then I'll do as you ask," I lied.

"I'll get the guards to..." he said in a high-pitched whine.

"You could, but that would make you look very weak," I said, he didn't like that.

"You have arranged to get Mrs Hughes home?" I asked again gently. He nodded.

"When?" I asked.

"Tomorrow. Twelve-thirty BA flight to Heathrow," he answered reluctantly.

"Are you happy with the arrangements? Will you be safe?" I asked this of Jessica.

"Yes," she said. "My office has been informed of all the arrangements. I will be accompanied all the way. It's legit." She replied as the cold, aloof Jessica that I knew. Her professional persona, I guessed.

"Why are you turning me over to the local authorities?" I asked Edwards.

"You murdered three men on a beach south of Essaouira. There was a witness. We have no choice but to hand you over," he said defensively.

So, the little bastard that got away from me on the cliff top was now officially a 'witness'. I wondered briefly, that if I had managed to kill him too, I wouldn't be in this mess. But concluded that another witness would emerge when they discovered their dead friends on the beach, so it wouldn't have made any difference in the long run. They'd still have me where they wanted me, in a Moroccan jail.

"Do you believe their story?" I asked of Edwards.

"It doesn't matter what I believe. We have no choice," he whined.

"We have no choice," I repeated. "That's what people say when they're too weak to choose the hard way."

I didn't like British embassies. They'd told me, 'we have no choice', when I came out of the jungle. They'd have preferred we all just died in that jungle and didn't cause them any problems.

"When will you hand me over?" I asked, moving around the room.

"As soon as you are declared medically fit," he said. "Which you obviously are."

"No, he is not," the doctor spoke up. "He'll need several days of monitoring to ensure there is no lasting brain damage, he could relapse any time. And he needs to be kept still for his wounds to heal."

Inaction and hesitation, I thought. I'd spent a year in my lonely glen dwelling on what I should have done, blaming myself for not acting when I had the chance.

I walked around the bed to the window, partly to see what was outside and partly to check how I was moving. Three days of sleep had allowed my muscles to recover from the exertion. The sharp pains from one side of my ribs and a shoulder blade told me where I had stitches, but they didn't hinder movement. I could walk OK, but the soles of my feet hurt like hell. I wouldn't be running a marathon anytime soon. My head ached but my thought process was as sharp as it ever got. My leg nudged a sort of utilitarian sideboard next to the window as I turned around to face Mr Edwards.

My hands were the main problem, I flexed them carefully in their white boxing glove dressings. I could use them, painfully, the backs of the fingers tight and sore. I had full feeling in the fingertips. But I wouldn't be throwing any punches, which would make things a little harder.

I continued my little tour and came to rest beside John Edwards at the foot of the bed.

"You can't get out," he said smugly, as if he was clever for deducing what I was thinking. "There are two guards outside the door. We're on the fourth floor, in a secure ward, there are Moroccan police in the lobby."

I was looking at the doctor's ID badge as Edwards spoke, it was on one of those little round retractable devices clipped to his belt. You wouldn't bother with the little device unless you had to frequently insert it or swipe it somewhere. The breast pocket of his white lab coat held a few pens and the distinctive round finger holes of a pair of scissors. Probably a set of those long-shanked scissors with short cutting blades and blunt ends so as not to cut patients.

I was really starting to dislike Mr Edwards from the British embassy.

"Does it bother you that I am obviously being set up?" I asked him.

"As I said. We have..."

"Yes. No choice. You mentioned that."

I looked at Jess. I couldn't read her face, but there was a lot going on behind that mask of hers.

"Are you sure you will be OK?" I asked her.She nodded. "And Claire and the girls?" Another nod.

"And you're sure about what you said?" Another nod.

Inaction and hesitation, I thought. Never again.

"Tell me," I asked Mr Edwards. "How are your guards intending to stop me when they don't carry firearms?" I took a stab in the dark.

"They carry stun guns and telescopic batons," he said in his self-satisfied way. "Which is more than they need to keep you in here."

"Thank you," I said.

He looked a little baffled at this, until I slammed an elbow up into his jaw.

Chapter 12

I caught him before he hit the floor and put him in the chair.

"Doctor, make sure he doesn't die. But don't make a noise or try to leave." He nodded.

I pulled the dressings and bandages off my hands so I could use them properly. They weren't pretty. I heard Jessica groan at the sight.

"May I?" I asked the doctor, plucking the pens and scissors out of his pocket. At the window I snipped all the cord I could from the slatted blinds. The thin metal slats fell on the floor flooding the room with light, I brushed them aside with my foot and opened the window.

It was about three-foot square, hinged at the top, with a mechanism on one side to stop it opening more than a few inches. Ten seconds' work and it swung wide open. I looked down to a roof two storeys below that looked like reinforced concrete.

I estimated distances and compared them against available materials. It would do.

I heaved the sideboard up and balanced half-in half-out of the window, resting on the broad windowsill. There was no wind so I hoped it wouldn't fall out too soon.

Doubling up the nylon cord from the blind I tied one end to the sideboard. The other end I carefully ran out to the heavy-looking metal-framed bed.

Tying a loop in the cord I slipped the pens through, wedging them across a right angle in the bed frame with a little slack in the cord. Maintaining the tension to hold the pens in place nudged the sideboard just past its tipping point. I tied the remaining cord to the sideboard and ran it gently out to the back of the door, added a couple of feet and fashioned a pair of nooses using running bowline knots.

Out of cord now I tied the bandages I'd taken off my hands to the bundle of pens, measured the bandage out to the back of the door, added a foot and tied it around my waist.

"Don't move. Don't speak," I said to Jessica and the doctor.

I put my ear to the door.

"Here goes." I winked at them.

I opened the door. The two guards were expecting no problem from inside the room and kept their eyes fixed on the corridor. I flicked a makeshift noose over each man's head as I took a purposeful stride forward and felt a tug at my waist from the bandage.

The bandage pulled the pens free, the loop of the cord slipped off them, the sideboard fell out of the window.

There was a second's delay and then I heard a pair of heavy thuds, scrabbling of feet and choking noises. I looked left, looked right, saw no one and stepped back into the room, closing the door.

They were both big men, had they not been taken by surprise, and by their necks with thin cord, they could easily have held the weight of the sideboard. As it was they were pinned to the wall below the window clutching their necks.

Reaching down for a stun gun in a holster on one of their belts, I studied the device as I'd never used one before and gave them each a good zap.

They both twitched uncontrollably but made no noise due to still being strangled. I checked out the window and cut the cord, the sideboard shattered on the roof below.

I turned back to the room.

Edwards was unconscious in the chair. The doctor was standing staring at me. The two men at my feet incapacitated, but not out cold. I retrieved some cord and tied them up.

"Well," I smiled. "That went better than I'd expected."

Jessica was staring at me wide-eyed, either amazed or stunned.

I stripped one of the men and donned his suit, shirt, socks and shoes.

I pocketed the two stun guns and took a telescopic baton from each man. I hadn't used these before either. I flicked one of the slim six-inch tubes and it extended with a thwack into a slightly flexible twenty-inch stick with a bulbous end. I swung it to get the feel of it.

"How did they know we would be at that beach that night?" I asked Jessica. "And who the hell were they?"

"Probably followed us from Essaouira," she said. "I don't know who they were, locals obviously."

"And who, exactly, are you?"

"I am a forensic accountant," she said defensively. "But my company is often sub-contracted by government agencies."

I digested this for a moment and then filed it away for later.

"They'll be watching airports, train stations, ferries. You can't use your passport," she said, which seemed to remind her of something. She reached for the drawer in the bedside table and threw my wallet, passport, wad of cash and the cheap pay-as-you-go Moroccan mobile on the bed. I was surprised it had all made the journey, especially the cash. Although the wad was a bit thinner than I remembered, but when I fished around in the depths of my wallet everything was there.

"Do you know who killed James?" I asked her bluntly.

"Not exactly, I'm just a tiny cog in a big organisation. But it's connected to what we've been working on. That's why I was sent out here."

"You were sent! Jesus, are you a spy? If your people think I know something useful, why are they throwing me to the wolves?"

"I'm sorry. I don't know," she pleaded now. "You need to run, find me in London. I'll tell you everything." She scribbled on a bit of paper and handed it to me.

As much as I wanted every last piece of information I could glean from her it was time to go if I was to avoid a Moroccan jail.

"Your access card please, doctor." He handed it to me. "Is this all I need to get out?" He nodded. "Describe the way out please." He did so and I raised one of the stun guns.

"No, no, please," he cried.

"Relax. I just need to put the marks of the contacts on you, so they think I stunned you too, otherwise they might think you helped me," I said. "Brace yourself." He screwed his eyes up. I jabbed him in the chest without pressing the button that would stun him. "That should do it."

"Now you," I said to Jessica, using the discarded bandages to tie her wrists gently to the sides of the bed.

I went to gag her.

"Ruraidh. I..." she started.

"Ssssh," I said as I gently put the gag in her mouth. "Can you breathe OK?"

She nodded.

"Get me the name of the man that killed James," I said. "I'll see you in London."

I turned to leave.

"You'd best lie on the floor and look stunned when they come in," I told the doctor. "And thank you."

I looked in the mirror before leaving and recoiled at my own reflection. I wasn't looking my best. I pulled the big white dressing off the side of my head to reveal a shaved patch of angry bruising and stitches. From the sink I splashed some water on my face and wetted my hair, smoothing it over in a dodgy combover to hide the shaved patch. It was the best I could do.

I stood up straight, squared my shoulders, adopted the posture of a person that belonged there and strode confidently through the corridors, through the security doors, down the stairs and out into the lobby.

The lobby was open and airy, a long reception desk down one side and a large seating area where I saw two local policemen sitting. They looked like they had been there a long time. I walked casually, hands in pockets, across the lobby, the policemen didn't even look at me as I entered the revolving door, thinking that it was all a bit too easy.

I walked out into the midday heat of Marrakesh and locked eyes with four men in the shade of a tree on the far side of the square, watching the hospital's main entrance intently.

OK, not so easy then.

Chapter 13

The hospital opened on to a large, landscaped square, maybe a hundred yards along each side. There were people about, but they were generally on the move. The four men in the shade of a tree stood out. I turned casually to my left and made for a line of taxis.

They were watching me, talking animatedly.

The dodgy comb over, the suit and the distance making them unsure of a positive ID.

As the taxi drew away, two men left the shade of the tree for a line of mopeds, we turned a corner and lost them. I soon saw them darting skilfully between lanes glancing in taxi windows. They were still behind as the taxi stopped at the corner of Jeema el-fna.

I walked into the square without looking back until I got to a convenient corner and paused. I wanted to escape, naturally, but I wanted answers more.

My current appearance had been enough to throw a little doubt on a positive identification at the hospital. So they hedged their bets and only two men had been dispatched to follow me and two had stayed put. That was good. In my weakened state I could handle two at a time if I had the element of surprise. The question was, what was their intention?

A quick glance around to get the lay of the land and I took off the dark suit jacket. The white shirt would be more obvious in the bright sunlight and I wanted to be seen. I peered around the corner, the men had reached the square and left their mopeds. They were looking around. I kept peering round the pillar, trying to look nervous, like a man being followed. I didn't look directly at them, but back down the street, watching them out of the corner of my eye. I waited until one of them noticed me and motioned to his friend. When they were both looking at me, I moved my nervous gaze in their direction, feigning surprise and fear when I made eye contact. I remained rooted to the spot, like a rabbit in headlights, as they spoke to each other and one of them pulled out a phone, I hoped it was to tell the other two that I was the one they wanted.

I shrank back behind the pillar as they started towards me. I turned and walked at a decent pace until I was sure they would have rounded the corner and could see my bright white shirt and then ducked into a deserted alley. I stripped off the white shirt as I went and put the dark jacket on again.

The alley was narrow, dark and lined with doorways, piles of rubbish and boxes. Thirty yards in I hung the white shirt just inside a half-open door, making sure it was just visible, retraced my steps and ducked inside another dark doorway. Seconds later the men walked past silently and slowly, like a man would when creeping up on something he was intending to kill. Both had familiar curved knives in their hands. They'd seen the slither of bright white inside the doorway. Their demeanour told me all I needed to know. They weren't here to make friends.

As they crept past I stepped silently out behind them and pressed a stun gun to each of their necks simultaneously. They convulsed and dropped to the ground.

I searched each man, pocketed cash and phones, throwing away the knives. I drew one of the batons out of my pocket and flicked it open. I didn't want these men chasing me when they recovered. Four smashed kneecaps and four smashed collar bones ensured they wouldn't.

One of them was out cold, the other was groaning.I am not a cold-blooded killer, but I genuinely believe the world would be better off without men like these. There is no need for them, they bring only misery and pain. Any crime they committed in the future would be on my head. I could prevent it, right now, easily, it would take practically no effort. But I needed them alive for the moment.

I put the shirt and jacket back on, grabbed a foot of each man and dragged them towards the entrance to the alley. One remained inert, but the other was moving and in danger of making too much noise too soon. I gave him a gentle tap on the head with a baton to quiet him down and left the bodies just inside the alley.

I sauntered around a few clothing stalls. Brought a non-descript beige shirt and dark cargo trousers from one vendor. A floppy bush hat from another, a canvas shoulder bag from another.

I carried on browsing around the stalls. Keeping the mouth of the alley in sight. As I went I haggled with stall owners and brought a few items for my new bag. A bottle of water, a little food, a couple of cheap gas lighters, a knock-off Leatherman multi-tool.

I found a secluded spot and changed into my new clothes. With a floppy hat hiding the stitches on the side of my head and hands in pockets to hide the dressings I continued meandering around like a tourist.

There was still no commotion from the alley, so I ducked into a chemist and bought some pain killers, dressings, tape and antiseptic.

One, or maybe both, had recovered consciousness, their shattered bones causing them to make a lot of noise and draw attention to themselves. Uniformed tourist police rushed over and a crowd started to build. The first well intentioned attempts at first aid were met with feral screams.

The crowd was getting bigger, you couldn't enter the market square without noticing it now, I blended in and waited.

The two men currently writhing in pain had indeed called their friends upon positively identifying me ten minutes ago. It took them longer than I'd expected to get here, but there were four of them now, they'd picked up reinforcements on the way.

They entered the square, stopped and swivelled their heads back and forth like meercats. Noticing the crowd, they marched over and barged through it. I heard an anguished howl as they tried to move one of their friends.

I gravitated further into the crowd, not pushing or shoving, just moving quietly so as to get a good look at the newcomers as paramedics turned up and the crowd parted to let them in.

I stood behind a tall American and watched over his shoulder.

The paramedics caused a lot of screaming as they assessed their patients and strapped each to a gurney before wheeling them away, whereupon the crowd started to disperse.

The four men didn't pay any attention to the crowd in front of them. It never occurred to them I might be in it, so I just slipped away unnoticed with the rest of the tourists. They eyeballed the far reaches of the market, not what was right in front of them.

Joining a queue for one of the food stalls I kept my back to them and watched their fuzzy outlines in the reflective surfaces behind the counter.

They were obviously locals. Two were young and non-descript but I'd recognise them again. Two were older. One with a gaunt hatchet face and deep scarring from childhood acne. The other had a square jaw and tufts of grey at the temples. The latter seemed to be their leader, the one they deferred to.

I guessed most people on the run would instinctively head for the souk. Not that I really knew anything about people on the run, but I reckoned it was the worst thing to do. These local criminals would know the maze-like market like the back of their hands. Every alley was lined with stall holders who watched the passing tourists for a living. A man running for his life through the souk would be pretty obvious. The men following would be, quite literally, pointed in the right direction.

The men divided into pairs and headed for different entrances to the souk. The leader with one of the young men went to the north-east, the other two headed for the north-west corner.

I did my best impression of a man deciding he couldn't be bothered waiting in the queue for food and ambled off in the wake of the hatchet-faced one and entered the souk a little way behind them.

I passed from the bright sunlight into the gloom. Into a labyrinth that would spell death to a man on the run. But I wasn't on the run. This maze was to be my hunting ground, they just didn't know it yet. The attitude with which you enter a situation is everything, I'd learnt that too late last time.

They spoke to stall holders as they went. Mostly getting shakes of the head, obviously asking if they'd seen a man in a suit recently.

They didn't look back once. They were looking for a man on the run, looking forward, moving forward.

I ambled along. Slouching slightly under the baggy shirt to narrow my shoulders and reduce my height. As they stopped to question stall holders I paused and added things to my bag from whichever stall I'd paused at. Some cord from one, a pair of cheap compact binoculars from another. I disposed of the suit jacket, shirt and trousers and replaced them in the bag with fake Levi's, a couple of shirts, baseball cap, cotton scarf and fake Ray-Bans. My wad of cash took a bit of a beating.

Once or twice I got a bit close and had to carry on past them as to stop suddenly would have looked wrong. They didn't even look at me when they moved on. I had by now acquired assorted items in my shoulder bag including a glass bottle of lamp oil. I pretty much lost my bearings. I reckoned we were not far from the leather tanning area of the souk, judging by the smell. The alleys were wider, there were fewer stalls and less people.

I was conscious of the time, for all I knew they'd called in a small army to scour the market for me. Besides, my feet were killing me, I felt like I was walking on broken glass. I couldn't keep this up for ever.

We entered a short alley that was empty of people, I picked up my pace and simply pressed the stun gun to the back of the younger man's neck with one hand and swung the baton, back handed, at the hatchet-faced man's head. The young guy twitched and dropped. The older man stayed on his feet. My blow had lacked real power being a short back hand. I corrected that and was pretty sure the second blow had killed him. I only needed one of them alive, the younger one was my first choice, he was probably more tech-savvy and I needed him to make a phone call.

I dragged them down a side alley, the backs of my fingers protesting and various stitches pulling, but none ripped. I searched them both. Taking cash and the hatchet-faced man's mobile. I smashed the younger man's kneecaps and left collar bone. His right hand and forearm were more developed, and his mobile was in a pocket on the same side, so I left his right collarbone intact and the phone where it was.

I'd dropped them where the roof on one side of the alley was only one storey high. I climbed up on to the flat roof where the usual Marrakesh roof top paraphernalia was lying around. I picked up a broom and moved a plastic chair over to the wall above the bodies below. Breathing a sigh of relief as I took the weight off my feet I popped a couple of painkillers with a swig of water and set to work.

I placed the glass bottle of lamp oil, a lighter, a rubber band and a telescopic baton on the low wall. Using the fake Leatherman I removed the head from the broom handle and leant over the wall to check the length. I sat back down and took out the two stun guns and checked the little screens, the tiny battery icons showed fifty percent left, which would do, so lashed them both securely to the end of the broom handle. Cutting a length of the Elastoplast tape I'd bought at the chemist I wrapped it loosely around buttons that activated them, then double checked everything and settled down to wait.

After a while the young one started groaning below, then made a phone call. Before long I heard the other two men run in to the alley. I silently peeked over the low wall.

The square-jawed leader and the other man, summoned by the injured young man's phone call. I moved directly above the four of them, keeping out of sight.

The lighters I had bought were of the cheap, disposable, pressurised jet-flame type. When you pressed the little black button down on top the gas came out under pressure, so you got a small, hot cone of flame. I stretched a rubber band from one end of the lighter to the other to hold it on. I held the glass bottle of lamp oil over the alley and smashed it with the baton.

Dropping the remains of the bottle I picked up the lighter and tossed it after the oil.

The lighter reached the oil as the oil reached the men and a sheet of flame engulfed them. I tightly reapplied the piece of tape around the two stun guns lashed to the pole and they crackled into life. I leant over the low wall and prodded each man with my six-foot long, improvised, cattle prod as they furiously danced in the flames. The stun guns soon sizzled out, batteries exhausted, but they'd done their job. Four bodies lay smouldering in the alley below.

I swung my legs over the low wall around the roof and, bracing myself for the bolt of pain from my feet, dropped to the ground. After smashing a few more kneecaps and collarbones with the baton, I hauled the leader up over my shoulder and walked off.

Chapter 14

Once I was well away from the smoking bodies I found a deserted-looking building and shoved open the door, a glance told me it hadn't been occupied for some time. It could have been a small workshop, piles of rubbish and a sturdy work bench being the only furniture. Not much light filtered in through the boarded-up windows.

I tied the man to the bench with old rope scavenged from the piles of rubbish. I took a long swig of water from a bottle then emptied the rest on his face. Compared to the other sensations he'd endured recently, being burnt and stunned, I wouldn't have thought a bit of water would have much effect, but he came to, spluttering.

He looked around the gloom, realised he was restrained and struggled violently. He froze when he saw me in the shadows, made angry noises behind his gag, strained at his restraints then fell still, glaring.

I walked slowly towards him, expressionless, with empty eyes and hopefully looking more than a little disturbing.

I spoke very, very quietly, which I've always thought more menacing than shouting and screaming.

"Can you speak English?" I moved the gag so he could answer.

He just glared at me.

"If you do not speak English you are no use to me," I stated simply.

He just sneered back at me, I replaced the gag and gave his left kneecap a good thwack with the baton.

I asked the question again, he sneered again, thwack.

I didn't have the time or the desire to go through all his two-hundred-and-six bones, one at a time, pausing to ask a question after each one, so I figured I'd just keep going till he stopped me. After the kneecaps I carried on to other bones, nothing too serious, tibia, fibula, ulna, radius, a few ribs, nothing that would kill him. I tried to look like I was enjoying my work and he didn't hold out for long.

I removed the gag.

"What were your orders?" I asked quietly.

He stared at me with all the hate in the world. "Kill you," he spat.

That was good, it meant I wasn't being unjustifiably hard on them.

"Who do you work for?"

"Don't know."

I raised the baton.

"No. No. Don't know. Call come from London. London all I know," he spat in stilted English. "London call, then cash come."

"How does it come?"

"Package. Address on. Nothing else."

London, that was interesting, but otherwise a dead end. But I needed one other question answered, for my own conscience.

"Were they your men at the beach?"

He stared at me with pure venom and nodded.

"Their orders?"

"Kill you," he snarled. "Tourist attack." I assumed by that he meant to make it look like a random attack on tourists for their valuables, or worse. We wouldn't have been the first and we wouldn't have been the last. Open and closed case.

"And the girl?" I asked.

"Didn't know about girl."

I stood beside him and looked into his eyes. The answer to this question would have a profound effect on his lifespan, but I didn't inform him of that. "What would have happened to the girl?"

He didn't answer. Didn't need to. The eyes told me all I needed to know, the corner of his mouth twitched up in a sneer or a smile, I couldn't be sure which. I replaced the gag.

None of the injuries I'd inflicted were life-threatening. He'd recover within a month and carry on doing what men like him do.

I looked down on him. "For all you have done, and all that you will do."

I saw the hate in his eyes change to fear, the same fear his victims must have felt.

Afterwards, the room was silent as I changed into the new jeans, shirt and hat. I tossed the old clothes in a corner as I walked out, pulling the door closed behind me. I wasn't worried about leaving evidence, it was a bit late for that. The only thing now was to get out of the country, but I wanted to check something first, just in case.

I headed east. Twenty minutes later I had to take the weight off my feet. The guard's shoes felt like they were full of warm water. It was blood, of course. From all the little cuts on the soles of my feet from the other night being aggravated. I didn't really want to leave a trail of bloody footprints, so found a quiet corner to sit down out of view. Pulling the shoes, socks and blood-soaked dressings off my feet almost brought a tear to my eye. I mopped out the shoes as best I could. Re-dressing my feet with the supplies I bought from the chemist earlier in the day and forcing the shoes back on. It was lucky they were black leather. Anything else might have shown up the blood. I popped a couple more pain killers before turning my attention to my hands. Keeping them in my pockets when around people wasn't always going to be an option. And the blackened, blistered skin was too memorable. I used the Leatherman to cut dressings to the right size and held them in place with lots of flesh-coloured Elastoplast tape.

I continued on my way rummaging through my bag and pockets as I went. Doing a stock check. A substantial roll of cash went into one pocket, seems the criminals here liked a bit of cash to flash. I checked each mobile phone, but none were what I needed. They were all cheap, not-very-smart phones. I stripped out SIM cards and batteries, disposing of them as I went.

I was heading in the general direction of the Ville Nouvelle, where the bus and train stations were. I wasn't going to use either, too obvious. The airport was also a non-starter, I didn't have the skills, knowledge or contacts to obtain false passports or plane tickets. I could loiter around the departures area in the hopes of finding someone looking similar to myself and relieve them of their passport and ticket. But that wasn't a great option, I wasn't a pick pocket, and there was a lot that could go wrong and cameras everywhere.

Logic dictated I had to go north and try to cross into Europe. Tangiers being the obvious choice. From there try and cross the straits of Gibraltar. Otherwise, there was the rest of the north coast of Africa. No shortage of people trying to cross the Mediterranean. I could lose myself amongst the thousands of refugees making the same journey. Although this was not without its risks, the news was rife with images of overloaded, capsized boats and dead bodies washing up on beaches around the Mediterranean. Many of these boats were intercepted by the authorities before they made landfall anyway.

North by road then. Hitchhiking wasn't a great option. Standing at the side of a northbound road with my thumb out?

Steal a car and drive north? A possibility. But not without its risks and I'd still need to cross the water into Europe.

Hide in a lorry or commercial vehicle? Probably my best option for going north, but that's what every migrant would think and the first place police and border control would look.

Nearing the Ville Nouveau the buildings were newer, taller, and in a good state of repair. The roads were all tarmac, wide and lined with newer cars. The shops and the average person on the street looked more affluent.

I checked my reflection in a shop window. Considering what I had been up to today I half expected to look like some blood-soaked maniac, but I looked pretty normal.

I singled out a likely looking café. Reasonably busy, plenty of younger people, inside and outside seating and no cameras that I could see. I took a stool at a high table with a good view of the whole scene and ordered a large glass of water, a couple of paninis and coffee.

My thoughts turned to the police. Were all police officers armed as standard these days in Marrakesh? So how much force was it reasonable for me to use in avoiding capture? After all they were just doing their job. As far as they were concerned I was a confirmed murderer.

Between the beach, the hospital and the market this afternoon I guessed I'd killed or assaulted, in various ways, thirteen people in roughly four days. And I'd been unconscious for three of the days.

With a body count like that, they'd probably shoot me on sight. Which was a problem, in more than the obvious way, as my slightly warped moral compass wouldn't allow me to harm them, too much.

I wondered if I'd made it on to the news? Twitter? The possibilities in today's online world were endless.

My order appeared.

I sipped coffee and scanned the café, noticing a couple of things. Most people used a six-digit number to unlock their phone and people still smoked in cafés in Morocco.

I'd spotted a young woman seated near the bar but facing the street, who picked up her phone every ten seconds, without fail, to respond to a beep or send a message.

I finished my coffee and walked to the back of the café, which allowed me to have a good look around, and bought a pack of cigarettes and a box of matches along with another coffee from the girl behind the bar.

Leaning against the bar I turned a little towards the room so I could see the screen of her smart phone when she held it in front of her, but her fingers were too fast to catch her PIN.

I had to order another coffee and fake smoke two cigarettes in the time it took her to pick up and unlock her phone enough that I was sure I had her code.

Whilst waiting I'd torn the end off the box of matches, folded up the small length of cardboard and slipped it down beside the matches in the box to act as a kind of leaf-spring. Taking the cigarette, which was about one third depleted, I pushed the filter end in amongst the matches. Held there securely. Leaning over the bar I picked up a paperclip that was lying in a shallow bowl amongst other miscellanea beside the till and pocketed it.

Walking unhurriedly towards the bathrooms in the back, holding the match box and a bunch of napkins in one hand, I dropped the lot through a swing-bin lid as I passed.

Carrying on to the toilets I entered one and slid the bolt to. I stood there for maybe thirty seconds, listening. There'd been maybe an inch of cigarette to burn down before it set off the matches.

Leaving the toilet, I took out a phone and studied it carefully, head down, walking slowly. Still nothing. I stopped and leant against a wall, intently studying the blank phone screen.

At last a faint wisp of smoke curled out from the swinging lid of the bin. I left it a bit longer hoping the fire would really take hold.

"Fire!" I heard someone shout, slightly hesitantly.

The bin didn't disappoint. As I flipped the lid off the air hit the fire with a whump and an impressive cloud of smoke rolled out. I stood back quickly, knocking into a table with a young lady sitting at it, lost my balance and tipped it over.

I scrambled to my feet and as people stampeded for the door amid shouts of "fire!" and even a couple of, "bomb!" which really got people moving. I went behind the bar to get a fire extinguisher I'd spotted earlier, pulled the safety pin and sprayed it liberally all over the café, which speeded up the exodus nicely.

I made sure to actually put the fire out before leaving by the emergency exit down the same corridor as the toilets, changing my shirt and hat on the way, I left the scene of my latest misdemeanour.

Pulling out the iPhone that I'd palmed as I toppled over the table I walked away and entered her code, the screen unlocked. I turned the phone off, straightened the stolen paperclip to poke in the tiny hole that pops the SIM card out. I replaced it with the one from my old phone that had sat in my wallet all this time and turned it back on.

The woman I'd swiped the phone off was young and, judging by the speed she typed, well acquainted with modern technology. I guessed she'd be up on the various apps with which you could lock your phone remotely in the event it was stolen. Whether they would work without your SIM card in your phone I wasn't sure, but I couldn't take the risk. I hoped by overturning the table and creating a stampede she might waste some time searching for her phone before declaring it missing in action and locking it remotely.

I stared at the screen, willing it to work. *Come on.*

The usual icons appeared, I let out my breath and scrolled back to the day my phone screen got smashed back in Scotland. To when I could hear the beeps of messages coming in but couldn't get them. I read the messages as though James had sent me the very meaning of life itself. Or the meaning of his death. I tended to look at emails on my Mac, but SMS, WhatsApp and so on came only to my old phone, which I hadn't looked at since the screen got smashed around the time of James's death. So, I scrolled through old, unread messages with some intensity.

"Oh, James," I sighed.

I extracted the SIM card, slipping it back in my wallet, then smashed the phone against a railing as, rounding the corner of a building, I bumped into an assault rifle.

Chapter 15

The assault rifle was strapped across the chest of a surprised looking policeman, he wasn't pointing it at me. Not yet. The man next to him was identically equipped. Both had handguns on their belts and body armour.

I instinctively took a step back.

I wondered if an apology and a quick getaway would work. We were far enough away from the café that they weren't aware of the commotion there and they seemed relaxed, they'd just been walking along.

The man I bumped in to looked me in the eye and whether he saw something there or recognised me from a photograph or description I didn't know, but as one, they started raising their hands to their weapons.

I stepped forward, clamped my hands on the man's weapon directly in front and gave a vicious shove. His upper body flew back until the sling came tight across his back, I yanked him back toward me and slammed the compact machine gun up, snapping his head back. Then slammed the gun butt to my right, connecting solidly with the second man's temple before he was able to swing his weapon around to point at me.

They both went down, but my dilemma now was whether to take their weapons. To do so was putting myself firmly in the shoot-on-sight category, as far as the police were concerned.

But I didn't want to leave them able to shoot me, I leant down and pulled out one handgun. Ejecting the magazine and locating the disassembly lever I pulled the slide off and tossed it away, removed the spring and barrel and threw them in different directions before dropping the remaining part of the handgun on the pavement, so they'd know I didn't take it.

I didn't want to waste time locating the relevant pins and levers to disassemble the unfamiliar machine guns. I just stuck each muzzle through the bars of a drain cover in the road, using my body weight to hold in place I forced each gun over. When I dropped the weapons next to the policemen the end of each barrel was almost comically bent at nearly ninety degrees.

It had taken less than two minutes to render two policemen and four weapons useless. I was feeling quite pleased with my efficiency when I heard shouting from the main street as two more policemen came around the corner and clocked the scene, which was me standing over two prostrate policemen.

They raised their weapons.

I ducked behind the corner and heard a volley of bullets hitting the wall where I'd been.

So much for not shooting me on sight if I wasn't armed.

I ran, wishing I'd kept the guns.

The adrenalin kept the pain at bay, but even then, I was nowhere near my normal top speed, which wasn't very fast anyway.

Angling towards the main road I found myself on the pavement of a busy street next to an older man sitting astride an idling moped at the kerb, chatting to a man on the pavement.

I gently lifted him off the seat and placed him on the pavement, he was too surprised to object.

"Sorry," I said, straddling his moped and twisting the throttle as the policemen burst on to the street behind.

I twisted the throttle as far as it would go and the moped gradually picked up speed as I weaved in and out of the traffic. I crouched down low, tucking in my knees and elbows to reduce the wind resistance, which had no discernible effect on my speed.

I heard sirens behind me. I wasn't going to outrun anyone on this moped, but it had given me a bit of breathing space. I carried on at its top speed of about thirty miles an hour, scanning left and right looking for better options.

I passed a junction and spotted my better option at the front of the waiting traffic on the other side of the road. I made a wobbly U-turn, amid much honking, and weaved my way through the stationary traffic, coming to stop next to a gleaming red motorbike with Ducati on the fairing.

The rider in black leather wore a futuristic-looking helmet with a tinted visor. I couldn't see the eyes, but the helmet turned my way, slowly looked my moped and me up and down, then looked away again in dismissal.

Kicking out the moped's stand I hopped off it and on to the Ducati behind the rider. The bike was idling in neutral and the rider was sitting with his hands on the handlebars. I wouldn't be able to dislodge him if he had a good grip, so I gave him a quick jab under both sides of his rib cage at the same time, not hard enough to do any damage, but enough so he instinctively let go of the handlebars and brought his arms back to protect his rib cage. As he did so I hauled him off his seat and dumped him on the road, not nearly as gently as I'd displaced the old man from his moped.

Sliding forward I took the handlebars and in one fluid movement depressed the clutch with my left hand, snicked the machine into first with my left foot, and with a twist of my right hand shot off the mark weaving through the traffic crossing the junction in front. First, second, third, fourth, the gear changes as quick as that, and within seconds left any pursuit far behind. Taking sharp turns at high speed with my knee down, practically fused to the high performance machine as I streaked through Marrakech in a red blur.

At least, that's how I'd planned it.

I did slide forward on the seat, grab the handlebars, put the bike in first gear and twist the throttle. But it had been a good few years since I'd ridden a motorbike, and even then, it had been mostly small engine scramblers. Nothing remotely like this.

The power caught me completely off guard as I twisted the throttle. The rear wheel span with a high-pitched scream, suddenly caught traction and nearly ripped my arms out of their sockets as the bike took off under me. The front wheel lifted and all I could do was hang on as it shot through the traffic crossing in front of me doing a wheelie. I got so close to a bus it ripped off a rear indicator. The bike veered into the oncoming traffic, still on one wheel, cars and mopeds dodged left and right.

My weight was so far back I couldn't physically untwist my hand on the throttle, and I couldn't let go, instinct wouldn't let me. I was past the point of no return and falling backwards when I managed to get two fingers around the brake lever on the handlebars and pull it as hard as I could, which did absolutely nothing. I recalled at that same instant the rear brake was operated by the right foot and stomped on it as hard as I could. The result was instantaneous. The brakes were as fierce as the acceleration and the rear wheel stopped dead, causing the front wheel to come crashing down to the road like a sledgehammer.

The front wheel slammed down with so much force I smacked my chest into the tank and my face into the instrument panel. The bike stalled and fell to one side.

I managed to plant my legs and catch the bike before it hit the road and stood there in the middle of the oncoming traffic with horns blaring and lots of abuse coming my way. My head hurt, again, and blood was streaming down the side of my face from a split eyebrow.

I may have slightly underestimated the power of a modern superbike.

The sirens were closing in behind me.

Starting the bike and slipping it into first I gently, very gently, twisted the throttle and took off smoothly. Moving up the gears cautiously, getting a feel for the bike. After a few blocks I shifted my weight to one side and made a reasonable turn. Straightening up, I crouched low and forward over the tank and opened her up just a bit. The front wheel stayed on the road and I gradually increased my overall speed as I gained in confidence and familiarity with the machine, soon enough I was enjoying myself.

A few minutes later I was halfway across Marrakech, with no real idea where I was going, on broad quiet roads around a beautifully landscaped park area to the south of the centre. I was just allowing myself to think I was well clear of the police and had slowed down to blend into the traffic when a pair of police motorcycles cruised past on the other side of the road.

I'd wiped the blood off my face and my eyebrow had stopped bleeding, so I thought I looked pretty normal and kept my eyes on the road ahead as I passed them. Seconds went by and I was feeling confident when I heard sirens blare into life behind me as the policemen performed a pair of perfectly executed U-turns and accelerated swiftly through the traffic to came up either side of me on enormous white BMW motorbikes, with large panniers and flashing lights. They handled their big machines with a practised nonchalance. The rider close on my right gestured for me to pull over.

With a sigh and a visible drop to my shoulders I raised a hand and nodded my head to indicate compliance, then lashed out my right foot and gave his handlebars a good kick. The big bike went down with a crash. We weren't going fast and he was wearing full leathers, so he wouldn't be hurt.

I veered to my left but the other rider was too quick and jinked out of range. Glancing back, I saw the first man stand up and try to haul the big BMW upright without success.

The second rider hung back, watching. He was older, maybe fifty, with an inscrutable expression. We were at a stalemate. He couldn't physically stop me and knew it, but he had a radio mic in front of his mouth, he just had to keep me in sight and relay my position to others who, sooner or later, would corner me. I couldn't let that happen. I gave him an apologetic shrug, hoped neither of us would get hurt and threw my body weight forward, opening the throttle to the stops again. Flicking up the gears I topped one hundred and fifty kilometres an hour before braking to take a large roundabout. Straightening up on a section of dual carriageway I focused on maintaining speed, throwing the bike hard over from side to side while looking as far ahead as I could to anticipate the traffic.

The motorcycle policeman stayed on my tail without any apparent effort, which was disconcerting as I had the faster, nimbler bike. He was just a much better rider than I was, that was all there was to it. Different tactics were needed.

Spotting a narrow road coming up on my left I slowed ever so slightly to let him come closer. When he was as close as I dared I threw my weight back and braked as hard as I could without being flung off the front of the bike. The rear wheel lifted, I feathered the front brake to prevent cartwheeling. The police motorbike shot past me, braking hard, as I dropped the rear wheel to the ground and threw my body weight far to my left to make the sharp turn.

The big BMW had lost ground by the time he'd made a U-turn and followed me but wasn't as far behind as I would have thought. I turned in to progressively narrower and narrower side streets using the smaller, lighter bike to my advantage.

Shouting at people to get out of the way and with the horn blaring constantly I scattered locals and tourists alike during my dash around the back streets and alleys. At one point the alleys became so narrow and congested I often couldn't make the corners in one go. My bike's smaller size paid dividends as I could manhandle it round the sharp corners and obstacles, often without dismounting. The big BMW had to shuffle back and forth in three- and four-point turns. The distance between us grew.

In the narrowest alleys I resorted to tipping over bins and stacks of pallets, rubbish, boxes and basically anything I passed, to slow up the man behind. Nothing stopped him, he was relentless.

Just as I thought I was creating some distance between us I accelerated around a corner into a busload of tourists. I slammed on the brakes, lifting the rear wheel up again as I tried desperately to stop in time.

Slowing, but not fast enough. I pulled the front brake harder, the rear wheel lifting dangerously high.

An elderly woman at the rear of the group was frozen in place, staring open-mouthed at my approach. My front wheel came to a squealing stop just touching the hem of her skirt. Tipped up on the front wheel my nose nearly touched hers before the rear fell back to the ground.

We stared at each other in relief.

I manoeuvred the bike through the crowd at snail's pace. "Sorry. Thank you," I apologised and chivvied them out of the way as I went.

Behind me I could hear the same thing happening to the police rider. He had the advantage of a uniform and flashing lights, the crowd got out of his way faster, but his bike was twice the width of mine, with the fairings and panniers, so in the narrow alley people had to actually squeeze past it.

We were now in a slightly surreal, super-slow chase. Both moving through the crowd at the same snail's pace about twenty yards apart.

I kept up my running apology as I went and finally broke out the front of the crowd, gunned the engine and shot off.

There were more and more market stalls. I had completely lost my sense of direction by now, but I knew I didn't want to be here. I took a left and planned to take a couple more. The motorcycle cop was far enough behind that he was just turning in to an alley as I was leaving it. I took another left and passed a stall on wheels piled high with baskets and bowls of colourful spices. I screeched to a halt, hopped off the bike and dragged the stall around so it was wedged across the alley just after the corner.

"Sorry," I said to the irate stallholder. Giving him some of the cash from the roll in my pocket.

I sped off just as I heard a muffled crash from behind. Looking over my shoulder all I could see was a multicoloured cloud of powder filling the alley.

I wound my way back out from the old town and on to broader streets, flashing past a police car which turned on its sirens and gave chase but soon fell behind. I was heading north and wondering where to go from here when I saw a multicoloured motorcycle and rider coming in at right angles from my left trailing a colourful cloud of powder, like a pastel comet. The police car would have radioed in my heading and the motorcycle cop had second-guessed me. He joined the road I was on a hundred yards behind me.

I was fast running out of options, the number of police cars was growing, I couldn't scream around the city on a bright red bike much longer without being cornered or crashing. And I was going to run out of fuel at some point. I spotted a flyover for the motorway coming up. I reckoned a motorway was just a long thin trap, all they had to do was set up a roadblock somewhere ahead. But I couldn't lose this police motorbike, so I had to try something. I flicked the bike over and accelerated up the on-ramp. The police motorbike a hundred yards behind, police cars way further back.

Once on the motorway, heading north, I opened her up as far as I dared. I couldn't see the speedo, my eyes were watering with the wind, and I was very aware I was wearing no protective gear. If I came off the bike now, I'd be a long red smear on the hot tarmac.

I had driven this motorway in the opposite direction a month ago. I knew the first junction was some way north of Marrakech, maybe as much as twenty kilometres. The police should have no problem making a roadblock there.

The motorway had substantial barriers between the north and southbound carriageways and on each side. When I was roughly halfway between the city and the first junction I pulled in next to the central barrier and killed the engine. The big police BMW had a lower top speed than the Ducati so had finally fallen back.

I heaved the bike over the central reservation. It was heavy, very heavy, and awkward. The engine and exhaust were red-hot. In a gap in the oncoming traffic I wheeled the bike over the other carriageway and heaved it over the next barrier. Straddling the bike and starting her up I glanced back at the motorcycle policeman standing motionless on the far side of the central reservation. There was not a chance the average-sized Moroccan policeman could heave the big BMW over it, as I had done with the smaller, lighter sports bike. His only options were ten kilometres in either direction. I gave him a slight nod before rolling down the dry, compact dirt of the embankment on to a graded road which took me away from the motorway.

Back on the outskirts of the city I entered an area of quiet suburbs and industrial buildings. I pulled into a row of deserted-looking business units and rolled up to a door that looked like it hadn't been opened in a long time, gave it a nudge with the front tyre and rolled the bike in. I killed the engine and with regret covered the bright red bike with an old tarpaulin. I gave it a pat, closed the door and walked away.

Now I was back on my feet the pain returned with a vengeance. I flagged down a passing taxi and hopped in. I needed some distance between the bike and whatever vehicle I stole next. Which turned out to be another bike, an old 125cc scrambler, a simple vehicle that looked like a thousand others on the roads. Unlikely to be reported stolen as I was probably the fifteenth illegal owner. Like most of the motorbikes around here it didn't have a number plate, and when I rocked it the sloshing in the tank told me it was nearly full.

Motorbikes are ridiculously easy to hot-wire, especially old ones without steering locks. Locate the wires coming out of the back of the ignition barrel, probably four. Strip the sheath off the red and black ones and twist them together. You can ignore the green wire because it's the earth, and the black wire with the white strip is the kill wire, touch it to the entwined red and black wires to stop the engine. Simple as. Even if you don't know the colour coding a little trial and error will get you going in no time.

But where to go, all logic still dictated north, it was the obvious option.

The canvas bag was still slung over my shoulders holding various things, including a road map now. I rumbled along on the well-worn tyres at a steady fifty kilometres an hour, a comfortable speed on this skinny motorbike, and settled in for the long night ahead.

Chapter 16

The next morning, I was sitting under the awning of an Italian-style café overlooking Agadir's marina. Two-hundred-and-sixty kilometres south-west of Marrakech, on Morocco's Atlantic coastline, sipping a very welcome espresso.

I had ridden the skinny scrambler all night, only stopping now and then to siphon fuel out of cars. Reaching Agadir early this morning I'd ridden around the deserted streets until I came across a decent-looking hotel not far from the centre of the town. It was a nice enough little place. No CCTV cameras and happy to take cash. But mainly it was laid out in such a way you didn't have to go through the reception to get to your room. After paying in cash, I went shopping.

During a much-needed shower I unwrapped the blood-encrusted dressings on my feet then set about dying my hair, which is not something I'd done before. Dark brown normally, an hour later and I was a kind of streaky, dirty blonde which contrasted a bit with the weeks' worth of stubble on my face so I had a very close shave. Filling my newly blondish locks with hair wax I styled it to hide the stitches on the side of my head.

I cleaned and dressed my feet and the backs of my fingers. Carefully applying the flesh-coloured Elastoplast tape to my fingers to look as natural as possible.

Donning a pair of tan chinos, a slim leather belt, cotton shirt, deck shoes and Panama hat, all fake designer stuff, I studied myself in the mirror and concluded I didn't look much like me and was confident I could walk around Agadir without a problem. No one would be looking for me here anyway, as I was almost exactly in the opposite direction that anyone with any sense in my position would be heading.

I swallowed more than the recommend number of painkillers and gathered up all the rubbish, leaving the room as empty as I'd found it.

A second espresso and it was time to tour the marina, all four hundred by three hundred metres of it, with the entrance in the south-east corner protected by a long breakwater. The other three sides of the marina had a broad promenade lined with shops, restaurants and bars at street level and high-end holiday apartments above.

There were maybe a hundred recreational boats in the marina, half were sail boats, the rest power boats, ranging from gin palaces to RIBs, like my deceased RIB, but smarter.

I wasn't much of a sailor; as a kid we'd had an old mirror dinghy that we used to sail around the loch below our cottage. As an adult I'd cruised around the Hebrides on friends' yachts now and then, but always with competent sailors in charge. I reckoned I could handle a single masted yacht up to thirty feet long, which narrowed down the choice in front of me to about a dozen. The next requirement was a proper yacht, something with all the necessary equipment for a long voyage, not a weekend playboat. That narrowed it down further. I could see a few possibilities and one of them was well placed for a quick getaway near the mouth of the marina. I couldn't tell what the hull was made of from this distance. Steel would be nice, GRP acceptable, anything flimsier was a non-starter.

She looked like she'd been lying there for a long time. Nothing on the deck and the mast and boom were bare. Just sun-bleached fenders protecting her and faded lines securing her to the floating gangway.

The first obstacle was the locked gate to get on the floating gangway. It was a large fan shaped creation of metal rods, designed so that people couldn't climb around it. The lock looked like a simple mechanical combination pad with a handle underneath. The whole thing more of a deterrent than anything because anyone could just swim out to the boats beyond it anyway.

I went for a slow walk along the dockside and had a good look at the gate as I passed, then stopped in a gift shop and bought a few things.

Back at the gate I positioned my body to hide my right hand passing through the bars and pushing the Leatherman's flat screwdriver blade in the gap between the door and the frame. As my other hand pushed numbers on the keypad, I pushed the spring-loaded latch into the lock and swung it open.

I strode confidently down the gangway to the yacht, looking like I owned it. Her name was *Sandpiper* and her home port was Portsmouth. Up close she looked and felt abandoned. If so, she might not be missed for a while. I guessed she'd been bought, sailed down here, maybe the first leg of an Atlantic crossing, and the owners realised sailing wasn't for them and flew home.

Stepping on board I had a good look at the fittings, winches, cleats, fairleads, chain plates, mast and stays. Everything was covered in a fine layer of dust or sand and more than a few seagull droppings. I crouched at the hatch to the companion way and pulled out one of the hair clips I'd bought at the gift shop, folded out the thin, flat, prong-like clasp and used it to shimmy up the pins in the barrel of the lock while applying torque with the Leatherman's tin opener blade.

It smelt musty inside but looked OK. I paused in the companionway for a while but heard no shouts. I had a quick look through the small cabin, galley and seating area then the compact engine bay under the cockpit.

I didn't know a whole lot about yachts. Most of my experience at sea was on large commercial vessels like construction barges, dive support vessels or salvage boats. The yacht looked good superficially, but I wanted to be sure, so I set about a thorough inspection of the little craft.

I took up every floorboard and piece of furniture I could to inspect the steel hull. The was a small puddle of scummy water in the bilges which had been sitting there for some time, judging by the well-defined line of green stuff around the edges, which meant there was no active leaks. The interior of the hull was clean, uncorroded and the plates were all neatly welded.

I checked and started the little engine to power up the systems. Electrics, water, bilge pumps, de-salination plant, radio, GPS, depth finder. I checked everything and found them fit for purpose. The little forward cabin in the bows acted as the sail locker with bags marked Main, Storm Jib, Spinnaker and so on. The fuel and water tanks weren't full, but I could remedy that.

There was a lot more I could and should check, but the basics were there so I wanted to buy some supplies and get underway. I'd work out the details as I went.

Chapter 17

It was blessedly cooler at sea than on land, *Sandpiper* was making six knots running in front of a south-westerly wind that had remained steady for days.

I was sitting with one hand draped over the wheel making small adjustments. The waves were substantial but a long way apart, the motion was relatively gentle.

I'd discovered the desalination unit was more of a backup unit than a primary source of drinking water, so I was rationing the remaining water, which meant doing as little as possible in the heat of the day.

The first couple of days had been nerve-wracking while I got used to the boat, convinced the Moroccan Navy and Coastguard would be bearing down on me at any moment.

But it turns out it is surprisingly easy to steal a yacht. After a couple of shopping runs, I'd started up the small engine, cast off, and puttered out of Agadir's marina in the late afternoon.

That was it, no dramas at all.

The waters around Agadir and Essaouira had been busy with small fishing vessels and as I sailed on through the night it required a constant watch and therefore not much sleep.

That was a while ago now and *Sandpiper* had made good time, much better than I deserved, considering my limited sailing knowledge.

There had been only one dodgy night when the weather got up and I was forced to reef in the main sail and jib. A more experienced sailor would no doubt have made better use of the stronger winds, but I had to play it safe and reduce the sail area to ride out the heavy weather.

I had fallen into a routine of sleeping in the cockpit with an alarm clock I'd found set to go off every hour when I would check the horizon with the binoculars, check my position on the GPS and plot it on the chart. All being well I would settle back down for another hour's cat nap. In this manner I'd caught up on missed sleep and felt hugely better for it while keeping moving twenty-four hours a day.

To begin with I'd been moving about the boat on all fours to keep the soles of my feet out of contact with anything. They were healing well and the last of the scabs fell off to reveal pink and tender skin underneath. It was harder not to use my hands, but they were healing ok.

In a calm spell I'd juggled a shaving mirror and the fake Leatherman to remove the various stitches, I was glad they used stitches and not staples. It had taken a while and a lot of swearing to remove some of the more awkward ones.

The days passed and if it weren't for the reason I was having to sail back to the UK, I would have enjoyed it. The days got longer as we travelled north and the wind stayed favourable, *Sandpiper* made good progress. I had read every sailing manual and instruction book on the boat and was gaining in confidence in handling the yacht. In the cooler hours of darkness, I was now taking as much exercise as I could on a small boat, which was mainly squats, sit-ups, press-ups and pull-ups on the boom.

Sailing back to the UK was a double-edged sword. I needed the time to heal, but I felt I was also wasting time. Getting back to the UK any other way would have been problematic, so I felt this was still the best option.

With time on my hands I thought a lot. Every person, every event was replayed in my head repeatedly. I called up and scrutinised every memory of each person I encountered. The faces, expressions, dress, mannerisms, demeanour, motives. But I simply didn't have enough to go on. It all hinged on what I'd find at home, if anything. And then there was Jessica, another unknown.

Three in the morning, *Sandpiper* and I were in the Celtic Sea, due south of Cork on the same latitude as the north-west tip of France. One hundred and fifty nautical miles to go until my first planned landfall in the UK.

It was a starless night and the seas had picked up as the forecast force eight gale materialised. I'd raised the storm main and jib in preparation, but all my newfound confidence suddenly dissipated in the face of gale force winds and waves. I felt distinctly inexperienced and could only hope it wouldn't get worse.

I'd been seeing the navigation lights of enormous commercial vessels passing far in front as they came and went from the English Channel. Even from this distance I could tell they were vast, creating mammoth bow waves which travel out for some distance, it was one of these that caught me out as the sea opened up and swallowed my boat.

I was wedged in the corner of the cockpit, eyes closed, dozing five minutes after my usual checks, which I'd shortened to every fifteen minutes with the channel coming up and the weather deteriorating.

The whole boat dropped, leaving me momentarily weightless. The bow reared up to near vertical as the wave's face caught us then dropped till the bow pointed straight down. Our forward momentum and the wind in the sails pushed the yacht past the vertical, she about to crash down on her deck. The mast would snap like a twig, likely wrecking the deck and cabin roof too. It was called pitchpoling, I'd read about it in one of the sailing manuals I'd found on board.

She corkscrewed slightly, which saved us, instead of pitchpoling she took the face of the next wave on the starboard rail. We were carried along pinned fast to the face of the wave, half-buried in it.

Unable to hold myself in the cockpit, the force of the water had hauled me forward over the cabin roof, I'd wrapped an arm around the foot of the mast and was hanging tight.

We started to slide down the back side of the wave, as the mass of water sheltered us from the wind the ballast in the bottom of the hull overcame the force acting on the sails and we started to right ourselves. I naively thought we were in the clear and started to make my way back to the cockpit on all fours.

But a boat that's heeled all the way over to one side doesn't just come nicely upright, it rolls straight past the vertical and almost as far over the other way.

The next wave caught us broadside and she was forced further over. When she went far enough the mainsail was pushed under water, the forces acting on the mast and sail would be enormous. It wouldn't survive much of this and even though my knowledge of sailing was basic, I knew I needed a mast.

The mainsail and jib were banging and tearing, mast bending crazily, lines were snaking about everywhere. I needed to get the sails down, but there was no way I could drop them properly, so clinging on to the deck as green water rolled over me I hauled the Leatherman out of a pocket and started cutting ropes and sails before *Sandpiper* lost her mast. In the darkness and the confusion I couldn't tell what was what, so just cut everything. It was the storm jib and mainsails I was cutting away, I still had the normal jib and main down below.

At one point the main sail ended up wrapped around the boat like a huge straitjacket with me pinned underneath. As I cut myself out the blade snapped, so I carried on with the saw blade, then pliers until both the boat and I were free of the sails and the motion of the yacht settled.

I crawled back to the cockpit, said a prayer to the patron saint of inept sailors and pushed the button to start the little engine. It coughed. I gave it a few seconds, and a few swear words, then tried again.

Put, put, put, it came to life. I turned the bows in to the oncoming waves and put a stop to the crazy broadside rolling.

The mast was still there. Ragged holes in the deck planks showed where some cleats and fairleads had been ripped out. The boom, like the mast, was made of extruded aluminium and was intact but a little bit bent.

The weather deteriorated through the night. Waves steepened, and the visibility reduced to nothing in the rain. There seemed to be huge vessels everywhere, coming and going from the channel. But my first encounter with these monsters had taught me a few useful lessons in seamanship. Unexpected waves appeared here and there but I had enough warning to take them properly and had no further dramas.

I'd also dug out the lifelines and was well attached to the yacht from then on.

The wind had turned to an unfavourable quarter but instead of endless tacking with little or no progress I ran the little engine flat out which meant I was burning through fuel. I'd been deliberating whether to make landfall in Devon or not. I needed help, and money for more fuel, and mostly I needed to check on Claire and the girls, but I knew they were being watched. However, I was not keen to involve anyone in a situation I didn't understand myself.

With the poor weather I was relying entirely on the readout of the GPS unit and had given up trying to plot our course on the chart as I daren't be away from the cockpit for the time it would take. I watched the GPS and the fuel level like a hawk until, at around one o'clock in the morning, endless hours after the first capsizing, I saw the coast of North Devon appear on the little screen of the GPS.

Woolacombe didn't have a harbour, so I headed for Ilfracombe to the north. The picturesque harbour looked like it belonged on the lid of a fudge tin as I puttered in on the last fumes from the fuel tank. I killed the engine and tied the boat up with the few remaining bits of rope I had on board.

I wanted to go below and sleep for a week. But knew I wouldn't, so wasted no time and stepped on to solid land for the first time in weeks and started walking on slightly wobbly legs. I had all I needed. The clothes I wore would be sufficient for tonight. My wallet, with a ten-pound note, bank cards I couldn't use, and some left over Moroccan rials, was sitting in its usual pocket.

The persistent rain of the last couple of days had cleared and the night was clear as I strode through the old harbour town. I was aiming for the highest point behind the town and passed no one on the way at this time of night.

Passing a shop window under a streetlight gave me a near-perfect reflection of myself. I turned square on to the window for a second, grinned and walked on.

I didn't have to worry about anyone seeing me. I didn't recognise myself in sun-bleached, salt-stained clothes, long streaky blonde hair, a thick beard on my face and deeply tanned skin everywhere else.

Upon reaching the high ground I got my bearings and struck out across the fields. The land was undulating and gentle so shortly after dawn I was approaching the town of Woolacombe on the coastal path. Despite the early hour I passed joggers and dog walkers as I strode along trying look like I was out for an early morning walk.

I descended in to Woolacombe with a good view of the long beach, a dozen surfers sitting on their boards a hundred yards out from the beach.

House number ten on Shore Road wasn't hard to find. It was also an easy address to remember from when Harry mentioned it prior to James funeral.

I knocked. No reply.

He'd said that he surfed, so maybe he was one of the bodies sitting on their boards out in the bay, I still couldn't picture him as a surfer. I'd give it two hours and move on if there was no sign of him.

I walked down to a cafe at the end of the road that had a view of the beach, ordered, paid for and ate the biggest breakfast they had. Afterwards, sitting with a bucket-sized mug of coffee I had pretty much decided I was going to leave. I was wasting time waiting for a man that may, or may not help. I started thinking about how to get my hands on some cash, for fuel and parts, or where I could steal them.

As I watched the beach, I saw a tall, lean, male silhouette emerge from the sea. He jogged along easily with a shortboard tucked under one arm. No mistaking the loping gait of Harry Stone.

I put down the mug and set off at a jog. I caught up with him as he bent down to withdraw a key from a small pocket on the lower leg of his wetsuit.

"Harry," I said simply.

He straightened and looked at me. "Ruraidh Maclean?"

"I've no right to come here and ask for your help, I'll undoubtedly bring trouble your way, but before I go, please check on Claire and the girls." I added, "I'll wait here."

He said nothing. Turned to his door, opened it and stepped inside.

I'd got it wrong. After all we had only really met properly at James's funeral a couple of months ago.

Harry's head popped out of the door, he looked at me as if I were a bit simple, indicated with a sharp nod that I should come inside.

The ground floor of his small house was open-plan, with wood floors and white walls. Harry leant his board against a wall, stripped off the top half of his wetsuit to pull on a T-shirt, flicked on a kettle and came to rest looking straight at me, without a word.

I did not at this time know about his personal life, pending divorce, wealth temporarily tied up by lawyers which was why he was living in this house left to him by his grandparents. All I knew was I felt he was a capable man I could trust, because James had. And he was geographically convenient. But would he believe me?

"James was murdered. It wasn't a random crime," I said simply.

"Please call Claire," I asked. "I need to know they're OK."

Without a word he reached for a smartphone, swiped, tapped and laid it on the kitchen counter.

"You haven't seen me," I said. "And ask after Jessica." He looked at me coolly. I added a "please."

"Hello," A young girl's voice answered.

"Hello. My name is Harry. I'm a friend of your mother's," he said in a gentle, rich voice. "Are you Lizzie or Emma?"

"I'm Lizzie. Emma is sooo much older," she replied tartly. I smiled. Harry asked to speak to her mum.

Footsteps came over the loudspeaker, a rustle and Claire came on the line.

"Claire, it's Harry Stone. I am sorry to call so early."

"Harry. How lovely to hear from you," Claire said. I barely registered the rest of the conversation so great was the relief. Claire and the girls were OK. Jessica was alive and in London.

After the call I briefly explained the situation, as I knew it, then allowed myself the luxury of a hot shower and soap, all the time wondering if I was about to walk downstairs to be handcuffed.

Harry was waiting on his own. There was a pile of clothes that he motioned towards for me.

He picked up a small holdall and handed it to me. "Spare clothes," he said, "I'll take you to Ilfracombe."

I followed him out, glancing up and down the street. We stopped next to an ancient Volkswagen Polo.

"Traded up?" I asked. The last time I'd seen Harry he'd been getting into a top of the range Porsche.

He merely glanced at me as I settled in the passenger seat, the engine cranked over for a good ten seconds before catching with a lurch and a belch of smoke from the skinny exhaust. Later he would tell me that his wife's divorce lawyers had the Porsche reclaimed.

Several brief stops later we pulled up on a side street near *Sandpiper* and ferried food, parts and fuel from the ancient VW to *Sandpiper*.

Harry stood on the pier as I filled her freshwater tanks from a convenient hose pipe with a sign on it saying For Yacht Club Members Only. I was trying to look nonchalant while watching the harbour looking for signs of the police.

I coiled up the hose, started up the engine and threw off the mooring lines.

I said thank you to Harry. He said nothing, just watched.

Sandpiper moved away from the pier, an inch, two inches.

I saw Harry look away from me and scan the surrounding harbour intensely.

Would he tell anyone he'd seen me - the police, Claire? Was he waiting for the police to turn up?

I opened up the throttle, started making contingency plans, couldn't think of any. I was on a boat going slower than walking speed. Not many options.

Then Harry took a decisive step.

Chapter 18

I would have landed in the water. Harry's long legs landed him on the foredeck as I pulled away.

He fixed me with a look. "Tell me everything."

Harry took the wheel while I raised the main and jib, turned on the GPS, then put the kettle on. With *Sandpiper* settled on course in front of the south-easterly I filled two mugs with coffee and took a seat across from Harry in the cockpit.

"Your mast is bent," he said.

"Yeah, I noticed that too," I said dryly. "So, do you want everything or just the highlights?" I asked.

"How long will it take to sail to Scotland?"

"Best guess? Forty-eight hours," I replied.

"Chapter and verse," he said.

Over the next few hours I gave him all the facts.

At the end he sat silent at the wheel. I trimmed the sails a little and checked our position.

"The offer still stands. We can turn around now. You can deny ever seeing me," I said.

"That won't be necessary."

"Thank you," I said.

"James was a rare thing. Totally honest. I hadn't really appreciated that in a person until recently."

There was a long pause.

"What's the story with Jessica?"

"I wish I knew, all I know is we can't trust her."

The rest of the trip was uneventful. I busied myself with running repairs to the boat while Harry kept us on course. We shared the watches through the night, having another person on board relieved the pressure of solo sailing enormously.

A couple of days later we were passing the Mull of Kintyre. The weather was blustery, but not unpleasant. We were running under sails alone, so I took the opportunity to service the little engine which had served me so well. I was becoming attached to this boat.

We passed Islay and Jura, then the small isles of Scarba, Luing and Easdale to starboard. The vista constantly changing, rugged and harsh one minute, then warm and inviting when the sun bathed the craggy landscape.

That next night was clear with a good moon and first light found us passing Duart Castle standing foursquare and ageless on its promontory, commanding the entrance to the Sound of Mull.

We motored through the narrows at Corran and up Loch Linnhe towards Fort William with the Moidart Peninsula to our port and the great mass of Ben Nevis to starboard.

Arriving at Fort William we tied up to the functional concrete waterfront and walked along to the pedestrianised high street to buy several pre-pay mobiles. We sat in a café above an outdoor shop to finalise our plans.

"I should come with you," said Harry.

"At the moment you have a certain amount of deniability. You're just on a sailing jaunt with a friend. You have no way of knowing I'm a criminal or that I stole the boat."

He looked a little forlorn.

"I'm just going home to get my post. What could possibly go wrong?" I asked innocently.

He just looked at me. I grinned back, and he passed over a wad of notes.

"How much money do you have?" I asked.

"My lawyers told me to cash in what I could before her lawyers could find it."

"How much are you worth? Millions?" I didn't expect him to answer.

"That's what the lawyers are trying to work out as we speak," he stated. Which made me wonder.

We shook hands and I left. Stopping briefly on my way out to buy a few things.

I caught a bus to Inverness, paid cash as I boarded and took a seat in the back, keeping my face away from the camera mounted by the rear-view mirror.

The bus took two hours to wind its way up the Great Glen past Loch Ness and into the highland capital of Inverness. As I got off the bus I quashed the urge to go and find Holly Shaw, whose paper was based in Inverness. A short walk brought me to the train station and after a breif wait, I boarded a local train heading south. I got off at Carrbridge, a small and picturesque village twenty-five miles south of Inverness.

I walked out of the station and took a single-track tarmac road which led back under the road and train line. It had been a while since I'd been this way, years in fact, but the lay of the land wouldn't have changed. The day was dry with enough of a breeze to keep the midges away. I had maybe eight miles to cover on easy ground through the woods, which was nothing.

Two hours later I was nearing the clearing in the woods that was home to Old John's farmhouse. I was down wind of it so Beetle caught my scent long before I got there and came bounding through the woods on a collision course.

He licked me, wagged his tail and jumped up and down until we got to Old John's house.

"I'm all for experimenting, but I wouldn't go with that look if I were you," he greeted me.

"Wasn't planning to," I assured him.

"You've been away longer than I expected," he said.

"Yes. Sorry."

"Not to worry, makes no odds to me and your hound's been too busy terrorising my civilised dogs to miss you," he said. "Cup of tea?" he offered.

I paused.

Old John looked closely at me for several seconds, coming closer and tilting his head a little from side to side as if trying to see into my head from different angles.

"Go on," he said finally.

I smiled a little, I'd always thought the man was a bit psychic. 'Second sight' old Scots called it. The gift of premonition.

"I am involved in something I don't yet fully understand. Being seen with me may bring some harm to you but I need to get to Mrs Leven's house and I need her kept safe for a while," I said. "Just in case."

Old John was silent for a second. "Is that all?" he asked. I nodded. "Jesus. I thought you had something serious to say for a moment."

I shook my head and smiled. With his mild and friendly manner, I forget sometimes that this old timer, much like my own late father, had seen and done a lot with their years. Nothing much would faze him.

I curled up with an excited Beetle on the floor in the back of John's green Land Rover. I knew where we were from the twists, turns and humps in the road. As we left the tarmac and started up the track that led to Mrs Leven's cottage I emerged from the tarpaulin.

We had quite a job convincing the old lady to stay with John for a few days. To his credit, he came up with some pretty good arguments and reasons. Claiming he needed someone around to keep an eye on a dog that would be producing puppies soon did the trick in the end and she went to pack.

My long-standing arrangement with the local postmen to leave my post here with Mrs Leven, who keeps it in a box in her porch, was paying dividends I'd never envisaged. I found a jiffy bag with my address in James's handwriting at the very bottom, it must have arrived just a day or two after I left to go to his funeral, and due to my phone being smashed I'd never got the SMS message from him telling me to look out for it.

Inside the small jiffy bag was a memory stick. Nothing dramatic, just an ordinary-looking black plastic memory stick.

Mrs Leven was of an age that she had nothing in her house that it could plug in to. I put it back in the jiffy bag and carefully zipped it into a pocket of my jacket. The nearest thing I could plug it in to was in my cottage, where I was heading anyway.

Helping Mrs Leven into Old John's vehicle I thanked him, reminded him to not talk to anyone about me, and they clattered away down the track leaving me and Beetle alone. As I watched his Land Rover recede, I briefly lamented the fate of my own Land Rover in Morocco. I figured it was either living life under a new identity or had been long since reduced to its component parts and sold as spares. Nothing I could do either way, so I focused on the present and started walking.

My cottage was less than five miles away, as the crow flies, but I wanted to approach unseen, just in case, so I was in for a longer walk.

I headed almost directly away from my cottage to gain a ridge dividing the glens. Once behind it, I could walk along the high moor for several miles until I was nearly parallel to my cottage. Creeping back over the ridge using the broken, rocky ground for cover I could crawl down the hillside using the burns and peat hags to a suitable point to lie up and watch my home to make sure nothing nasty was waiting for me. Overkill? Maybe. But someone knew who I was and wanted me dead. For once I'd be cautious and stay ahead of the game.

After several hours of walking and the last hour sliding down the hillside on my belly along burns and hags, I was holed up watching my cottage. Beetle was well used to stalking deer in these hills with me, he'd walk to heel when needed and when I crawled, he'd lie on his belly and do a kind of leopard crawl alongside me.

"Stay," I said quietly to him.

He happily curled up in a ball for a nap while I very slowly raised my head over the lip of the hag, just enough that I could look through the heather to my cottage a few hundred yards away.

I carefully raised a set of pocket-sized binoculars to my eyes. I took care not to let the sun reflect off the lenses.

The cottage sat there. As it had for more than a century. No movement. No smoke from the chimney.

Nothing.

I watched for hours, just to be sure. I debated whether I was being overcautious and reminded myself grimly that the last time I was naïve it preceded months of misery. Besides, if somebody wanted me dead or wanted what I knew then my home was an obvious target. So I kept watching, just as my father had taught me to all those years ago. Silent, still, alert yet completely relaxed.

I could see the loch far below my cottage, a few tourists milling about on the shore. One or two trying their hand at fishing for trout and others taking selfies with the ruined castle and island as the backdrop. They seemed perfectly natural, and all left as the afternoon wore in to the evening.

I scanned every inch of the glen as I waited, and wished I had my expensive, good quality binoculars and telescope that were sitting in the cottage below, instead of the cheap ones I'd bought in Fort William this morning.

No lights came on in my cottage as the sun dropped, and I knew for a fact that the inside of the cottage became dark long before it did outside due to the tiny windows in the thick walls.

I watched every inch of the hillside and woods as the light faded. Nothing.

I hunkered down in the hag with Beetle and begun rubbing dark peat into my face, hair, hands and clothes. I'd bought new clothes in the outdoor shop in Fort William as well, at Harry's expense, all muted khakis and greens in preparation for this.

I had a word with the dog. "Keep low, be silent."

We crawled off through the peat hag. I knew exactly where I was going as this hillside was basically my garden as a child. I found the burn I was after and followed it down. It hadn't rained for a few days, so the burn was just a trickle. It still didn't take long for my front half to get soaked through.

It was slow going, crawling silently, watching constantly for gravel or rocks, anything that could make a noise. The burn ran near the south side of the woods which were in turn to the south side of the cottage. When I knew we were far enough down that the woods would cover us, I stood and headed for the trees.

The films make it look easy, walking silently. They just seem to walk like normal and make no noise. The reality was very different, especially in woodland, where the ground is covered in twigs, small branches and old pine cones. The lack of rain in the last few days meant everything was dry and cracked noisily if stood on. I scanned the ground constantly in the dark and felt with each foot as I placed it carefully and lightly, gradually putting weight on it, stopping if I felt anything that might snap and trying again a little to the side.

At times I reached down and cleared the ground before moving. Beetle padded silently along beside me. Lighter and with four paws with sensitive pads he had no problem being quiet, but obediently matched my snail's pace through the wood.

My eyes were as well adjusted to the darkness as was possible, but even so, I slowed the pace even more, scanning both the ground and the forest ahead for the first glimpse of the cottage.

The first thing I saw was the faintest glint through the trees of a pane of window glass. I froze. I stood on the spot for ten minutes. Looking straight at things is not always the best way to see them, especially at night. Your peripheral vision picks out contrast better, something to do with how the rods and cones are positioned in your eye.

I moved to the next tree, stopped, and did the whole thing again. At the next tree I was on my knees. At the next I was lying prone and crawling imperceptibly forward.

I was edging towards the old shed, which was half-embedded in the woods. Once in its cover I stood up and silently made my way round the back of it, pausing to pick up the now rusty key I'd put under one of the rocks. Not a very ingenious place to keep a spare key. But a cottage with a flimsy wooden door, and a forty-year-old lock, in the middle of nowhere doesn't really warrant extensive precautions. I carried on round the back of the shed.

By the time I got to the windowless gable end of the house I was sure there was no one there. If there was, they had superhuman patience, or were dead. I'd been watching the house for hours and seen nothing. My only worry was that we'd approached upwind of the cottage, so Beetle wouldn't be getting the scent if anyone were there.

I stood silently next to the wooden door that led into the kitchen, listening. It was very unlikely I had been seen by anyone inside. In fact, I'd be downright annoyed if they had. Unless they had night vision of some kind.

That stopped me dead. I thought about night vision. But there was nothing I could do about it now. Besides, if they had night vision and wanted me dead, I would be dead already.

As I listened I was watching Beetle carefully. A dog's nose is something like a thousand times more sensitive than ours.

I edged further over, put the key in the lock and turned it gently.

And I knew I'd been had. It was already unlocked and as it opened the merest crack a deep vibration emanated from Beetle's chest as he caught the scent of someone in the darkness inside.

Chapter 19

"Home sweet home, Beetle," I said loudly to the dog, swinging the door open, and flicking on the kitchen light.

The tiny kitchen was empty. The doorway through to the sitting room was dark.

So far so good.

I hadn't been shot.

There'd be no point in trying to sneak away, the key turning in the lock had made an unmistakeable noise that whoever was inside would have heard, so I took a chance they wanted me alive, at least for a while.

I motioned Beetle to sit, which he did, unhappily, his eyes moving continuously between me and the direction of the dark sitting room.

"Let's get some heat going," I said to him.

I reached into the wicker basket of logs, kindling and paper I kept next to the Raeburn in the kitchen.

I made plenty of noise while lighting the fire in the old range. Once lit I kept the door slightly ajar to let plenty of air in to get a good blaze going. The kitchen was so small all I had to do was spin around on the spot to reach everything I needed. I cleared a space on a shelf at head height, laid an old tray on it so that it was overhanging the edge in line with the firebox of the Raeburn. I placed a juice carton on the back edge of the tray, half-on the tray, half-on the shelf. On the overhanging portion of the tray I poured the contents of a packet of flour in a neat pile.

With a kitchen knife, I put a small hole in the bottom of the juice carton, palmed the knife and swung the Raeburn's fire box door all the way open, then the front door of the cottage all the way shut, leaving Beetle on the other side looking very pissed off.

From entering the cottage to moving into the sitting room took little more than a minute. I flicked the sitting room light switch as I went in. No light came on. I made a show of flicking the switch a few times and sighing exasperatedly while pretending not to notice that an old armchair had been moved across the room. I moved to the wood-burning stove as if going to light it and reached down for the log basket.

Snick. A faint, but distinct metallic noise came from the armchair.

"Stand up, drop the knife. Turn around." A London accent.

If he wanted me dead, I would already be, so I did as ordered and a bright torch blinded me.

This man with the slight cockney accent was either very, very patient, or he had been asleep in that armchair all day.

"Ruraidh MacLean." A statement, not a question. "We've been waiting a long time for you to come home," he said.

"You should have put the kettle on and watched a bit of TV."

He turned on a table lamp, illuminating a matt-black handgun. I was no expert on handguns, but it looked new and a large calibre, judging by the diameter of the muzzle pointing my way. His finger was on the trigger.

There was a mobile lying on the table. "Get much of a signal?" I asked casually. His look told me no.

Next to his phone sat a framed photo.

It normally sat on the desk. James, Claire, the two girls, Rebecca, me and Beetle smiled out of it. That sunny day on Loch Ness nearly two years ago.

He wouldn't have moved a random photo if it meant nothing to him. There were a lifetime of photos lying around, but he didn't recognise anyone in the rest, just that one.

The man followed my gaze.

"You have information I need."

I just stood silently.

"Listen man," he said. The gun didn't waver as he spoke. "You look pretty tough. I can respect that. I can shoot bits of you all night long, but I don't think that'll work. Will it?" He was thirtyish, compact, with the flat nose of a boxer.

His eyes hardened. "The wife," he said, indicating Claire in the photo. "Likes sensible underwear, cashmere jumpers and Lancôme moisturiser. The two girls share a room. Pink wallpaper with ponies on. The beds are painted blue, the light shade has rainbows on." He paused. "Do you get where I'm coming from?"

I did. So did the deep, dark, primordial part of my brain. I felt a tremor start in my fingers, hands, arms. Not fear. Anger. Ancient and basic.

"They won't be touched if we get what we want."

I said nothing, just waited.

He sneered. "The man didn't die well." He nodded in the direction of the photo again. "Don't make the same happen to the others."

I waited.

I heard a clatter in the kitchen, his eyes moved fractionally, but not the gun.

Then a monstrous *whoomph* shook the cottage and a burst of flame rolled out of the kitchen doorway behind me.

I knew it was coming.

The man didn't.

He instinctively turned away from the wall of flame. I lunged forward, got my left hand on the gun and rammed him into the

147

wall behind as I wrenched the gun back, snapping his trigger finger and loosing off a shot that buried itself in the roof.

I thought I had the advantage, but he was on me before I could turn the gun round in my hand and bring it to bear.

My head was snapped back by lightning jabs and my ribs pummelled. I'm not sure how I lost the gun, but it skittered away across the floor. I brought my arms into my sides, hands up protecting my head as he rained blows on me. I tensed every fibre of muscle I had to absorb the blows without sustaining damage.

If I threw a punch he saw it coming a mile away, deftly avoided it and planted stinging jabs in my exposed ribs or head.

He was a trained boxer, too skilful, too fast for me and we both knew it. But I was stronger, and much angrier, so I accepted the pain that was coming and hoped he wouldn't break anything I needed.

I shot out my left hand, which he assumed was another attempted jab. As usual he landed a lightning-fast fist in the ribs I'd exposed, but this time I grabbed a handful of his clothes, just below the collar.

He saw what was coming and upped the tempo, jabbing furiously, but I had him now at arm's length, literally. I made no effort to cover up, no effort at tactics, just hauled my right arm back to its fullest and let fly the hardest punch I could muster as I held him in place with my left hand.

I'm not a trained fighter, of any kind. But I recalled someone from my school days telling us that you aim past what you want to hit. I aimed somewhere in the next county.

His eyes widened and in the last fraction of a second, he stopped throwing punches and put his hands up.

I don't know if it's possible for a man's sternum to make contact with his spine, but it can't have been far off. He went limp instantly with a great expulsion of air and snapping sounds, ribs, I guessed.

He was still conscious. I landed the next blow in the centre of his face. Driving his nose flatter than it already was and feeling the bones under his eyes give. The only thing holding him up now was me.

Just for threatening James's girls, let alone killing James himself, I would have kept going till I'd killed him and buried him on the moor, but I needed answers. I would bury him after. But I didn't need him mobile, so I stamped on the outside of his right knee, which gave with a wet crunch. As he slumped to that side I span and threw him across the room, he landed in a heap against the far wall as I saw, through the window, lights flash over the tree trunks on the far side of the gravel parking area outside the cottage.

Damn. I needed time alone with this man. It was midnight, whoever had just arrived wasn't going to be friendly.

I scrabbled around for the gun but there was no sign of it.

I risked a look out of a window and saw a single silhouette in a SUV.

Beetles was barking.

A shot rang out.

Everything was silent except for a faint crackling from the kitchen, something was on fire.

I feared the worst till I heard the barking resume, but further away.

The newcomer was armed. And I was stuck in a house with one door.

I was a deer stalker's son, born and raised right here, hunting the land for miles around this cottage. That was where my advantage lay. Out on the open hill with a rifle where I could see what was coming on land I knew like the back of my hand.

As a young boy my father kept the tools of his trade, shotguns and rifles, on a rack above the fire. But gun laws changed, and they now resided in a discreet gun safe hidden in the tiny room he'd used as a study. I darted into it and fished the key out of a crack in an overhead beam where I kept it and swung the safe open.

Everything was there. A neat row of my father's old guns, all traditional blued steel and polished wood. The last in the row was my rifle. Standing out starkly with its modern look. I took it out along with a box of ammunition.

I considered disabling the remaining guns, but didn't have time, and I couldn't take them all with me. I locked the safe, putting the key in a pocket. Using the butt of my rifle to break the glass in the small window I reached through to lean the rifle against the wall outside and then dived through, rolling to my feet on the grass outside. I felt, more than saw Beetle join me and we ran in to the darkness of the moor.

I heard shots behind as we ran. I hoped they were from handguns, we were already a hundred yards away, well beyond the accurate range of handguns, as far as I knew.

At two hundred yards I dropped into a peat hag, rolled over and started crawling up hill. If they had seen where I took cover then I wanted to be somewhere else.

Fifty yards uphill I peered back and could see no movement. The little window to the kitchen was dark, which was good as it meant the cottage wasn't on fire after my flour bomb. I couldn't see their vehicle from where I lay.

I back-tracked down the hill, crawling down the gullies and dips of the peat hags until I could get a look at the gravel area at the other end of the cottage.

There was a sleek black Range Rover Sport sitting there. It was not the type of vehicle I took much interest in as I would probably never own one myself, but it looked brand new and top of the range.

All my father's old guns in the safe I'd just taken mine from were very traditional weapons with blued steel work and wooden stocks. I preferred modern precision, probably the engineer in me. I'd often earnt money in the university holidays working on local estates, carrying annual deer culls. Although I hadn't done this for some considerable length of time, my rifle was still as good as anything you could buy now. A Swedish manufactured superlight synthetic and stainless steel rifle with a ridiculously expensive and powerful Swarovski scope on top.

It was chambered for .243 Winchester, which was a relatively small calibre for shooting large deer, but the accuracy of the set up more than compensated for it.

The other great thing about modern optics was the light-gathering abilities, which meant that the picture I saw through the scope was brighter than I could see with the naked eye. I loaded the magazine and worked the bolt to push a round into the chamber.

I rubbed more peat into my hands, face and hair, especially the hair as the blonde highlights were not what I need at the moment, then eased ever so slowly over the lip of the peat hag and rested the rifle gently on the folded-out legs of the bipod. I settled myself in position behind it and scanned the cottage.

No movement. The windows were black.

I didn't want them calling reinforcements, so the landline had to go.

I was two hundred yards away. The telephone wire was attached to an old cast-iron bracket on the corner of the cottage. Only in the movies could you hit a wire with a rifle bullet at this distance, but the bracket was a realistic size target. I turned the ballistic turret on top of the scope to compensate for the two and a half inches the bullet would drop in flight. I turned a turret on the side of the scope that compensated for the effect of parallax.

I settled in behind the rifle, relaxed, breathed in and out steadily.

I was aware that as soon as I fired I would give away my position. The cross hairs moved across my point of aim with each breath. I paused an exhalation and squeezed gently.

A muffled boom, a slight jump of the scope and I saw the first loop of phone wire fall away. Seeing as I'd given away my position anyway I worked the bolt and put a round in each of the Range Rover's tyres and two in the engine. Five shots in five seconds.

I flicked the safety on and left the empty casing in the chamber while I crawled back the way I came. I heard two muffled shots. I assumed they had been firing at where I had been. Beetle followed me around in his own version of a leopard crawl as if this was just another day, albeit one where he got to stay up late.

They couldn't drive away and couldn't make a phone call. Now I just needed to work out how to take them alive as I wanted what they knew because, frankly, I didn't know anything at the moment.

Chapter 20

The man had been sitting in the chair when I walked in. If he'd seen or heard me coming, he probably wouldn't have been sitting quietly in a chair where he couldn't see the only door that led into the house. That didn't make sense. So, he was just waiting in case I turned up, then I walked in.

If he didn't know I was coming, then the vehicle was there for some other reason. Maybe a shift change. One man couldn't sit there twenty-four hours a day on his own, not indefinitely. Maybe they did twelve-hour shifts. Midday to midnight, midnight to midday. The Range Rover had arrived at midnight.

If there were more men coming, I'd see them and as long as it was dark I could simply melt away into the moorland at will. But in the meantime, I had to somehow catch them alive.

Knowing I was out on the hillside with a rifle they wouldn't come out of the cottage, and I couldn't storm the cottage with a long rifle. I could get to it unseen by creeping up on the uphill gable end as it had no windows. But once there I had few options. Two men with semi-automatic handguns in a dark house had the advantage against one man with a long, unwieldy, bolt action rifle in a confined space that only had one realistic point of entry and exit. The windows were a possibility, but required crawling or diving through, so weren't ideal.

As I lay in the dark and studied my house, I came to the sad conclusion that my only option was to smoke them out.

I could probably get to the shed unseen and there was more than enough material in the shed to make a couple of Molotov cocktails to toss through the windows. Then all I had to do was hide up somewhere convenient and put a bullet in them when they came out, somewhere non-lethal. Shame it involved torching my own house. But things had moved on. This wasn't about avenging James. It was about keeping Claire and the girls safe.

I needed their attention on this side of the cottage so a crawl back down the hill took me to a suitable point. I edged the rifle over the lip of the shallow gully I was in.

A moderator does what it sounds like - moderates the noise, muzzle flame and recoil of the shot. A six-inch long, two-inch wide tube screwed on to the muzzle. On this occasion, however, I wanted a good tongue of flame coming out of the muzzle and a loud bang to let them know where I was and keep them looking out of this side of the cottage for the next while, so I unscrewed it.

I settled behind the scope and took aim. Removing the moderator would affect where the bullet hit, but I didn't know how much as I'd never fired this rifle without the moderator in place. I aimed at the centre of the sitting room window as a target and fired off a shot.

It smashed the glass two inches high of where I was aiming, which was interesting. I worked the bolt for a second shot just to make sure they were looking this way, as I pushed the bolt forward I saw another windowpane smashed out and a muzzle appear. I recognised that muzzle.

I gave up on the bolt and dived back into the main peat hag, landing on Beetle and forcing him into the ground with my weight as a dull thud sounded very close by followed by the booming of my father's old .308 Mauser.

Keeping hold of Beetle, I crawled deeper into the hag in a minor panic.

A .308 was a big round, half as much lead in it again as my .243. I'd never put it to the test, but I'd wager it would go through a good few feet of peat without a problem. And I'd seen many times what those .308 rounds did to a twenty-stone stag. I kept going until I was well away from my last position.

I came to a stop deep in the hag with Beetle still clutched to me in a death grip.

"Sorry," I said and let him go.

Well, that was a game changer. I really wished I had taken time to sabotage the guns I'd left behind. I wondered idly if they'd known they were there all along, if so, why hadn't they sabotaged them? The man waiting when I'd turned up knew I didn't have a rifle, so shooting at them with one had probably told them I got a rifle from in the house and the study, my obvious point of exit, was the first place they'd look. Damn. Maybe those two muted shots I'd heard after shooting out the phone wire was them breaking into the gun safe.

I screwed the moderator back in place. No more giving away my position.

Dad had always preferred a .308 for red deer. He was very traditional. He'd had that rifle longer than I'd been alive. The scope was a Schmidt and Bender, the best you could buy back then. It had a fixed magnification of six times which was state of the art for sporting rifles four decades ago. I'd used it a lot in my youth, shot that first stag on my own with it, but hadn't touched it in years. I kept his old guns out of sentimentality.

Now they had a rifle. They still couldn't see me if I didn't give away my position. Their scope was old and didn't have the light-gathering properties of my modern scope, when they looked through it the image would be darker than they could see with their naked eye.

I still had the advantage. And I still reckoned plan A was the way to go. But maybe I could reduce their number by one beforehand. Give them something to think about.

I had a brief think about this as, frankly, not all my ideas had gone well recently. After a minute or two I decided it was worth the risk as it meant I might not have to burn my cottage down.

I pulled one of the cheap pre-paid mobiles out of my jacket pocket and hunkered down in the deepest, most overhanging bit of the peat hag I could find and turned the phone on under the cover of my jacket so that no light seeped out. I scrolled through the various menus until I found the alarm settings. I chose one for thirty seconds time and locked the phone.

Thirty seconds later the screen flashed brightly, under my jacket, perfect.

I found a good location not far from where I had last been and propped the phone up on the lip of the hag in such a way as it would illuminate the heather around it. I wanted them to see a vague indistinguishable glow rather than a blatantly obvious mobile phone screen flashing in the darkness. I set the alarm for ten minutes time and started the stopwatch on my old G-Shock watch which had a backlit digital readout.

I moved back up the hill twenty yards and found a good spot. The night was still dark, but time was racing by; the sky would start lightening before long and with it much, if not all, of my advantage would be lost.

As I lay behind my rifle scanning the windows I considered my decision. Because the windows in my cottage were small, and the walls thick, it meant I couldn't be too far away from the phone when they took a shot, otherwise I wouldn't be able to see in the window or get an angle for a shot, which meant I had to be disconcertingly close to where they were going to place another .308 slug.

I took comfort in the fact that their last shot had been close, so they and the rifle were accurate. I just hoped the old scope they were using would let them see the glow in the heather.

The next question was whether they would still be shooting out of the same window. All three windows on this side had their glass smashed out by now and if they had the sense to stay far back in the room I wouldn't know which window they were using until they took a shot.

I checked my watch, zoomed in the scope to the maximum and studied each window in turn. Nothing, they weren't giving themselves away so easily. I rotated the ring around the scope and brought the magnification back to the point where I could see all three windows. One in the centre of the cross hairs and one at each extremity. It wasn't ideal for taking the shot, but if I didn't see where to put the bullet, there was no point to the whole exercise.

I tried to relax my eyes and not focus on one spot to allow my brain to concentrate on three things separately. I didn't know if that was possible, but I knew if you focused intently on one point you often wouldn't see anything else.

I didn't look at my watch again. Partly so I didn't risk missing anything and partly so the tiny backlight didn't affect my night vision.

Waiting. My watch alarm beeped quietly.

It must have gone off by now. I wouldn't hear the phone on vibrate mode and I wouldn't see the glow from here, although the phone was only twenty yards away, because... *Flash. Boom.*

They were in the sitting room, the muzzle flash lit up the inside of the room for a split second.

The shooter was too far inside the room. In the residual image that was temporarily burnt on my retinas in the dark I could make out the rifle and the first half of the scope. The rifle was resting on the back of the armchair. I could make out a vague shape to the shooter's left. A man standing slightly behind him and to the side, crouched over slightly to look in the same line as the shooter. It was an inch or two of his shoulder I was seeing. Half a second after they fired I put a bullet in to the darkness where the image of his shoulder had been.

I heard a faint noise from inside the cottage. I hoped it was a scream. My shot wouldn't have killed him if it had hit his shoulder, but it would have made a hell of a mess; I was using expanding ammunition designed for deer.

I almost felt sorry for him. But not quite.

The chances were that the man behind the rifle was a late arrival because I'd broken the other man's trigger finger, amongst other things. Which made it likely that it was the already injured man I had just taken a shot at.

Plan A was still looking good. Creep up the hill in the dark and circle into the gable end, torch my house and shoot them in the legs as they came out.

I'd moved up the peat hag a bit from my last shot as even with the moderator back on the end of the barrel there would have been a bit of a flash to give away my position and it was vaguely possible they'd seen it. Although one of them was going to be slightly preoccupied at the moment.

A stun grenade would be ideal. Better than burning my house down.

I ran through the list of flammable contents in the shed, considered their properties and either shortlisted or dismissed them. Top of my shortlist was the acetylene cylinder, same as the cutting gear I'd used earlier this summer in Ullapool, but much smaller. Acetylene is a very flammable gas.

I could flood the cottage with gas. If I got the amount right I could cause a big enough bang to stun them and allow me to take them easily.Of course, if I put too much gas in the cottage I could blow it sky high and kill both men instantly.

There were cans of WD40 in the shed, they might work.

I filed the idea as plan B.

By the time I got to the shed I'd probably be on plan W.

I made to slither back down into peat hag and start making my way up hill and around down to the shed. Just before my head dropped behind the heather and peat I saw a faint glimmer through the sitting room window. I brought the rifle back up and looked through the scope. The sitting room was very slightly illuminated from inside, as were the other two windows on this side of the house. A flickering glow, as it increased in intensity it dawned on me: They'd set fire to the cottage. Bastards.

Why?

They were still in it, which seemed a bit self-defeating.

They were planning to leave the cottage. Obviously. But where to? The woods behind my cottage? Had to be. The Range Rover wasn't going anywhere, but did they know that? They may have heard my shots from inside the cottage, but they wouldn't have known it was their Range Rover I'd been disabling.

They were either going to make a break for it to the woods or make for their vehicle to discover that it wasn't going anywhere and then their only option was to hide in the woods.

The cottage was burning fiercely now, each window a solid wall of flame, so unless they voluntarily burnt to death they were already in the woods.

The next question was whether they'd hide deep in the woods, unlikely, it would be a poor tactical decision as they would have no field of view in the woods. More likely they'd stay on the edge of the woods where they could see the cottage, and me, if I approached it, or them. They wouldn't be downhill of the cottage, they'd want the high ground. Both instinct and training would dictate this, and I assumed men in their line of work were ex-military.

So I knew where they'd be, because it's where I'd be. Trouble was I couldn't approach over the open moor from my current position now they were in the open, I'd be in their field of view and I'd be a sitting duck when the sun came up soon.

I strapped the rifle to my back and ran north, directly away from the cottage. I needed to be in position when the sun came up. They wouldn't see me in the darkness past the still-burning cottage, so I dispensed with caution and focused on speed.When I judged I was far enough to the north I started angling up toward the ridge that ran around the top of the glen. Aiming for a gulley that would allow me to get to the high ground without being silhouetted against the sky.Once well over the top on to the flatter moor I turned south. Roughly a mile would bring me parallel to my cottage over the ridge and halfway down the hill to the loch. Another five hundred yards further would bring me to the same burn I had crawled down yesterday to watch my cottage. I ran on. Beetle was running circles around me and expending plenty of energy, which was good, as I needed him calm and quiet for the next stage.

I took the same line as I had the afternoon before, into the burn that led down the hillside towards the south side of the woods. The horizon to the east was light now, half an hour, maybe less until the sun was up.

As before I stopped regularly to look over the lip of the burn, but this time I had the powerful magnification of my rifle scope as adverse to the poor-quality pocket binoculars. I scanned the ground to my right until I found what I was after, a way to traverse the hillside above the woods without breaking cover.

After twenty minutes I was level with the north-east corner of the woods and two hundred yards up the hill. That meant I was looking down on to the front edge of the woods, where my cottage sat.

The cottage was now just four blackened walls with a smouldering pile inside. The shed was no more, just a pile of ashes with some twisted black metalwork sticking out here and there. It had burnt fast. I put it out of my mind.

The edge of the woods I was looking along below me was not a straight edge; it was slightly wavy and undulating. I knew where they'd be because a hundred yards or so above the remains of my cottage there was a slight mound in the edge of the woods with good cover. It's where I would have lain if I'd torched the cottage to drive them out.

I spoke quietly to Beetle, telling him to stay put in the hollow. He curled up and settled in for a nap.

I crawled diagonally forward. Very slowly.

It was the rifle's muzzle that gave them away, the slightest gleam of dawn on blued steel. They were where I had thought they would be.

I couldn't see the men themselves, so I still had a way to go, but knowing they were there took a whole lot of strain off the situation. I kept on my original course, not for an instant taking my eyes off them, just slithering quietly through the heather until I could see the rifle, scope and the men's heads. The rest of their bodies hidden by tree trunks, rocks and roots. Three hundred yards uphill of them. I settled behind the scope.

They were lying at the edge of the woods. Two of them tucked just far enough back not to be easily seen but to have a good view.

At a shade over three hundred yards my rounds would drop ten-and-half-inches below the point of aim. I slowly and gently turned the scope's turrets accordingly. The faint breeze was coming from the south-east, so the woods would be sheltering the bullet for most of its flight, I made no adjustment for windage. I settled the cross hairs on the head of the man nearest me, the one lying there with my father's .308 in his hands.

At this distance, in these conditions I couldn't miss. That wasn't arrogance, I knew well what I and my rifle could do. But I still wanted them alive and with our relative positions I only had head shots at the two men, the rest of them hidden from view and now it was fully light I didn't want to risk moving again. I'd wait till they moved. They wouldn't stay there forever. At some point they would decide I'd hightailed it over the moor and come out of cover.

I waited. The sun rose, it was going to be a glorious day. The wind died a little, just a faint breeze now where I was lying on the open hill.

I smiled grimly.

Where the men lay in the lee of the woods the breeze would be non-existent. The midges would be out. As I watched through the scope I could see them twitching from the faint cloud of the little beasts around their heads. It wouldn't be long now. No one can withstand the dreaded highland midge for long. They'd soon decide I'd left during the night so they could get away from the midges. As soon as they moved away from cover I'd put a round in each of their legs, have a quiet chat with them, then bury the bastards on the moor. And for the first time this summer I might have some idea what was going on.

A glint in the distance caught my attention. I'd been keeping an eye on the remainder of the glen, purely out of habit, since the light came up. A few cars had passed along the road in the distance, but none had come around this side on the single lane track. It was still early, the tourists wouldn't come this way for hours yet.

The glint had been the low sun reflecting off a vehicle. I watched it come almost to a stop on the main road, miles over the far side of the loch. I willed it to carry on and not turn off.

It turned off.

It was just a speck but as it slowly drew nearer I saw it was dark red with a white roof, a van, not a car. I watched it with a sinking feeling as it wound its way closer through the undulating moorland.

Chapter 21

It was Holly Shaw. The reporter. In her old red and white VW camper.

There was no chance she was just out for a drive, she was coming up here, to the cottage.

She was about to disappear into the blind spot where my track starts. Next time I saw her would be as she pulled up next to the Range Rover.

The old .308 was more than good enough for an accurate shot from where the men lay. Would they kill her outright or try to take her as a hostage? I couldn't allow either, so the thought was irrelevant.

I hadn't moved as I watched Holly's van, so the rifle was lined up, scope adjusted, all I had to do was slip the safety off and squeeze the trigger. But the only targets I had were their heads, they wouldn't be telling me anything after all.

Breathe in, out slowly, pause.

A muted boom rang out across the moor. My right hand worked the bolt unconsciously, the cross hairs not leaving the next target. Pushing the bolt forward and down, breathe in, out, squeeze.

Barely a second between shots. That's how long it took to extinguish two lives.

Purely out of habit I worked the bolt and seated another round in the chamber as I looked for movement. Nothing. I glanced over my shoulder and saw Beetle's head above the heather where I'd left him. I raised a hand, *stay*, he wasn't happy, but he stayed.

I'd seen my shots land. There was absolutely no need to watch these men in case they required a follow up shot, but it gave me an excuse to just lie there for a moment. The long night was over, but I hadn't learnt anything, other than that they had killed James.

I heard the underpowered old camper van strain up the last incline and come to a stop next to the Range Rover.

I sighed. The heather was comfortable, springy, the sunlight was warm. I could easily close my eyes and fall asleep but upon seeing Holly, Beetle had reached his limit of obedience and bounded past me at a full gallop.

I groaned, worked the bolt to remove the live round and closed it on the empty chamber.

This was going to be awkward.

I stood up and started wearily down the hillside.

Holly was just standing there, staring at my cottage. She walked up and looked in the door at the pile of black, gently smoking debris. The shed had suffered the same fate, made of wood it had caught light and burnt to the ground.

She turned to look around and noticed Beetle on a collision course, he knocked her back into the wall with his paws on her shoulders. She didn't seem to mind, and I could see her rubbing his flanks as she looked around.

She saw me, still a couple of hundred yards up the hill and waved. I returned the wave with little enthusiasm, not because I didn't want to see her, just not under these circumstances. Which was a shame, as even from this distance she looked good.

Her hair was bigger and blonder than I remembered. The figure was better than I recalled. Strong and athletic. A tomboy in a pair of jeans.

A hundred yards from the cottage I stopped. Working quickly, I removed the men's jackets, wrapping them tightly around their heads. I was somewhat satisfied to see one of my towels from the cottage wrapped around the boxer's shoulder. I'd scored a hit through the window earlier, but a glancing one by the looks of it. I hoped it'd hurt, for James.

I gave them a quick frisk and took their handguns and reclaimed my fathers rifle.

Holly was circling the Range Rover, looking at the bullet holes. Beetle glued to her leg.

I swung the .308 off my shoulder and laid it in the bonnet. Lying my own rifle down I took out the two handguns I'd just picked up and inspected them.

Beretta 92Fs. I'd used them at a shooting range in South Africa when I worked down there a long time ago. I released the magazine and pulled back the slide to eject the round from the chamber. The nine-millimetre round popped out of the ejection port, I caught it and slipped it back in the top of the magazine and laid them both on the bonnet. I repeated the procedure for the second Beretta.

"Been rabbit hunting?" she asked innocently, waving an arm over the assorted guns. "And come home to find your house burnt down by a freak lightning strike and someone's delivered a bullet ridden car?"

"Hello Holly," I said.

"Hello Ruraidh."

"As much as I am happy to see you, and I am, it's not really a good time. I don't suppose there's any chance you'll leave and forget you ever saw me?" I asked in my most convincing tone.

She shook her head, very slowly. "Nooooo."

"It really would be for the best."

"What's up there?" she asked, indicating up the hill where she'd seen me stop to pick up the guns from the two dead bodies.

"Ummmm."

Holly walked around the vehicle and stood in front of me, hands on hips.

"I really, really need you to leave."

"I'm not going anywhere," she replied. "What happened in Morocco?"

It was still early but we didn't have long before the first tourists might arrive at the loch below. I ran through options in my head. Leave the men and run. Bury the men on the moor, I could bury them OK, but not their car. If the bodies were found, they would no doubt make the news and whoever had sent them would know I was back in the country. Holly and her van were now an issue; if anyone saw them in the area she'd be linked to the crime.

"Ruraidh?" she said, still awaiting an answer.

"Walk away, now," I told her.

I recognised a stubborn woman when I saw one so tried another tack.

"I'm wanted for murder in Morocco and I seem to be wanted dead in this country. Being seen with me will put you in a danger I can't protect you from. And I cannot live with that. I will tell you everything as long as once we are away from here, you let me take you someplace safe until this is over."

She nodded.

"You can't write about a word of this."

She nodded again.

"OK." Time was getting on. "Do you have any duct tape?"

"Of course," she replied, as if every girl carries duct.

I walked back up the hill and dragged the bodies back down. Holly looked a little unsure as I dropped them at the back of the Range Rover and went through pockets till I found the keys to their vehicle and blipped it open.

"Don't feel sorry for them," I told her. "The day we met in Ullapool they'd beaten my oldest friend to death. Two little girls lost their Dad." I picked up each one in turn and tossed them into the boot and slammed the door on them. "They would have killed us both."

I sat in the driver's seat of the Range Rover, it wouldn't start, my two shots into the engine had done their job. I shifted it in to neutral.

"Do you have anything to use as a tow rope?"

The front end of her van and the back end of the Range Rover were both flat. It might work.

Between us we dragged the mattress off the bed in the back of the camper and folded it in half.

"How did you know I was here?" I asked as we taped the mattress to the front of the van.

"Mrs Leven told me."

I glanced questioningly at her before I ducked my head to look under the front of her van.

"You did say you'd get in touch when you got back, you never did, so I came up here a while ago. You weren't here so I checked up on your neighbours," she said.

"You can't see Mrs Leven's house from the road or from here. How did you know she was there?" I asked, standing up.

"I am an investigative reporter," she said haughtily. "And I can read a map."

"She shouldn't have said anything to you," I said, concerned she'd spoken to other people.

"I'm irresistible," she shrugged. "She phoned me late last night and told me you were back and she'd been bundled off to stay with a friend." I was going to have to have a word with Old John and Mrs Leven.

"Hop in." I held her van door open. She brushed past me as she got in the seat, she smelt good.

"Did you..."

"No," I replied too quickly. "Back it up and put your nose to the Range Rover's back bumper."

"What happened in Morocco?" she asked again out of her van window as she manoeuvred to get behind the Range Rover.

I put all the guns in the back of the camper van then recounted the events in Morocco as I attached the tow rope from the front of Holly's van to the back of the SUV. There was no reason not to tell her, she was involved now, and it meant someone else knew the story if anything happened to me.

"Drag me back and then nudge me down the track," I said as I opened her van door and held it in open with a bungee cord stretched to the front bumper.

"What's that for?"

"Making sure your doors stay open, so you can jump out," I said.

"Eh?"

"Once you've nudged me down the track you'll have to stop us rolling out of control down the hill and crashing. I've got no power, no brakes, no engine," I told her. "You've got a tiny engine and not very good brakes, so if it gets away from you, jump out and take Beetle with you."

"Is there a better way of doing this?"

"Probably, but we don't have time."

She looked a little unsure. "Don't worry. It'll be fine," I told her.

"Then why have you just tied my doors open?"

"It'll *probably* be fine," I said. "You know how to use engine breaking?" She looked daggers at me from under the blonde fringe.

"Just checking."

I ushered Beetle into the van and slipped behind the wheel of the Range Rover.

Holly made a good job of it and we were soon rolling down the track. I heard Holly's van engine rev as she let the engine breaking do its work. And it did to begin with, but as the heavy 4 x 4 gained momentum we got faster and Holly's engine revved alarmingly, unable to restraint the weight of both vehicles. I had kept my door ajar, just in case. I now swung it fully open and held it there with a foot.

We sped up quite a lot, I had to haul harder on the wheel, forcing it around against the resistance of the powerless power steering system. In the rear view I could see Holly's face - pale, eyes the size of tennis balls and her nose practically against her windscreen.

I gave her an encouraging smile as we passed the halfway point and noticed the van's wheels were locked up now, having given up on engine breaking and stomped on the brakes, and the whole thing was being dragged down the track by the weight of the Range Rover with a bow wave of soil and stones in front of each of her wheels.

The 4x4 was towing Holly's van down the track so it was cutting the corners a little on each turn, at one point the van had two wheels quite high up one of the banks on the inside of a turn and looked near its tipping point.

As my wheels hit the tarmac of the road at the bottom of my track my vehicle stopped. I let out a little breath of relief and then Holly shunted us from the rear. I walked back to her.

Her little fists locked in to place with white knuckles.

"I. Did. Not. Enjoy. That." she said slowly, still looking straight ahead through her windscreen.

Beetle leant over from the passenger seat and gave her a friendly lick.

"That's the worst over," I said, gently unpeeled her hands from their death grip on the steering wheel. My hands were big and dirty compared to hers. Which reminded me I had been rubbing peat into my face, hands and clothes all night.

I turned one of her wing mirrors round and had a look at my face.

"Yeah. It's not a good look," Holly said, recovering.

I looked like a coal miner, a good look for last night, not so good for being incognito during the day.

"You'll need to drag me back round and push me down to there." I indicated a small bay a little way along the shore of the loch.

With a lot of revving and a bit of jolting we made it and I untied the tow rope between us.

"Give us the best shove you can," I pointed.

A good shove would see the SUV roll off the tarmac, down a grass slope and into the loch. I knew from swimming in the loch as a child it was quite shallow for the first twenty yards then dropped off to fifty feet or more.

I stripped off as quick as I could.

"Uh. Why?" Holly asked.

"I'll have to keep pushing once it's in the water to make sure it gets to the deep bit before it sinks," I explained.

"Unless you'd like to..." I offered, with a hand gesture towards the loch.

She shivered dramatically. "I'm just aiding and abetting. You're the master criminal here," she told me.

"Master?"

"It wasn't meant as a compliment," she said. "The only thing criminal about you is that hair."

"It's a disguise."

"Did you do it yourself?"

"Can you tell?"

"OK. Shove her in," I said, before she could reply. "Then drive over there and make your van look normal."

Holly eased her van forward until it made contact and dropped the clutch. The Range Rover rolled forward into the water and floated gently away from the bank. I waded in and pushed it to keep it moving. It floated better than I had hoped. It was past the shallows and floating out over the deep water.

But it wasn't sinking.

It seems Range Rovers were well made, not many holes and gaps for water to get into the passenger compartment.

"It's not sinking!" called Holly helpfully, as she hauled the mattress back into her van.

I duck dived and scrabbled around on the sandy bottom for a useful-size rock. Swimming out to the bobbing 4x4 I smashed the windows and grabbed a roof rail to tip it enough that the water started pouring in over the top of the doors. I pushed off in case it rolled over and watched it slowly sinking.

I trod water while it sank out of view. After a minute passed I dived down for a look to reassure myself it was deep enough. It was at the limit of my lung capacity to get down far enough to see its murky outline in the peaty coloured water of the loch. It was settled on the bottom, sitting upright. Streams of bubbles rising from it.

I surfaced and rubbed my face and hands to clean them up a bit and realised that the streams of bubbles from the submerged car were surfacing and bursting in a large circle all around me. It was a flat calm morning with barely a ripple on the loch, so they were very obvious, and obviously not caused by me.

"Ruraidh!" Holly called out. "Police."

Chapter 22

"Hide the guns."

The bubbles were bursting all around me.

"Come and swim with me!" I shouted.

She looked at me blankly for a second then she was a blur of movement in the back of her van and emerged from the side door in a sports bra and tiny shorts. Tanned and toned she waded into the cold water with Beetle in tow until waist deep when she dived in and cleaved the water with a strong front crawl.

"This wasn't really what I had in mind this morning," she said.

"You sure it was a police car?" I asked.

A white and blue car with blue lights and 'Police' on the side appeared next to her van.

"Pretty sure," she said.

"Pretend we haven't noticed them and splash lots," I said. Turning around to look the other way.

"Oh yeah, that's convincing."

"Got a better idea?"

In answer she came around in front of me and wrapped her arms around my neck and her legs round my waist. Her face close to mine.

"Keep treading water," she said.

Her lips were nearly but not quite touching mine. Her head at a slight angle so she could see past my head and her eyes almost, but not quite closed. From the shore there would be little doubt as to what we were doing.

"They're getting out." She ran her hand over the back of my head. "Come on, pretend you're enjoying this."

It was hard work treading water vigorously enough to keep us both afloat, but to her credit, it was disturbing the water surface enough to hide the bubbles as my arms and legs worked furiously to keep our combined weight up.

"They're looking at us." She tucked her head in a little closer to mine, a hand on each side of my face, as close as you could be without touching.

"They've turned around and are looking at the hills," she said, pulling back slightly. We locked eyes from about two inches away. I am not sure what she was thinking, I know what I was.

"How do they look?" I asked.

"Relaxed. Like they're out on a wild goose chase. Not chasing an international criminal."

"Master criminal." I reminded her.

"In your dreams," she said and brought her face back down to mine. "They're looking this way." As she spoke her lips brushed mine, so lightly it could be my imagination. I wondered if it was on purpose. I scanned the water around us, it looked like the worst of the bubbles had escaped.

"You're breathing hard, you must be out of shape, I'm not that heavy," she said with a little smirk.

I went to contradict her but she narrowed her eyes and cut me off by squeezing her thighs hard together, I lost my rhythm and dipped below the water and came up spluttering.

"They're waving," she whispered. "I think our time's up."

We heard a faint "Hello," coming over the water. Holly raised her head towards the sound as if she hadn't noticed them before and waved back.

"So how was it for you?" she asked out of the corner of her mouth as she smiled and waved towards the police.

"Bloody hard work," I replied.

She put her hands on my shoulders, unwrapped her legs and pushed off me, pushing me under water. I surfaced spluttering, again, and watched her swim away as if she was born to the water.

The police did look relaxed from this distance. A man and a woman. I trod water for a few seconds checking the bubbles had stopped, before heading in with a leisurely breaststroke.

Ahead, Holly had reached the shore. Cold water streaming off her body. Even from this distance I could see the male PC make a valiant effort to keep his eyes on her face, and off her body, as I heard Holly say a little sheepishly, "Good morning officers. Sorry, we didn't see you. We were...ah."

"No problem, ma'am," said the policewoman. "Did you camp here last night?"

"No," replied Holly easily. "We're just passing through."

"Have you noticed any fires?" the taller policeman asked. "We had a report from a motorist."

I waded out of the water myself at this point and their eyes turned to me. "No. We haven't noticed any fires."

I noticed Holly smirking as the policewoman blatantly looked me up and down. Holly turned to her van, slid open the side door and threw a towel at me.

As they spoke to Holly I looked them up and down. They were dressed head to foot in black, stab vests festooned with black nylon pouches carrying everything from phones to notebooks and radios. I could see no evidence of weapons other than pepper spray. But they each had a small, round camera lens strapped to one shoulder of their vests.

"Nasty scar," the policeman said, looking at my chest.

"DIY accident," I replied.

"He's pretty accident-prone," said Holly, as she came over to me and put an arm around my waist. I responded with an arm round her shoulders. We fitted together well, naturally. Somebody said something, but it didn't register as my brain was grappling with something else entirely.

Holly ran a hand up my back, then down again, and paused. Her fingers traced a faint diagonal line across my back under the towel. She looked up at me questioningly as the line she was following with a finger was crossed by another, and another. You couldn't see those scars anymore, especially under my current suntan, but she could obviously feel a slight difference between the old skin and the scar tissue. Not something I'd thought about as I never felt my own back and hadn't had anyone do so since I'd acquired those scars over a year ago.

"Where are you heading?" he asked.

"Aviemore, no particular plans, bit of a road trip."

Beetle emerged from the loch and greeted the police with a vigorous shake, covering everyone present in a shower of cold water.

"Sorry," Holly said, reaching down to fondle the dog's ears.

"That's alright," said the female officer. "I have dogs myself. Is it a lab?"

"Just about."

I started pulling on my clothes as Holly slowly patted herself dry under the watchful eye of the policeman, whom she looked at dolefully.

The policewoman shook her head at him, "Well, thank you. Have a good day."

"You too," replied Holly sweetly.

They walked along the track looking up at the hillside. From down here all you could see of my cottage was the top of the gable end nearest the loch. It looked like just another ruin.

Now I'd been seen in this country. Alive and well. I didn't think my new look would fool anyone for long and Holly had been seen with me. They had bought our story and hadn't bothered to even ask our names, but they would have Holly's number plate, and our faces on their body cams.

"We need to get going."

"Ready when you are," she replied.

I turned around. She was back in her jeans and crop top with a towel wrapped turban style around her head.

"Do you mind if I drive?" I asked.

The old camper belched smoke as we rolled off along the single-track road around the loch. We gave the police a merry wave as we passed them standing at the bottom of my track, looking up it a little uncertainly. Their vehicle was a standard estate car which wouldn't like my track, especially with the extra trenches Holly's van had recently created. They didn't seem to relish the idea of walking up either. I hoped they wouldn't bother.

I glanced at my ruins in the rear-view mirror. My father's ruins. All my material possessions and memories were a pile of ashes. Mother. Father. Rebecca. I didn't have even a photograph of any of them.

I pushed it out of my mind, they were just material possessions. Things. Objects.

James had lost his life. His girls had lost a father. Possessions didn't matter.

"Ruraidh," Holly said. And I realised her hand was on mine on the steering wheel.

"Ruraidh," she said again.

I made a conscious effort to relax and bring myself back to the here and now.

"I'm sorry about your house," she said with genuine sympathy.

"I was needing to renovate anyway."

She gave me look. "Your back..." she said quietly. "Were you...?"

"We have to get rid of your van," I told her. She accepted the change of subject without pushing.

"You are not drowning my van in a loch," she told me, crossing her arms.

"It's OK. I know a place we can hide it near here," I told her.

We headed towards Aviemore, just as we'd told the police a few minutes ago. After several miles I checked there were no vehicles within sight and turned off on to an old dirt track that was in poor repair. To the best of my knowledge no one had driven this track in many years as it was all part of the estate that was still in dispute. It led only to a small wooden barn, we opened the sagging doors and drove the van in.

"It's an easy walk to the train station in Carrbridge from here."

I slid open the side door to let Beetle out and retrieved the guns from under the mattress.

"We can't take all of them with us," she said.

"We'll hide them in the woods as we go," I replied.

"Why not leave them here?"

"Kids might find them."

"Seriously," she said. "You've killed two men already today and you're worried about kids finding guns in a van in the middle of nowhere?"

"Yes." It made sense to me.

She paused, looking at me. "OK," she said holding a hand out. I passed her the Berettas which she held at arm's length between forefinger and thumb, as if they'd bite.

"Do you know how to use a gun?" I asked.

She gave me a look. "Do I look like I know how to use a gun?"

"I'll show you as we walk. Tuck them in your belt, they're perfectly safe, chambers are empty."

Holly locked her van after taking a few items for disguising ourselves. We buried the keys a little way from the shed and started walking.

She easily kept up with my pace taking long, strong strides, arms swinging, barely breathing hard. As we went I stripped the rifles down as far as I could without tools and stashed them under rotten logs and rocks. Soon enough all we had left were the two handguns in Holly's waistband.

Holly had pulled a little ahead of me as I stopped to hide the last rifle. As I stood up and carried on walking, I was admiring her rear view in the snug jeans as she turned around and caught me.

"Really?"

"Just making sure you still had both guns," I said innocently.

"Sure you were." She took them both from the back of her jeans and held them up. "Maybe you should take them and then you'll have to find another excuse to stare at my butt."

"OK," I said compliantly and went to take them.

"On second thoughts, I think I like being the only one of us that's armed."

I took one and showed her the basic functions, she caught on quick.

"So. Can I?" she asked, like an excited kid.

"Sure," I said. Who knows, she might need to shoot someone before this was over. I placed a chunk of rotten wood the size of a watermelon on a fallen tree ten yards away. We were miles from the nearest road and she'd be shooting deeper in to the woods which would muffle the sound of gunfire.

"Plant your feet wide and lean into the gun, good, now cup your..."

Boom. The chunk of wood jumped in the air and landed on the ground. *Boom*. It jumped again and came to rest a few feet further back. *Boom*, another hit.

Holly grinned, slipped the magazine out, racked the slide back, caught the round that jumped out, slid it into the magazine and the magazine back in the gun.

"It really is as easy as it looks in the films," she winked, turned on her heel and walked on.

I stood, staring after her, not sure whether I was utterly smitten, or a little bit scared.

She spoke over her shoulder. "Now you know I can use this gun, stop staring at my arse."

I followed her, trying and failing to neither laugh nor look.

As we neared Carrbridge we stashed her phone and she donned a baggy flat cap, which she tucked all her blonde hair under, and a long shapeless jumper made her less distinctive.

"Now you," she said.

"This is my disguise," I said indicting my beard and hair.

"Mmmm." She took a hair band off her wrist and pulled my hair in to a manbun, it was just long enough by now.

"Really?"

The plan was to split up to arrive at the station separately and board the next train to Inverness where I'd follow Holly at a discrete distance to the meet with a friend of hers. I was loathe to involve anyone else, but I needed to see what was on that memory stick and Holly assured me this man was worth meeting.

I took the one remaining Beretta and tucked it in my waistband.

"You go first," she said, "so I can watch your... gun."

Chapter 23

She made it easy for me to follow her through Inverness, never looking my way but making sure I saw which way she was going before she went out of view. I followed her to an unremarkable looking back street bar.

There was a boy sitting at a table in a dark corner. He looked about twelve years old. Skinny as a toothpick. Dark hair shaved up the sides, long and lank on top. Painfully thin with piercings in places I didn't know could be pierced and the complexion of a person that might burst in to flames if exposed to sunlight.

"Muzz. Ruraidh. Ruraidh. Muzz," Holly said by way of introduction.

Muzz?

I leant across the table and stuck out a hand. The child took it tentatively and up close I noticed the eyes were much older than his look suggested. The sheer skinniness of the guy was misleading. Holly looked positively Amazonian sitting next to him.

"Muzz," I said carefully. "I don't know what I'm in to, but people have died because of this." I held up the memory stick. "You can walk away now. I wouldn't blame you."

The geek sat there looking at me wide-eyed for several seconds. He swivelled his head slowly to Holly, who just shrugged.

"Dude. Lighten up," he said, took the stick and plugged it in to a laptop covered in stickers for computer games and skateboards.

Without looking up he said, "The Northern Constabulary are not currently looking for you."

I looked at Holly."You can trust him," she said, reading my thoughts.

"The cops in Morocco, however, would love a piece of you," he said.

I winced. "What do you know?"

"Lots. But not everything, how'd you get into the UK?"

"Borrowed a yacht and sailed back."

"Smart," he said thoughtfully. "But slow."

"The time came in handy."

"For what?"

"Healing."

"Ah." Then, "It's tracked."

I sat up.

"Chill," he said. "It's child's play to block the signal. But it's encrypted, we need a key. Any ideas?"

I gave him the obvious ones James might use. Names, birthdays, special places, but we came up blank.

"No probs, I can crack it, but it'll take a while," he said with a nonchalant shrug. "There's been a lot of traffic searching for you. Most of it is innocuous. But one search has left no footprints."

"What does that mean?"

"They hid the fact that they searched. No IP, nothing."

"If there's nothing to show they searched, how do you know they did?" I asked.

He gave me a look that said, "I could explain, but you wouldn't understand."

I leant in close, "Humour me."

"You look like an outdoorsy guy. Imagine looking at a map drawn in pencil and then tracing your route through it with a rubber, technically there's nothing there, but you can still see the route because there's nothing there."

"Who?"

"Government," he stated simply.

"As in police?"

"Intelligence."

Jessica had said her company often worked for government agencies.

"Wouldn't a person that works for the government doing this sort of thing be good enough to know to hide the blank spaces?"

"Some will, some won't. It's like any big organisation. They might employ a thousand programmers. Some will be brilliant, some average and some crap. Depends who got tasked with this search and whether they were having a bad day."

"How much do you know of the police's ability to protect witnesses?" I asked them both.

"Protect from who?" Muzz asked.

"Anyone who may intend them harm."

"Ah," he said. "None."

"None?"

"All they'd do is provide a convenient way to locate you."

"Then we need to make you disappear," I said, looking at Holly. "As agreed."

I pulled out one of the pre-paid disposable phones which Muzz promptly took off me and pulled apart. He gave us a lecture on making untraceable phone calls, then I called Harry.

"Do you know much about facial recognition, CCTV and generally not being seen?" I asked Muzz.

"Facial recognition generally uses recognition algorithms such as principal component or linear discriminant analysis, elastic bunch graph matching and multilinear subspace learning models to compare statistics." This rolled off his tongue without any apparent forethought.

Holly and I just looked at him.

"It's not like the Jason Bourne movies. There is no magic computer programme that will instantly recognise your face when it appears on any one of the five-and-a-half million cameras in the UK. Most facial recognition software is less than five percent effective. Someone who knows what you look like needs to be looking at the right camera, at the right time, otherwise surveillance cameras are only really any use for working out where you have been. Change your appearance, don't look up, keep moving and don't go back to the same place twice."

This geek could be very useful.

"Are you busy for the next couple of days?"

"I'm available twenty-four hours a day for my clients," he stated.

"How much do you charge for this service?"

"You don't want to know," he said simply. "But if you live through this you won't begrudge the bill."

He was probably right, and it looked like I was going to need his help. I'd been lucky so far, but I couldn't continue to walk and sail everywhere to avoid being seen.

"Who are your clients?" I asked. "Typically."

"There is no typical," he said with a look at Holly.

I'd noticed he rarely went more than a few seconds without a glance in her direction. Not a complete geek, then.

"We should go," I said.

Muzz handed us each an old, simple mobile phone, a charger and plug in earpiece and a warning to follow his instructions when it came to illicit communication.

Holly leant down and put a hand on his shoulder. "Thanks," she said with a sisterly peck on the cheek.

"Thank you." I stuck out my hand again. "Can I have that back?" I indicted the memory stick.

He pulled it out of its slot and gave it to me. "I've copied it. If you plug it in to anything they'll know where you are immediately."

Twenty minutes later we separately entered Inverness bus depot and boarded a coach for Fort William. Holly sat at the back with Beetle. I sat just behind the driver, where I could see to the back of the coach in his large rear-view mirror, and anyone getting on had to pass me.

I studied each person that got on at the stops. I saw nothing alarming until a man around my age entered and took a seat halfway down the coach.

He didn't fit the type. He didn't look like he was on holiday. He was of an age where he should be working at this time of day. While I'd been watching him in the mirror I'd seen him turn his head in Holly's direction numerous times. There wasn't much else to look at down that end of the coach. When he stood up and walked to the back of the bus I followed. As he got to Holly he stopped and placed his hands on the seat backs on either side of the aisle, lent down and spoke.

"Hi. I'm sorry for interrupting," he said. "Is this seat free?"

Was he chatting her up?

I was standing practically on top of him, about to stick a handgun in his ribs.

"John. Hi. I thought that was you sitting down there," Holly said loudly and enthusiastically, standing up. Great, she knew him. It couldn't get any worse.

Then I realised she was looking past the man at me.

"Sorry," she said with a smile to the hapless man as she stood up and squeezed past him to give me a hug.

"It's been too long. I hardly recognised you," she said to me.

We all did an awkward shuffle in the aisle as the now red-faced man made his way back to his seat. Holly kept herself pressed hard to my side, the side with the Beretta in my hand under the jacket, until he'd passed.

"Come and sit with me. We'll catch up."

Once sitting, she leant close and said quietly, "You looked like you were about to kill him."

"I was."

"Jealous type?" she smirked.

"Protective type," I growled.

"What now?"

"Corran Ferry. Where Loch Linnhe narrows about ten miles south of Fort William. Harry will pick you up and you'll disappear till this is over."

"I still think I should come with you," she said.

We were quiet for a few minutes until Holly said, very quietly, "After Ullapool I asked Muzz to do a search for you, he found a photo from a small local paper in a place called Puerto Laterna, dated a little over a year ago."

She was a reporter, Muzz was a hacker, of course they'd come up with something between them.

"It was poor quality. Half a dozen people in rags on some kind of river boat in the jungle. Your name was there, but I couldn't see you."

I smiled sadly. I could name everyone in that photo.

"Third from the left," I told her.

She turned in her seat to look at me, eyes moved from the top of my head to my feet. Shaking her head. "No, the men in that picture were skeletons. I mean, look at you." She poked my bicep to make her point.

"Yeah, they didn't feed us much. But protein shakes and weight training fixed that," I said. Not quite true, the first few months had been a cocktail of drugs to rid me of disease and infection.

"Puerto Laterna is little town on the Orinoco in Venezuela. I was working on a project building bridges in a bid by their government to open up transport links to remote areas. Rebecca came out to visit, we went climbing, one of the rock spires that juts out of the jungle." Having avoided talking to anyone about this in the last year I was surprised at myself for how easily it was coming out now.

"What was she?" Holly interrupted gently. "To you."

"Fiancée."

"There were no women in that picture," she said, almost in a whisper.

"No," I said slowly.

We were close to Fort William now, the bulk of Ben Nevis took up the sky to our left and both our phones beeped simultaneously, saving me from further explanation.

A message, from Muzz, presumably.

I had forgotten how small the buttons were on these old phones. I used the tip of a fingernail to navigate through the basic menu, much to Holly's entertainment.

"You look like a Gorilla trying to thread a needle," she said to lighten the mood. "The police are on to us."

I finally got to the message myself. The Northern Constabulary wanted us both for questioning. There were mug shots of us both, obviously taken from footage from the police officers' chest-mounted cameras this morning.

There was no mention of murder, hidden bodies or Morocco. Just that we were wanted for questioning in a suspected arson case.

Still, it was bad enough. It was now public knowledge that I was in the country and Holly was now associated with me.

"You'll be safely out of sight on a yacht within a few hours. I'd hoped to get a taxi to Corran but I think it might be best to stay out of sight now."

"What's the plan?"

I pointed to the hill on the south side of Fort William. The suburbs of the town extended up the slope and stopped a couple of hundred feet short of the low wooded summit. A path winding its way up the gentle hill was clearly visible.

"We'll say goodbye like long-lost friends, you'll get off first. Keep off the main street. Buy water, it's a warm day. We'll meet at the top of the hill and walk. It's eight or ten miles in a straight line so with a bit of effort we'll get there in time."

The coach pulled to a stop. The door hissed open and the few passengers started shuffling off. We stood and Beetle stirred at my feet, stretched, farted and looked up expectantly.

"You'd better take him. You got on with him, the driver might remember," I told her.

She stood up. "Well it's been great to see you again. John," she said loudly and stretched her arms around me in a farewell hug. "We really shouldn't leave it so long next time." Her body was pressed to mine along its full length for a few seconds. I put one arm around her shoulders and held her to me briefly.

"Any chance I can have the gun?" she whispered.

"Absolutely none."

She pouted and strode off down the aisle with Beetle.

I watched her go while faffing with my jacket to buy a little time. I stepped off the coach as she disappeared around a corner forty yards away. I headed leisurely in that general direction.

I shadowed the girl and the dog through the streets of Fort William and up the hill, as in Inverness earlier, she made it easy. I joined her at the top, pausing long enough to take a swig of water from the bottle she'd bought on her way through the town.

"We need to get moving."

"What's Harry like?"

I thought for a moment. "Do you know those stone faces on Easter Island? The ones no one knows who made?"

"Yes."

"That's Harry," I said. "Let's go. We'll follow that vague ridge."

I walked fast. As fast a pace as I could maintain indefinitely, too fast for comfortable conversation. Head down, arms swinging, legs pumping. The sun beat down on us. Loch Linnhe shimmered far below us as we marched along the high ground parallel to it. It was a stunning day. One of those days you find it hard to believe; the Highlands are usually swathed in mist, cloud, rain or snow.

I pushed the pace relentlessly. Not out of malice. Out of the knowledge that the safest place for Holly was on that yacht with Harry, hidden away from the eyes of the world.

I could hear Holly panting behind me. Still keeping up well after the first hour.

I was carrying the bottle of water and paused briefly and often to offer it to Holly who gratefully took a long swig. We never paused long enough for conversation. Beetle ran around us gleefully.

We were well in to the second hour before I was satisfied we would make it and eased the pace a little. From our high ground we could see down the length of Loch Linnhe and the narrowing at Corran Ferry was obvious.

We came to a stop in a clearing in the woods above the little village of Corran. I thought I could see *Sandpiper* coming up the loch under power. It was just a little too far away to be sure. Holly stopped next to me and flopped on the ground, catching her breath.

"Well," she panted. "That burnt more calories than your average Pilates session."

"That's Harry," I said, indicating the yacht moving up the loch leaving a white V of a wake.

"He'll pass through the narrows and swing in close to the pier. You'll have to let him know I sent you. Tell him to use the binoculars and he'll see me. That should do it. Call me only if you have to. Otherwise it's essential calls only and stick to what Muzz said."

Holly was still lying on the ground. "You need to get going," I said. She said nothing just raised an arm for me to help her up, which I did. She came to her feet in front of me without letting go of my hand. Her shoulders glistening with perspiration.

Harry was just coming up to the narrows. He'd pass through and turn around, if Holly wasn't there he'd carry on.

I turned her gently in the direction she needed to go.

Beetle looked back and forth from Holly to me. "Go," I told him and he trotted after her. Leaving me in the clearing feeling strangely alone.

Holly paused, turned, and ran the few steps back up the hill to stand toe to toe with me. Harry was getting close. Holly had five hundred feet to cover between us and the pier at Corran.

I reached around her, lips brushing, and slipped the Beretta into her waistband against the small of her back.

"Now you need to run."

I watched her go. Beetle chasing her heels as she skipped through the broom down to the main road, which she ran across with a glance each way and on to the pier just as Harry drew up to it.

Holly waved. I saw Harry take up a pair of binoculars and look in my direction. He scanned the hill till he found me, I looked straight at him and nodded.

Harry replaced the binoculars, angled *Sandpiper* into the pier, and passing within a foot of it Holly and Beetle leapt aboard.

From the clearing I watched the tiny figures. I suddenly wanted very much to be on that yacht. Then I saw two little girls dressed in black, standing in the rain beside their father's grave.

I turned on my heel and kept walking.

Chapter 24

I pushed my glasses up my nose, straightened my tie and strode confidently across the plaza outside Euston train station in London, wearing a light grey suit.

After leaving Holly, a brief burst of energy had allowed me to cover the five miles across the hill to Ballachulish, where I borrowed an old Ford Fiesta from a back street and drove through Glencoe, leaving the little car hidden in Tyndrum, where I caught the train to Glasgow's Queen Street station.

I had a few hours until my next train so went in search of a barber shop.

"What will it be, sir?" the old boy asked.

"Short and neat."

He picked up a strand of dirty, matted, streaky blondish hair with a look of mild distaste.

"Excellent choice," he said politely.

I was washed, trimmed, clippered and even hot towelled.

At the end of it he swung the chair round to face the mirror with a flourish saying, "I think you'll agree that's an improvement?"

My hair was very short, neat, and back to its usual dark brown, almost black. Not a hint of blonde remained. A tidy parting on one side. My beard had been trimmed to within an inch of its life and gave me a far better jaw line than I had naturally. Hot towels had softened and cleaned my face to the point that I looked civilised, and younger. He'd even done some gardening on my eyebrows.

Next stop had been a department store where I picked up a black cabin-size wheelie cases, filling it with a new suit, hat, and reading glasses amongst other things. Then I made my way to Glasgow's Central Station where I settled into a cabin on the Caledonian Sleeper service to London, booked under a false name by Muzz.

At twenty-three minutes past seven the next morning I arrived in central London looking nothing like myself. I had the remains of a wad of cash in one pocket, a memory stick in the other and trailed the little black wheelie case behind me.

"Trafalgar Square, please," I said.

The cabbie didn't even look at me. A few minutes later we pulled up, I paid him and stepped out, walked another couple of blocks and hailed another cab in a different direction. After a good couple of hours of this I had deposited all the dirty old clothes in various bins across the city and replaced the them with things I would need for the day. I'd visited phone and electrical shops, newsagents, chemists, hardware shops and a couple of back street stalls. All in a seemingly random, zig-zagging path around the city.

I was currently near Leicester Square and a few minutes' walking found the kind of spot I was after: a small, quiet, courtyard with several cafés.

I walked casually around the area for ten minutes to get to know the lay of the land before circling back in to the square and walking in to the first café I had passed erlier. A nice little place, not one of the big generic chains. I chose a small leather armchair near one of the front windows and took a seat.

A waitress came and took my order. I laid my jacket on the seat and a *Financial Times* on the table. Picking up the wheelie case I walked towards the back of the café, passing the waitress I asked her to keep an eye on my things. The jacket pockets were empty, and the paper was just a paper, but the seat was in the right place, so I didn't want to lose it.

I spent a few minutes in the bathroom and reclaimed my seat by the window as an espresso and croissant arrived.

I ate the croissant, sipped the espresso, paid my bill then slipped a small tablet out of my case. Using the ear bud and phone Muzz had given me yesterday I called him, as we'd arranged.It rang briefly, stopped, no one said hello at the other end.

"Ready?" I said.

"Yes."

I pushed the little button on the side of the small tablet I'd bought that morning and waited for it to come to life.

I searched through the menus until I found what I was after and reeled off a long number, very carefully.

I waited.

"Good to go."

The long number was the machine's IP address, which Muzz had found and was now tracking.

I pulled the memory stick out of a pocket and pushed it in to the tablet's USB port.

I counted ten seconds in my head, gave it a few extra seconds for good measure and pulled it out.

"Done." I ended the call.

I wiped my fingerprints off the tablet and slipped it under the cushion I was sitting on, finished the espresso and left.

In the square outside was an old-fashioned bin against the wall into which I dropped a brown paper bag from my case and then walked into another café, going through a similar routine as before.

I sat down in a window seat and placed the case on the floor next to me, opening the zip on the top and slipping a hand in. Satisfied, I opened the *Financial Times* and pretended to understand it while sipping another espresso. I smiled to myself at what James would have said seeing me in a suit, in London, reading the FT.

They were quick, which was worrying. Barely ten minutes had elapsed.

Four serious-looking men in suits walked into the courtyard and paused. The man in front had his hand to his ear and fixed his eyes on the first café I'd been in. I saw his mouth move and three of the four men marched into the café while one stayed outside. I carried on reading the paper whilst watching the café out of the corner of my eye. From this angle I could only see the corner I had been sitting in by the window. After a few minutes one of the men came into view, checking under furniture and behind plant pots as he went. It didn't take him long to find the tablet under the cushion.

I'd bought it with cash and a false name.

Several minutes later they walked out, one man carrying my tablet. Presumably it took those minutes to satisfy themselves the owner of the tablet wasn't there and to ask whom had been sitting in that seat fifteen minutes ago. I had purposefully bought a not very well-fitting suit to disguise my frame and look average, forgettable.

The leader paused outside the café and looked around; he was looking high. For cameras? He'd see none, as I had. I dropped my hand in to the open zip of my case, resting my finger on a toggle switch.

He turned on his heel and marched out of the square without a word to his men who all followed obediently. I withdrew my hand from the case with relief.

I finished my second espresso of the morning before donning my jacket, zipping up my case and walking out of the café. As I passed the bin I pulled out the brown paper bag and put it back in my case.

I left through the other end of the square and took a left, a left and a left. No sign of them.

I redialled Muzz on the phone.

"Vehicle. Head west," he said.

I walked west, pulling out an old-fashioned paper A to Z of London.

I hailed a taxi, "Notting Hill, please."

"Still going due west," Muzz said.

"Bayswater. Still going," he said a minute or two later.

I followed his updates with my left forefinger on the A to Z. My right forefinger kept track of our whereabouts. Old school, but I didn't have a smart phone or any other gadgets to do it for me.

"Holland park. Still moving," Muzz updated.

"Stopped. One hundred metres west of Hyde Park," he said a few minutes later.

"Sorry," I said to the cabbie. "Could you make it the north end of Hyde Park, please?"

"Sure," he replied.

I paid the fare and walked into the park.

"Signal gone," Muzz said, giving me a house number and road name. I located it on the A to Z.

"Cameras?" I said.

"On it."

I walked south-west through Hyde Park. It had been many years since I was last in this part of London. From a stall near the entrance I bought a cheap fold out map of the park and orientated myself.

There were a lot of people about, walking, taking pictures, lying on the grass picnicking and sunbathing. It was turning in to a scorcher of a day.

I guessed the western half of the park was roughly a kilometre square. Wide paths crisscrossed the grass, the London plane trees and horse chestnuts in full leaf, thick and impenetrable.

In the centre of Kensington Gardens, I came across the *Physical Energy* statue where several paths met. The statue of a prancing horse and rider stood about fifteen feet tall on a rectangular plinth. I looked around. It would do.

I wandered the area like a tourist, admiring the statue from different angles dropping paper bags into different rubbish bins. I studied my map and walked south of the Round Pond towards Kensington Palace.

I spoke to Muzz via the ear bud.

"What have you got?"

"Basic view of the front only."

"Can you see the driveway, gates, cars?"

"Yes, yes and yes..."

"Anything in Kensington Gardens around the *Physical Energy* statue?"

"Nope." I hadn't seen any cameras either.

I strolled back to the statue and lay on a patch of unoccupied grass with the case next to me, unzipping it I arranged a few things inside and took a last look around.

"OK. Put me through."

The ring tone went on, and on. I was starting to get a bit worried. Muzz had just dialled the number Jessica had given me in the hospital room in Morocco. I hoped the call was as untraceable as Muzz believed.

"Hello." The cut-glass English voice was level and measured.

"Hello Jessica," I said.

There was a long silence.

"Ruraidh?" A little incredulity was obvious.

"I have what they wanted. Where are you?"

There was a longer pause. "London," she said. "Where are you?"

Interesting. If she was on her own, she'd be asking all the natural questions: Are you OK? Where have you been? What happened?

The cool, considered replies and long pauses suggested she was not alone.

"The *Physical Energy* statue. Kensington Gardens. Twenty minutes. Come alone," I said, very clearly, and ended the call.

"You watching?" I asked Muzz.

"Course."

Barely five minutes later Muzz's voice came through my ear.

"People coming out." A pause. "Shit!"

"What?"

"A seriously hot woman, six thugs in suits with and a middle-aged man leaving the building."

The hot woman could only be Jessica. "Five-ten, burgundy, looks like a supermodel?"

"Uh-huh," he replied.

"Describe the man."

"Fiftyish. Lean. Salt and pepper. Distinguished."

So what did that mean? Did she work for them? Was she one of them? I had to find out where she came in all this for Claire's sake.

"They're getting in to two black saloon cars." A pause. "Turned left out of the gate." Another pause. "Lost them."

A left took them to Kensington High Street, the nearest entrance to the statue was Queen's Gate.

A few minutes passed. Long enough for them to cover the distance. I saw Jessica stride up to the statue on her impossibly long legs. She moved well, no sign of her injury from the beach, but many weeks had passed. I focused on everyone but her and spotted a man trailing her that fitted Muzz's description of the older man. He walked slowly, looked around casually and took a seat on one of the benches, not acknowledging Jessica in anyway.

I couldn't see any thugs in suit. Plenty of men in suits, like myself, but they all looked natural. I didn't know how these men were trained to go about a situation like this. They probably had some kind of a procedure to follow. Maybe they were to form a loose ring around the area and close in. Maybe they'd make a defensive ring around the meeting point looking outwards for signs of trouble. Maybe there was one positioned up each path to grab me when I passed. Maybe, maybe, maybe. Basically, I didn't have a clue what they were going to do, didn't have a clue about the whole situation in fact. I was making it up as I went.

I let time stretch to the full twenty minutes before calling again.

"I said come alone."

"I am alone," she said. I could see her head swivelling, looking for me.

"Let me speak to him." I could see indecision in her body language. "He's sitting on the bench to your right."

She walked over and handed him the phone.

"Mr Maclean. I presume." His voice was authoritative, but warm.

"And you are?"

"Mr Drake."

"I want to know why James Bradbury was killed."

"It would be easier to explain face to face."

"I'd prefer to keep a little distance between us."

"Perfectly understandable."

OK. Wasn't expecting that.

"James Bradbury. Why?"

He sighed. "I was hoping you could help us with that."

He was good, very smooth, he was drawing me in to a civilised, urbane conversation about a man's brutal murder, presumably to stall for time. And I was letting him.

"Have you looked at the contents of the flash drive?"

"As this morning proved, it's tracked."

"Ahh," he said. "Did you do that on purpose? Clever."

I'd learnt all I could here, I had a name and knew what he looked like, I could carry on this conversation on the move. There were still six thugs somewhere.

I drew my feet in to stand and a shadow fell across me.

"Excuse me. Sir."

Too late.

Chapter 25

I don't think he knew I was the one they were after, he wasn't acting with like a man who has cornered his quarry. They must have been approaching likely suspects for a closer look.

From the angle I was looking up at him from, I could see the strap to a shoulder holster. He clocked the direction of my eyes, something changed in his face and I knew this wasn't going to end well. In the process of drawing my legs up and feeling his shadow fall across me I'd slipped my hand in the open zip of my case and flicked the little toggle switches.

One second.

"Sir." Two seconds. "Stand up please." His hand moved to his jacket. Three seconds, four.

"As I said before, Mr Maclean. It is something better explained in person," Mr Drake said again through the ear bud.

Five seconds.

I didn't bother replying.

It shouldn't take this long.

Boom. A sharp explosion rang out, pandemonium erupted in Hyde Park.

Boom. A second explosion. The first got people's attention, the second had sent them running.

The man above me crouched and turned to the noise, hand on his gun to see rubbish raining down like confetti from the little DIY bombs I'd put in the bins. I'd bodged them together from tins of lighter gas, jet lighters, cheap remote-controlled toys as the trigger and lots of duct tape. Noisy and distracting, but they wouldn't hurt anyone, the small blast would be directed straight up by the metal bins.

The man above me was taking a second to compute what happened. I knew it was coming so was already moving.

With my legs under me now I grabbed his ankles as I stood up and yanked them upwards, so his upper body went down. Once he was on his way to the ground I dropped his ankles and fell on him with a very ungentlemanly knee to the groin and delivered a fast jab across his jaw.

I glanced around and slipped the compact handgun from his holster to my case, emptied his pockets and hurried off to join the throngs of people high-tailing it out of the park.

I headed in the direction I figured they must have left their vehicles. I couldn't see Drake or Jessica, so sped up as they'd have a head start. I stood on a bench briefly to look further ahead and spotted Jessica's distinctive head of hair. A burst of speed narrowed the gap between us. As I passed between a couple of trees with low-hanging branches I ducked in to their cover and took a second to look at the gun, a Glock. I checked there was a round in the chamber and worked out the safety features before tucking it in the small of my back. I slung the case over a shoulder on its strap and set off.

I closed the distance to Jessica and spotted Drake walking purposefully next to her. There were two men in suits, one in front and one behind. Were the remainder staying in the park? Searching for me?

I followed the small group at a distance and closed the gap as we neared Queen's Gate.

My plan was somewhat flexible, due to not really having one, but for the moment I knew where they were, and they had no idea I was right behind them.

As we got to Queen's Gate I saw two black Jaguar saloons, double-parked and facing east. I checked behind, no sign of the rest.

A really bad idea started forming in my mind. I felt the corners of the case I'd been wheeling around all day, the bottom corners were of hard plastic, they were pretty solid.

At the Jaguars one suited man stepped into the road to go around the far side, presumably heading for the driver's door. The remaining three stayed on the near side. The second man opened both doors on the pavement side of the car and stood aside. Drake lowered himself into the front seat, Jessica descended gracefully into the back.

I was five yards away.

Would that last man get in after Jessica or walk around the back of the Jaguar and get in the other side? He closed both doors and started round the back of the Jaguar. I walked forward as if to cross the road just behind the car, he opened the rear passenger door, which blocked much of what the driver could see in his wing mirror.

The man was getting into the car in a typical manner. Facing forward, he lifted his left leg and put in in the footwell behind the driver's seat. With one hand on the top of the open door he pointed his backside towards the seat and let gravity do the rest.

When he was half-in and just ducking his head, I took two swift steps and jabbed the hard, plastic corner of my case into his skull just behind the ear. He slumped into the seat, unconscious. I just sat in his lap, closed the door, slid into the middle seat between Jessica and the unconscious man and placed the muzzle of the Glock against the driver's head.

The driver froze, staring at me in his rear-view mirror. Jessica was doing her best to become part of the upholstery, eyes huge, I don't think she recognised me until I winked at her.

I leant forward and pulled a Glock from under the driver's jacket and a third from the unconscious man next to me.

Drake was looking out of his window towards the park and hadn't yet realised what happened.

"Take us back," he said, without turning his head.

The driver looked nonplussed. Jessica looked terrified, I gave her an encouraging smile. The driver picked up some courage and cleared his throat with an *um-hum* noise.

Drake turned to give the driver a stern word and froze as he saw a pair of Glocks. His eyes swivelled further round and took me in.

"Drive," I said quietly.

The driver didn't move a muscle. "I won't ask again," I whispered.

He didn't move.

These were well-made luxury saloon cars with excellent sound proofing. I lowered a Glock to the man's lap and fired. He yelped like a puppy and the only reason he didn't knock himself cold on the roof was his seat belt. He stared down in horror, assuming the worst.

He realised the bullet hadn't even touched him and buried itself in the thick seat under him. It was just the hot gases burning his inner thigh that he was feeling, I hadn't shot off anything irreplaceable.Without further hesitation he jerked out into the traffic.

"Steady. If we don't get away from here cleanly I will hold you responsible," I said quietly into the driver's ear.

He nodded in understanding. We passed the Royal Albert Hall and he took the next right down Exhibition Road, taking us away from Hyde Park. Another right and I recognised the Natural History Museum. A left turn and I was happy he was taking us away from Hyde Park.

Things were progressing better than I'd hoped. I'd found them, got Jessica and her boss on their own, and it wasn't even midday yet.

Drake was watching me carefully.

"Do you carry a gun?"

He smiled pleasantly, "I do not."

"Prove it."

He loosened his seat belt a little and lifted his suit jacket up high and turned left, then right, in his seat. No holsters or guns.

"Ankles."

"Very thorough," He said, showing me black socks and a few inches of pale skin above each ankle.

"Are your men in the habit of carrying ankle holsters?"

"No. They are not. They each carry a standard issue Glock only," he said, still watching me carefully.

"Hands on the dashboard, don't move," I told Drake.

Keeping one gun up I reached down and felt the ankles of the unconscious man. Nothing.

To the driver I said, "This car's automatic, so if I see you drop your hands lower than the indicators bad things will happen to you. Nod if you understand." He nodded.

"Do you mind?" Drake said, indicating his hands on the dashboard.

"Put them on your knees, if they move, I'll put a bullet in your thigh."

"What's your name?" I asked of the driver.

He looked at Drake, who nodded his assent, "John Sowers."

"Which pocket is your phone in?"

"Inner left jacket."

"Take it out very slowly, pass it back to me." He did so.

"Mr Drake?"

"Outer right," he said.

I tossed them all out of the window, including Jessica's, who was sitting unnaturally motionless and subservient.

"Turn south at the next opportunity, John." He did so.

"I take it this car is tracked?"

"I would have thought so," Drake replied amiably.

I rummaged in my case, pulled out a device that looked like a car charger socket with an aerial and stuck it in to the twelve-volt socket, a little green LED lit up.

GPS signal jammer. I'd read an article on a long-haul flight a while back. These jammers are very popular with drivers of company vehicles who don't want their bosses to know their every move, for various reasons. Perfectly legal to buy in the UK and readily available.

"Now. Why was my friend was killed?"

"Mr Maclean, may I say something before we continue?" Drake asked in his smooth, reassuring manner.

"Be brief."

He turned to face me. "You believe we are the enemy. Understandable, given the evidence as you see it, but I assure you we are not. We have been looking for you since you disappeared in Morocco, for your help."

"Who killed James?"

"The man you seek is Wotjek Banyaki. He is, ultimately, the man behind your friend's death. From the country that was known as Yugoslavia when he was born in it, since then it's had a different name after each conflict, it's currently Bosnia and Herzegovina. He is the product of such a place, a narcissist, a sociopath, but a very clever one."

Definitely didn't see that coming.

"In the eighties his ambition outgrew his homeland, he moved to London to expand, he's operated under the radar ever since."

"East," I said to the driver.

"It wasn't until recently he was even identified. Hundreds of seemingly random, isolated crimes over the years are possibly attributable to this one man. He's careful, compartmentalised, and far removed from his activities. We started piecing his empire together as we always do, by following the money, but the scale of the investigation soon became enormous. Which is where Mrs Aitken's company came in. You know what she does for a living?"

I nodded.

Drake continued smoothly. "Two months ago a commercial conveyancing company discovered a discrepancy whilst carrying out standard checks on a property prior to a change of ownership. Naturally, Banyaki's name is red flagged. When emails started going back and forth within this company with his name on we took note. The emails were about historic records of ownership that showed little or no money changing hands for substantial amounts of real estate. These things have to be reported nowadays, some fraud law or other, regardless of the amount of time that's passed. It wasn't much, but it was enough. It was only those first few months in the country in the eighties that he put his name on anything, he soon learnt to use other people as fronts. This was his only crime that we had absolute proof of, enough to convict him, to send him to jail for long enough to take apart his organisation. We had a chance to cut off the head of the snake and let the body die."

I couldn't breathe, had James been trying to tell me? Prepare me? With all that information he would send about property.

"Our computers are trained, if that's the right word, to look for connections. James Bradbury was the solicitor in charge of the property that had flagged up Banyaki's name and he is, of course, the brother-in-law to one of our sub-contractors, Mrs Aitken here, who was involved with the financial side of the investigation."

I looked carefully at Jessica, nothing, not a twitch. She knew all this? And said nothing?

"The conveyancing company was requested to gather all the information related to Banyaki and place it on secure flash drives, of which many were handed out and most, somehow went missing. Mr Bradbury was to supervise the gathering of information. His flash drive went missing, it reappeared this morning, with you. They're quite special flash drives apparently, they record the information and then delete its source, so that stick possibly holds the only remaining copy of many incriminating documents."

James must have known he was going to die and his last action had been to send me the reason why. And I'd left it sitting in old Mrs Leven's cottage all this time.

"Morocco?" I asked.

"Of course." He gathered his thoughts. "We wouldn't usually involve a sub-contractor," he indicated Jessica. "But being aware of the connection we asked for her help. Just routine stuff, talk to his friends, work colleagues, anything that might shed light on what happened. You were obviously a close friend and someone James would turn to. You went to Morocco straight after the funeral. Whilst you were there we'd spoken to everyone else of interest and come up with nothing. You were the last one and we didn't know when you were coming back to the UK, so we asked Mrs Aitken to visit you in Morocco, as she'd planned to anyway. She is not a trained agent in any way, but as I saw it, she was just going out to see a friend, which she had been going to do anyway, so no harm could come of it."

I was looking at Jessica as he spoke. She didn't contradict or confirm any of what Drake said verbally or physically. She also wouldn't meet my eye.

"Mrs Aitken reported back that you knew nothing. But..." He paused, looking pained. "We seem to have a leak. Someone inside is, was, passing Banyaki information. It's the only explanation."

I was starting to get a headache.

"We think that informant is not high enough up to have access to everything, but enough. This same mole must have informed Banyaki of what Mr Bradbury's company found, as much of that information was subsequently destroyed in a break-in and some very clever work by hackers which makes that flash drive all the more valuable. The fact that we sent someone out to Morocco was given more significance than it deserved, and he assumed you had, or knew of, the whereabouts of this flash drive. Banyaki acted to eliminate a potential threat. Which is entirely in keeping with his brutal MO."

"The hospital in Marrakesh. I was going to be turned over to the Moroccan police, why?"

"Ah. Yes. That was a..." he paused, "complete cock-up. Basically. My fault entirely. I thought the threat of a Moroccan jail would have you telling us anything you knew. But I underestimated you. I didn't know about Venezuela at that point."

"What do you know?"

He knew everything.

He knew that several weeks after Rebecca's death I recovered sufficiently to be able to function again, weakly, but function. I was in a basic wooden cage surrounded by jungle. I could hear and smell their camp nearby but not see it. Once a day a rough looking guerrilla fighter in quasi-military uniform with a rusted AK47 would give me a bowl of sludge to eat and a bowl of water to drink and take away the previous day's bowls.

Once I had my wits back I'd easily escaped my filthy cage, as it was poorly made, and had a look around in the darkness. I discovered there were several other cages like mine, each hidden from the other. Another half a dozen people held in them.

After that I left my cage regularly and watched the guerrillas' camp with the patience and stealth of a deer stalker. Always from cover and always near enough to return to my cage if anyone went that way.

Over time I discovered that once a week half of the dozen fighters left for two days to fetch supplies. Like clockwork.

Their camp was a circle of rough huts around a fire pit where they would sit and drink at night before going to their huts to sleep. There was no guard. They were confident the cages and the pitiful condition of those inside meant they couldn't escape.

When the time came that half of them left on the supply run and half of them were snoring in their huts, in the darkness I simply crept into the huts one by one.

Before that I'd never killed a human, never had reason to, but I found it disconcertingly easy. They'd allowed Rebecca to die in my fevered, unconscious arms in that filthy cage then just dragged her body out in to the jungle to rot. I'd felt no remorse as I went about my work silently.

Having released the others from their cages we searched the huts and sat around the fire pit to eat as we studied maps. They were all male, white, from various countries and all in a poor physical state, some had been held for many months and were little more than bags of bones.

There was no radio at the camp, but we knew where we were from the maps. The nearest tributary to the main river was five miles away, may as well have been a thousand with the state they were in. They'd start walking and make a raft when they got to the tributary. I was going to stay behind and buy them some time. The six men away getting supplies would be back the next night. Fit, well-fed and used to the jungle they'd follow our trail and catch up to us in no time.

I was would to stay behind and slow them down, the others didn't argue, they were past caring and just wanted to get away.

I kept one assault rifle, grenades and a knife. The remaining weapons from the dead captors went with the escapees.

It was a simple job to booby trap the well-worn path the returning guerrilla fighters would take. My father had taught me all about trapping as a child, and when they came along it the next evening their deaths were almost an anti-climax, too easy, too quick. I'd wanted them to suffer, as she had.

So, Drake knew it all. Somehow. That I was a twelve-time murderer.

"OK," I said, lowering my gun. "Where do we go from here?" I asked Drake.

"Lunch?"

"If you're paying," I said and sat back.

He'd explained himself, now it was my turn.

Chapter 26

Drake passed a heavy A4 envelope over the crisp linen of the table.

"Not for the faint hearted," he said quietly.

I opened it to find a half-inch thick stack of glossy A4 photographs.

The first photograph wasn't too bad, it looked like a pile of old clothes on the ground in a vague likeness of a body. The man had been considered a threat to Banyaki in some way, apparently.

I was listening to Drake as I slipped the first photo to the bottom of the pile and froze. My brain took a second to process what I was looking at.

"That is what happened to the man's family," Drake continued.

I slipped the photo quickly to the bottom of the pile whilst looking at Drake. I lowered my eyes very slowly to the next photo with the cold dread you feel when you don't want to look at something awful, but you have to, it's inevitable, unavoidable.

I felt sick.

I looked away. Jessica was watching me from the bar where Drake had told her to wait. She was looking concerned. I couldn't even muster a reassuring smile or wink.

"These are genuine?" I asked Drake.

"Afraid so," he said very quietly. "Banyaki is singularly merciless in sending messages to his competition." I took a deep breath and went to the next photo. And the next, and the next.

Drake spoke now and again, giving background information to the photographs.

"That is a shipping container," he said. "The shipment was compromised; they were killed so no one could talk. They would have known nothing of use anyway. Whether he was making a point or just being careful we don't know."

My throat stung with bile, some of the bodies were so small.

"Sending this man to jail for a while is not enough. I know what you did in Venezuela," he said again, as if to make a point. "I know what you're capable of. I want you to cut the head off the snake. Literally. I want you to do what we can't, give us a chance to tear apart his organisation. To stop this," he indicated the photos.

I took a moment.

"James's murder seems quite mundane in comparison to these," I said calmly, although I felt anything but, as I indicated the photos.

"His saving grace, and his family's, is that they live in the UK. A scene like some of those you've just seen would be sensational in this country. Part of the reason he gets away with what he does is where he chooses to locate his businesses, far away in countries more corrupt and less developed than ours. On his home turf, here in London, he's very careful. Besides, it's hard to find men capable of carrying out such acts in the UK. There are plenty of contract killers in the country, but none that would do those things to order. Too conspicuous, they wouldn't stay in business for long."

"What are you? British Intelligence?"

"Yes." He said. Not specifying which.

"Do you not have your own people to do this?" I asked.

"Yes, but I have to seek permission and answer for their actions. Permission will not be given for this, not if there is some chance of bringing him in lawfully. But I believe the end justifies the means and this man deserves nothing lawful. And I'm not asking you to do anything you don't want to do. Am I?" He asked. "This is what you came here for, the name of the man that killed James." Exactly the last words I'd said to Jessica in Morocco. "And you have proven quiet adept, both in Venezuela and Morocco, at this line of work. Who'd have thought being a deer stalker's son and an engineer would make such an interesting skill set in a properly motivated man?"

"How do I find him?"

Drake sat back and smiled a little. "Scotland."

"Well... that's convenient."

"Yes, isn't it? It turns out that this narcissistic sociopath enjoys fly-fishing," he shrugged. "He goes all over the world chasing salmon. He's currently in your backyard, on the Spey."

He passed over some photographs and a map that covered the river between Grantown on Spey and Aberlour. The stretch he was fishing marked, and a circle around a building I knew to be the main house for that estate, another grand old Victorian hunting lodge.

"I know it." A popular stretch of water for salmon fishing if you could afford it. I had drifted down it many times as a kid in kayaks and rafts.

"It needs to look like an accident. An assassination would put everyone associated with him on alert, making our job much harder. So, no three-hundred-yard head shots."

"An accident will take more planning."

"You have seventy-two hours. After that he'll be back in the city."

"How do I get hold of you?"

He passed me a card.

Outside, once I'd turned a few corners I put the ear bud back in.

"Did you get all that?"

"Dude, I've got British Intelligence asking you to assassinate a man," Muzz replied excitedly. "That's... shit, man... that's gnarly."

I'd never cancelled our call, just slipped the ear bud in a pocket.

"Are you busy?" I asked Muzz.

"Depends."

I outlined my plans.

"No probs. Oh, and I cracked the password on the memory stick. It's as they said, Banyaki's names there."

I was horribly, horribly out of my depth. Organised crime, murder, British Intelligence, assassination.

I was in the same position as James had been in. Life-threatening information. But who to turn to? I felt deeply for my old friend.

Who could I turn to? The police? They'd arrest me on the spot. Knock on MI5's or MI6's door with a madcap conspiracy theory?

I could think of only one person that might help, that I had some minor connection with, that might listen to me, but it was a long shot. Muzz found me the address.

"General Mackay. I'm Ruraidh Maclean. We met in Ullapool," I'd said by way of greeting on the pavement in central London several hours later, just as he was about to duck into a Bentley.

He looked at me hard for a second. I was prepared to run, which was why I'd chosen to approach him on the pavement, not in a building.

"Indeed, we did. Get in," he said, indicating the Bentley.

Chapter 27

That evening I was in the driver's seat of an old but serviceable Ford Transit, found on eBay, paid for in cash to an owner who didn't ask any questions.

I was heading north through the night after acquiring some supplies.

The M40 eventually became the M6 which dragged on through the dark hours. By morning I was driving up the A9 north of Perth, sipping coffee bought from the last services. The day was looking typically Scottish - a little misty and a light drizzle but it looked like it would burn off with the sun.

I turned off at Aviemore. It felt odd to be heading in the direction of home but not going there. My thoughts dwelt on the pile of charred remains within the thick stone walls. Then memories of Holly that day came to mind.

I pulled to a stop in front of a house in the woods. Muzz had been busy. Amongst other things he'd hired this holiday cottage according to my requirements. It had to be isolated, have high ground around it with cover, be available as a last-minute rent for the rest of the week, be un-serviced so no one would come knocking and have mobile phone signal.

Getting out of the van I stretched, answered the call of nature and went for a walk. I circled the house several times at various distances until I was happy. Muzz had arranged for a key to be left for me. I unlocked the front door and had a good look around. It would do. The simple, cheap construction of the place would lend itself nicely to my plans.

I put the kettle on, retrieved some bags from the van and sipped coffee as I walked around. Feeling the spring in the floorboards gave me an idea. I took a minute to think it through, changed the plan in my head a little and got to work.

A few hours, and a lot more coffee and I was done. I piled everything back in the van and went for another walk. I circled the woods around the house several times then walked down the mile-long track to the road. I walked through the woods close to one side of the track on the way out and came back through the woods on the other side on the way back. Nothing much to see. The woods were uniform. A plantation of Scots pine planted around fifteen years ago judging by the size of them.

Back at the house I had one very careful walk around before shutting and locking the door with its new lock, just in case, for various reasons I didn't want the holiday home owners letting themselves in and getting a surprise.

I drove down the track and stopped at the road, got out and had a good look at the track behind the van, memorising the pattern of my tyre tracks in the soft, muddy bits of the track. When I came back later, I'd want to know if anyone had been this way.

I knew from Drake which stretch of river Banyaki was due to fish and checked an Ordnance Survey map of the area before parking the van out of sight. I packed a rucksack with some of my new purchases and set off for the river.

The river Spey, the second longest river in Scotland at ninety eight miles from source to sea, traditionally considered the best Salmon river in Scotland, meanders through a wide glacial valley at this point. The road I'd been on wanders down the same valley coming near the river in places and a mile away in others. I approached the river through fields and woodland.

The banks were lined with trees, grass, bushes and scrub of varying thicknesses. Most of the fishing on this stretch was accessed from the far side.

Banyaki's beat of the river started a little upstream. I started heading carefully upriver with the binoculars around my neck like a bird watcher. There was no one on the stretch of water between the beats so I moved fairly quickly until I got to the bottom end of the section I was interested in. I stopped and took out the map, memorising the features.

I moved on carefully and passed by an empty fishing hut on the far side and several pools that weren't being fished until I came to a long sweeping bend and saw cars parked on the track on the far side. One was a ghillie's vehicle, a short-wheel-base Land Rover with a substantial rod rack clamped on it. Every beat here came with its own ghillie - a combination of fishing guide, companion and supervisor for those fishing the section of river he was responsible for.

I crept on until I could see the entire scene and settled down in thick cover with the binoculars and a telescope. There were two very shiny Range Rovers, similar to the one I'd recently put in a loch, and six big men in suits. The ghillie spoke to the older man and indicated various bits of the river, no doubt telling him where to get in and how best to fish this pool.

I watched them carefully as they entered the water in their chest waders and moved out towards the middle of the river. The ghillie moved easily and surefootedly, as you'd expect.

Banyaki a little less so, but still perfectly capable. The photos I'd been shown were a good likeness for Banyaki. No mistaking him. I hoped he wasn't the kind of fisherman that liked the ghillie at his elbow all day long, if he was, things were going to be a little harder, but I doubted it, he didn't look like a man that required small talk or encouraging words.

I swapped the binoculars for the telescope and Banyaki's brutal, raw-boned face jumped into view, close and sharp, thanks to my new, eye-wateringly expensive telescope.

He was a good fly fisherman, his double spey casts were a thing of beauty, the line flying out straight for fifty yards before settling gently on the water. Better than I was, I conceded begrudgingly.

I didn't let his fly-casting prowess distract me.

I watched them all day as they moved from pool to pool. They fell into a pattern. The ghillie would arrive at the head of the convoy, the two Range Rovers following. One vehicle had four of the bodyguards in it and the other held Banyaki and two bodyguards, one of them driving.

On arriving at a pool, the ghillie would take Banyaki's rod off the racks on his vehicle and give it the once over, changing the fly if he saw fit. There'd be a brief conflab between the ghillie, Banyaki and one of the suited men after which the ghillie would lead Banyaki into the river. A pair of bodyguards would head fifty yards upriver, a second pair in the opposite direction. One would stay with the vehicles and one, the leader, would be on the bank somewhere near Banyaki.

The ghillie would stay in the water with Banyaki for the first few minutes or so and then retreat to the bank, leaving Banyaki alone in the river, but be near enough to help if needs be.

As I sat on the far bank of the river watching them from a safe distance I thought the bodyguards were doing a pretty lousy job. They were all on the far side of the river for a start. The fact that I'd been creeping around this side of the river all morning without a problem showed up their weak point. I was well camouflaged though. The trekking trousers, walking boots, fleece and waterproofs were all muted shades of green, khaki and beige, bought to blend in.

After a few hours I'd reconsidered my initial thoughts on the bodyguards' competence. I realised they didn't stand a chance against a sniper, so weren't taking any precautions against one. There was so much high ground, so much cover that there were a thousand places to take a shot from. And Banyaki was the perfect target, standing in the middle of the river. Each time he took a cast he stood motionless for up to a minute, as the current brought the line around before he cast again. The trees and plants gave plenty of information on wind speed and direction. It would be child's play.

Banyaki had caught two salmon by lunch time. He had played them competently and calmly, expending their energy, until he reeled them in to the long-handled net wielded by the ghillie. I watched him throughout the process and at no time did he show any actual enjoyment or satisfaction.

He reeled in his line after his last cast and waded back to the bank. Must be lunch time.

I stood after they'd departed, stretched and walked upriver to the very top end of this section.

If it weren't for the grim reason I was here, I'd be enjoying the day. It was sunny and warm by the river. But I had a job to do so I pulled out the little GPS unit. It took a few seconds to warm up and find itself and displayed a simplified map on its little screen. I programmed in the top of the pool as the first way point on the little unit and walked the length of this section of the river, programming the top and bottom of each pool.

I passed the fishing hut, on the far bank, on my way down the beat and moved carefully past it so as not to be seen and spent a few minutes watching them. The bodyguards were spread out around the hut and I could see a third Range Rover had arrived. Through the windows of the fishing hut I could see a young blonde woman sitting at a table with Banyaki having lunch.

The ghillie was nowhere to be seen, he'd live near enough to go home for lunch.

I carried on to the point I'd leave the riverbank to walk back to the van and programmed in the last way point on the GPS. Shrugging off the rucksack I ate and drank a simple lunch of my own before tipping out a camouflage patterned wetsuit along with matching neoprene boots, hood and gloves. They were popular with spear fisherman, apparently. When I'd walked into the diving and water sports superstore near London I'd been pleasantly surprised at the sheer variety of camouflage wetsuits available. I striped off my hiking clothes and pulled on the neoprene.

I strapped two empty divers weight belts around my waist, the type that have a row of six nylon pouches into which you put bags of lead shot for weight. They were empty at the moment leaving a total of twelve Velcro pouches strapped around my waist, I slotted the GPS unit in to one of them. It was supposed to be waterproof to ten metres. I hoped the claim was true.

I strapped a substantial dive knife to my calf, just in case.

Picking up a pair of black fins, a mask, gloves and a small pony bottle I set off upriver. Within five minutes I'd stopped and stripped off the top half of the wetsuit before I expired from the heat. Luckily my upper body was deeply tanned from the weeks on the yacht, so I didn't have to worry about a white torso giving me away. I carried on up the river. The fishing hut was empty, so I carried on and found them further up. I crept on until I was upriver of Banyaki and his entourage. I found a comfy looking patch of grass in thick cover and settled down to wait.

I waited all afternoon. Banyaki fished his way through several different pools. He caught one fish all afternoon. Each time they moved pools I repositioned myself upriver of them and waited. And waited. The afternoon passed.

At around six they all headed down the river. I wondered if they would go back to the lodge for dinner or eat at the hut. I was hoping a keen fisherman like Banyaki would have a quick dinner at the hut and keep fishing. And I really hoped he'd swap his fifteen-foot salmon rod for a smaller trout rod and try his luck for some sea trout, that generally only took a fly when it got dark. If not, I had a problem, because my plan would be harder in the daylight tomorrow. Not impossible, just harder.

I wandered carefully down the riverbank until I could see the hut and found a safe spot to keep watch.

The sun was getting low and my stomach was rumbling, I was glad I was upwind and couldn't smell their dinner, which arrived in a small white van with the estate's name emblazoned on its side. A bevy of young girls came in with platters and laid everything out on the table before withdrawing under the gaze of the bodyguards.

I tried not to nod off after having driven through the previous night.

After an hour the ghillie's Land Rover reappeared. He walked to the line of rods leaning against the hut, selected the same fifteen-foot salmon rod he'd used earlier and a smaller, nine-foot trout rod.

They left the hut in the usual convoy and headed upriver. The blonde left in the other Range Rover.

I took up position above whichever pool they were fishing and settled in to await darkness. Banyaki caught a salmon in the failing light which the ghillie landed for him without drama and they moved up the river as it got fully dark.

By the time I caught up with them the ghillie and Banyaki were wading out into a long pool with thick trees on my side and a clear section on their side where the trees had been removed to make casting easier. They waded out about halfway before Banyaki started casting, lengthening his line with each cast until it was nearly reaching this bank and the fly was covering the water that the sea trout were likely to be moving up through.

The night was dark and still, the water just a little rippled as it moved down the pool. The ghillie stayed with Banyaki for the usual ten minutes and then retreated to the bank. I could see the silhouette of one of the bodyguards and the ghillie, the remaining men were out of sight, I assumed they were in their usual locations up and down the track.

I studied where people were standing in relation to each other. I tried to gauge how long it might take for one man to get from one place to another. I watched the speed of the water, where it rippled, swirled and eddied as it passed over rocks below and where it sped up in the deeper channels.

I was stalling. I'd been watching the river and the people all day. I knew all I needed to.

I pulled up the hood of my camouflage wetsuit, then the gloves. I double checked the weight belts were secure. I took the pony bottle in one hand and slid silently into the water under the cover of overhanging branches. I lay in the shallows allowing the cold river water to seep into the wetsuit and warm up. As I waited, I started slipping rocks in to the pouches on the two weight belts I was carrying tightly around my waist. I filled all eleven pouches to breaking point. I needed to be as heavy as possible for this.

A pony bottle is a miniature SCUBA diving cylinder, just one litre in capacity, with a rubber mouthpiece screwed to the neck. You just held it in your mouth and breathed normally. One litre didn't give you much air, but I didn't need much, and I didn't want the bulk and hassle of full diving gear. The pony bottle was bright yellow when I brought it yesterday, I'd since wrapped it in black insulating tape.

The rocks I was carrying, in lieu of the normal lead, were to keep me pinned to the riverbed, using my hands and feet I traversed the river underwater. It took a few minutes, moving slowly in almost complete darkness. I breathed shallowly and let each breath out very, very slowly, so the bubbles didn't disturb the surface above me.

I moved into the shallows on the far bank of the river, roughly level with where I'd set out and surfaced silently under overhanging branches.

The pool he was fishing had the trees cleared off the bank to allow an unobstructed back cast for the fishermen. No more branches hanging over the river for cover. I judged the direction and strength of the current, checked the ghillie's and bodyguards' positions, whispered quietly, "For all you have done and all you will do," and slipped under the water.

Using the picture in my mind as a guide I pulled myself diagonally downstream across the riverbed.

When I judged I was lying just upstream of Banyaki I started downstream an inch at a time. Studying the darkness in front of me. I carried on until I saw an indistinct vertical feature. His legs. I was a couple of feet off to one side so shifted over. I couldn't afford to hang around at this point, as I had to hold by breath so he wouldn't see my bubbles break the surface.

I mentally rehearsed my next move.

Nothing fancy.

I yanked his boots out from under him, so he landed on his front in the water as if he had slipped on a smooth rock. He flailed wildly and what visibility I had was lost in the churned-up water.

The ghillie would be on the move already. I had thirty seconds at most. Working by feel alone I positioned myself under him, facing up and held his wrists in my neoprene gloved hands.

All I had to do was hang on. All the weight I was carrying was pulling me downwards and hanging on to Banyaki's arms was keeping his face in the water. Five seconds and his struggles had decreased in intensity enormously. The lifejacket burst into life, but I kept him face down in the water easily enough. I worked my fins to ease us into the deeper water, gently enough that no one above would notice the slightly unnatural direction of our drift. Each foot further away was an extra second before the ghillie or a bodyguard got to us.

Banyaki was motionless now, the world went quiet and I could hear a frantic splashing noise through the water, but I couldn't tell how far away they were. I held on to the last second, just to be sure. I let go only when I felt his body jerk as someone got a hand on it, I just let go and dropped smoothly away to the depths of the riverbed.

As I lay on my back looking up I started emptying out rocks from the pouches of the weight belts. At the point where I achieved neutral buoyancy the current took over and I felt myself moving gently downstream. I could see nothing in this deeper water, so I relaxed and went with it.

I took my best guess as to when a couple of hundred yards had passed, emptied out the remaining rocks and finned gently into the river bank on the opposite side to Banyaki's fishing group. I surfaced carefully.

I crept out of the water and made my way back up stream. The headlights from the Range Rover were illuminating the track where Banyaki's body lay. Any attempt at resuscitation had ceased. His body was lying on the dirt track, much like James would have lain in the woods till he was discovered.

Chapter 28

They weren't acting like a group of men who thought their employer had just been assassinated. They were acting like a group of men whose boss had just slipped and drowned in the river. There was a lot of shouting and finger pointing and I could see the white-faced ghillie making a phone call.

I watched for a while, just to be sure Banyaki didn't make a miracle recovery then moved back down the bank until I was out of sight around a bend in the river, slipped back into the water and just floated down the river. Easier than walking in the dark.

The GPS unit I had carried was in case I needed to navigate under water. If I had been forced to do this in daylight I would have stayed submerged far more to avoid being seen. Hence programming in the top and bottom of each pool and the point where I left my clothes and rucksack. As it was, I had no need for it.

I stripped of, dried myself, dressed, and carefully put everything in the rucksack, mentally ticking off each item so I knew I hadn't left anything in the dark.

I swung the pack on my back and walked through the dark back to the van. Just as I pulled away I heard sirens in the distance. I picked up the mobile and made a call, as arranged.

At the end of the driveway to the holiday house I hopped out and checked the ground for signs of fresh tracks. Nothing new.

I drove up to the house with the Glock from London in my hand and using a headtorch examined the frame of the front door. The tiny splinters of wood I'd placed between the door and the frame were still there. No one had opened the door while I'd been away. I took a walk around the house, no signs of anyone passing this way.

I took out another burner phone and keyed in the number Drake gave me.

A ring tone sounded once, twice and Drake's voice came on.

"Yes," he said curtly.

"It's done."

"That was quick."

"I had an opportunity. I took it. What now?"

"Are you somewhere safe?"

"Yes."

"Then lie low. Don't move if you don't have to. I'll be in touch."

"Understood," I said, and he hung up.

I tossed the phone on the dashboard of the van, it was a GPS enabled phone. I left it turned on. From the back of the van I donned some extra layers, more natural colours that would fade into the background on a night like this, and shoved everything else I'd need in the small rucksack.

I walked away from the front of the house and found the spot in the woods I'd identified during my meanderings earlier and holed up.

Lying totally still and silent I let my eyes adjust to the near darkness. After twenty minutes passed I smiled as the rabbits started appearing from their burrows around the edge of the clearing around the house. I had spotted their burrows earlier and was counting on the little creatures to be my early warning system. Now they were out I could relax.

I raised the binoculars to my eyes to see how much light they were gathering and got a surprisingly good, monochrome image.

I listened carefully as I waited. The spot I had chosen in the woods was high enough up the slope to give me a good view of the house and clearing below. There was a slight rise behind me which hid me from view of anyone approaching from that direction. I had collected dry pine cones and little sticks on my recce of the woods earlier and sprinkled them liberally on the ground behind me, adding to the detritus already there, making it next to impossible for anyone to approach silently from behind in the dark.

Over an hour had passed when I saw several rabbits twitch, some looked towards the track leading to the road and then, as one, they all disappeared down their respective burrows. I very slowly raised the binoculars to just below my eyes and waited.

The minutes passed in silence. No movement, no noise.

I waited.

I caught the slightest movement near the end of the track where it opened out into the clearing. Just a slight change in the depth of the darkness

There were two of them. Dressed in black from head to foot. One on each side of the track close into the trees. They paused for a long time at the end of the track before moving in opposite directions around the edge of the clearing and meeting up at the far side.

I watched through the binoculars. It was too dark for any real detail, but they were both carrying automatic weapons tucked into their shoulders and a bulge on their thighs hinted at a holstered handgun. The silhouette of their heads looked normal, so no night vision goggles clamped on, hopefully.

They approached the front door of the house, pausing, one of them knelt and picked the lock then they moved through the front door, one high, one low, silently.

The door swung closed behind them due to the spring I'd screwed in place earlier. I stood and was closing in on the house when I heard a loud *whooshing* noise and bright flashes of light lit up the windows.

I ran the last few steps to the corner of the house and trained my Glock on the front door. They didn't come out. I grabbed a couple of things out of the rucksack and dropped it. Moving forward I crouched low beside the door and listened. Nothing.

Donning a dive mask and breathing through a second pony bottle I put my key in the Yale lock, twisted the door handle and slipped through, moving to my left and sweeping the Glock back and forth.

Nothing. Totally black. I reached up and flicked the light switch on the wall behind me. The light revealed a total whiteout in the house, dense clouds of white powder in the air. I crept forward.

I headed towards the bedroom. The powder was settling slowly, the ceiling above now visible but everything below a complete whiteout.

I stumbled over one of the bodies before I saw it. No movement. I got closer, not wasting time looking for a pulse and threw the man's weapons away. I carried on and stubbed my toe on the second man who lay just inside the bedroom door. After removing his weapons also, I grabbed each man by a foot and dragged them out of the front door to the fresh air.

Out in front of the house I stripped off my dive mask and pony bottle and breathed in the night air. Keeping my Glock trained on the bodies I gave each one a, sightly harder than strictly necessary, kick in the ribs. Nothing. Leaning down to each one in turn, feeling for a pulse in the neck whilst keeping the gun handy. Both were alive, unconscious and covered head to foot in the white powder from the carbon dioxide fire extinguishers I'd rigged to go off when they stood on certain floorboards in the house. I secured them with tie-wraps.

I'd recalled from a firefighting course I'd been made to attend years before, when working briefly at an oil refinery, that carbon dioxide extinguishers, as well as being good for electrical fires, would cause unconsciousness followed by death in confined areas.

I entered the house again to open all the windows and doors to let the powder disperse, which it did quickly with the breeze.

Retrieving the two automatic weapons and handguns I dragged each man back into the house. With rope from the van I strung them up to one of the beams running across the open-plan living area. I searched them and made a pile of their belongings. Other than the weapons there wasn't much - no ID, one phone between them and a Jaguar key fob.

I picked up one of the automatic weapons and had a good look at it. Heckler and Koch MP5. I spent a minute familiarising myself with the weapon. It was light, short, manoeuvrable, fitted with a suppressor and chambered for nine-millimetre rounds. A handy little weapon at very short distances.

I turned off the lights and left.

I holed up in the same place as before. In case they had backup in the area. And if not, it would let the men in the house regain consciousness and sweat a bit.

I left it a good long time before approaching the house again. If anyone was waiting for these men nearby, they would surely have investigated by now.

I flicked the lights on as I went in. The man on the left was older with a greying crew cut and the unmistakeable countenance of a soldier. He watched me carefully.

The second man was the polar opposite. Younger, with a narrow weaselly face and the eyes too close together. He wasn't happy.

"I'll rip your throat out!" he screamed at me. "Who do you think you are? If you knew what I'd do to you when I get free you'd..." Every word was punctuated with a profanity.He carried on in this way until I landed a heavy blow into his solar plexus, driving the air out of his lungs.

"Are you alone?" I asked, very quietly.

The weaselly one opened his mouth. "You can fu-"

He stopped abruptly as the butt of the Heckler and Koch knocked out most of his front teeth.

He opened his mouth again. I gave him the benefit of the doubt, but the first word he uttered confirmed he was not going to say anything useful, so his nose went next, crushed flat.

When he'd recovered enough to listen I spoke quietly. "Not a quick learner, are you?"

"Are you alone?" I asked again, my voice flat, cold.

He had enough sense to stay quiet this time. Blood from his nose and mouth trickling down the black clothes he wore.

"Last time, after this it gets messy," I growled. "Are you alone?"

No answer.

I raised the automatic weapon in both hands, tucked into my shoulder, aimed at the fleshy part of his thigh and squeezed the trigger. The selector was on single-shot, so a single nine-millimetre round skimmed the quadriceps muscle. I swung immediately to do the same to the other man amid the screaming.

"Wait," said older man, perfectly calmly. I eased the pressure on the trigger.

"We are alone," he said.

"Pussy!" the bleeding man spat. "What you doing?"

The older man ignored his weasel-like partner.

I lowered the H&K but kept it tucked into my shoulder, ready.

"Your orders?" I asked him.

The weaselly one started, "Don't you f-" I silenced him with a sharp upward blow of the H&K's steel butt under his chin which snapped his head back, unconscious.

"Your orders?" I repeated.

"I can't tell you that," he said simply.

"You were obviously sent here to kill me. Why?" I asked.

"We're not told the reasons," he said.

"Your orders came from a man named Drake?"

"I cannot divulge that information," he told me.

There were quicker ways than this and I needed to make a call anyway.

I punched in a number. It rang once.

"It's done. Two turned up. I have them secured," I said. "Can you tell them to talk? I'd like to know whether to expect more."

I held the phone to the man's ear. I couldn't make out the other side of the conversation but the man hanging in front of me said lots of 'Yes, Sir's whilst staring at me and nodded when the conversation was over. I put the phone to my ear, the line was dead. The General had hung up.

"Who are you?" he asked. I ignored the question.

"He told you to cooperate?" I asked. He nodded. "How long have you been in the area?"

"Weeks," he said. I raised an eyebrow at this and thought hard.

I slackened off the ropes holding him up to the beam, as a sign of good faith, but I didn't loosen them to the point he was a threat.

"Have you been to a cottage above a loch near here?" I asked. He nodded.

"When?"

"Two days ago."

"Tell me what you found."

"A burnt-out cottage on a hillside."

"And...?"

"Evidence of a shooting." I made a carry on gesture and started pulling up floorboards. "We were told to find out what happened to two men who were supposed to be there. We took a walk around and insect activity drew us to an area of blood and brain matter in the edge of the woods above the cottage. The direction of the spatter told us the shots came from up the hill so we recced the area and found a pair of empty .243 cases." He paused. "Yours?"

It was my turn to nod ever so slightly. "You reported this to Drake?"

"Yes."

"Did you say how far the shot was?"

"Yes, three hundred yards," he said. Drake knew two of Banyaki's men were supposed to be waiting at my house. He shouldn't have known that, only Banyaki should have known he'd sent men to wait for me. I carried on removing floorboards and pulled out paracord and springs.

"You booby-trapped the house?" he asked. "You knew we were coming?"

I knew someone would be coming, because I knew Drake had lied to me, I just wasn't sure who, how many or how well-armed they'd be. Hence the booby trap. But I couldn't kill them, which was a shame. It would have been infinitely easier to just blow up the house than to take them alive. Carbon dioxide poisoning was the best, non-lethal idea I could come up with on the fly that didn't involve me getting close to men with guns.

I removed all the bits and pieces of my booby traps as we continued our conversation, filling in some blanks in my knowledge of events.

"Mostly we've just been on standby until the others arrived," he finished with.

I rounded on him. "What others?"

Six more men had arrived yesterday. A few hours ago they had received their orders. Two men to eliminate me. Two men to eliminate a young man in Inverness. And four to eliminate a man and a woman on a yacht. Drake was tidying up loose ends, all of them.

The bottom dropped out of my world.

Chapter 29

I dialled a number. "Muzz?" No need for avoiding names now. Somehow, he knew everything.

I heard heavy breathing on the other end. "Muzz!" I shouted down the line. More heavy breathing.

"Oh. Sorry dude," he panted. "Hang on."

"Muzz, you OK?"

"Yeah. Couple of serious-looking dudes came to my flat, been on the move since then," he said.

"How'd you get away?"

"Video doorbell."

"Good lad. Got somewhere to hide?"

"Yeah."

"Another four are going for Harry and Holly. Where are they?"

"Dunno exactly. They've been good at keeping comms to a minimum. I've been trying the phone, nothing yet."

"Last known position and heading?"

"They kept it vague, as agreed."

I quizzed the man hanging in front of me none too gently. The four men tasked with disposing of Holly and Harry were sent to Fort William to await their exact location, they knew they were in the Hebrides, but not exactly where. With a decent car they'd be at Fort William already. I was hours behind.

Each team reported to Drake only, they had no contact between teams. Drake was micromanaging, it seemed.

I pulled out the phone, hit redial, and told the general of this latest development.

"Can you call them off?" I asked.

"No. Drake took a swan dive out of his apartment window rather than face the music when he knew we were on to him. He kept this operation very close to his chest, and his chest is being scraped off the pavement as we speak."

"Can you send someone to stop them?" I asked.

"Not in time and I don't know who he sent or how to contact them. You're looking at several hours mobilisation even after I've convinced the army or marines to help."

"Well... shit."

"If you want something doing..."

"Not helpful," I snapped.

"Yes, it is. Focus. Use that brain of yours and think up something ridiculous. Let me know when you've found them." And he hung up.

I shook my head at the general's unorthodox pep talk.

How do you search a huge area of water for a small yacht in amongst the islands, inlets, bays and channels of somewhere like the west coast? I had a rough idea of the area they'd be. Harry wouldn't stay in Loch Linnhe, it was a dead end. He'd sailed south from Corran Ferry after picking up Holly. I reckoned he'd be somewhere east and maybe south of Mull. Probably not as far down as the isles of Jura and Scarba. He'd be somewhere with options, plenty of possible headings, not trapped.

I grabbed a large dry bag from the van and threw in all the weapons and anything else that could be useful.

The man watched me silently. Before I left I tightened his ropes.

"Sorry, sure you understand," I said flatly. As an afterthought I asked his name.

"Westerby," he said reluctantly.

I held up the Jaguar key fob I'd taken from his pockets earlier. "Where's the Jag?"

It was a good car, identical to the one I'd been in with Drake in London, must be their standard company car. The electronic driver's aids, not me, kept it on the road as I sped along narrow single-tracks. Luckily, there was nothing else on the roads in the middle of the night. I barely slowed as I passed through Aviemore. Five more miles of narrow back roads and I skidded to a stop with the headlights illuminating the doors of a small hanger in the middle of a grass field.

I examined the padlock holding the big sliding doors of the hanger together. It was a proper piece of kit, I couldn't pick it so shot it off. Sliding the doors back the Jaguar's headlights illuminated four slender, shiny white gliders crammed in the hanger. At the front, facing out, was the small red and white plane the gliding club used to drag their gliders in to the air on summer weekends.

I was already hours behind the four men dispatched to the west coast and even in the fast Jaguar it would take me hours to drive to Fort William, and then I had a huge area of water to search for *Sandpiper*. They had the advantage of satellites to track down the yacht. I didn't.

Searching from the air was the only option I could think of. There would be planes at Inverness airport. But small as it was, it still had fences and security. If I stole a plane from there it would be known instantly, I wouldn't get far.

This airstrip, behind the hamlet of Feshiebridge was just a hangar in a field with a grass runway. The nearest house was miles away and only a padlock between me and a plane.

The only problem was that I couldn't really fly. Rebecca had given me a trial flying lesson as a birthday present a few years back. I'd spent a happy hour throwing a Cessna around the sky. Flying a small plane was surprisingly easy. The take-offs and landings were the tricky bit, and we hadn't really covered those in the one lesson I'd ever had.

I had a close look at the little plane. It seemed in good nick. Clean and shiny. There were two fuel caps, one on each wing, a look inside showed them to be full. Robin DR 400 was written on the side, which didn't mean anything to me. It had a sliding glass bubble over the cockpit instead of doors, which was currently slid all the way forward. I climbed into the tiny cockpit, settling in to the seat the first thing I noticed was that there was just a metal stick between my legs. The Cessna, the only other thing I'd ever flown, had a wheel. This definitely wasn't going to be one of my best ideas.

I scanned the instrument panel in front of me. I had no idea what half the instruments were for. I recognised the artificial horizon, altimeter, climb rate indicator, directional compass, fuel and oil pressure. That would be enough to get me going, I'd work out the rest on the way. There was a well-thumbed file wedged between the seats which I hoped was a manual.

Usefully, a small, laminated bit of paper was stuck to the instrument panel with the heading "Start-up Checklist." I followed the instructions, locating the relevant switches as I went, the only sticking point was that it required a key. For some reason I didn't think planes actually needed a key. I fished out my head torch and contorted myself into an upside down position in the cockpit to look under the instrument panel and discovered a light aircraft was easier to hot-wire than a motorbike. I striped out the few wires behind the ignition with a Leatherman, a genuine one this time, and after a little trial and error twisted the right wires together. After following the remainder of the start-up checklist, the little engine wheezed into life and settled down to a smooth idle.

I stowed the dry bag from the car behind the seats. After checking the wind direction, I drove the car to the far end of the grass runway, spun it one hundred and eighty degrees with a handbrake turn and came to rest shining the head lights down the grass runway in the direction I would be coming from.

I ran back down the runway, strapped myself in, slid the canopy back and locked it in place. I pulled out the throttle and the plane started shaking alarmingly and rolled forward, the noise deafening in the hangar even with the radio headset on.

Luckily, the gliding club had pushed the plane in backwards, I had only to roll forwards on to the grass. I tentatively pushed on a pedal with my foot and the nose of the little plane swung slowly to one side. I experimented a little with the pedals and throttle until I got the hang of it and made a couple of quick figures of eight on the grass before lining up at the end of the grass runway pointing at the headlights, which suddenly seemed not very far away.

I waggled the stick between my knees one way and looked at the wings before waggling it back over the other direction. Forward and back came next, I noted the response in the flaps on the wings. I already knew what the pedals did.

With the basic controls sorted I faced forward. The pedals are used to keep the plane in the right direction as it rolled along the ground, simple enough. Stick to the left or right to keep it level. I had no idea what the take-off speed was. And I was sure there was a specific flap setting for take-offs and landings, but I couldn't see any useful marks on the flaps lever saying 'take-off', just up and down arrows. I reckoned the flaps had to be up as that would effectively push the nose up and the tail down which was the attitude one was looking for in a taking-off aircraft, so I slipped the lever in to the first notch in the up direction. If we didn't take off I'd just push it the other way. I was quite literally winging it, again.

There was too much I didn't know. But I did know that four armed men were well ahead of me, I knew that Holly and Harry had no idea they were coming for them.

I checked what instruments I knew and pulled the throttle all the way out. The little aircraft started shaking as the engine note rose to a scream.

The plane bounced so much I could barely keep my feet on the pedals and the stick steady. The instruments were a blur and I focused on the headlights in the distance to give me a reference point. As the torque of the propeller acted on the plane it wanted to veer to one side. I counteracted this with the opposite pedal and kept it aiming at the lights. As the speed picked up I started to feel a little lift from the wings and then a tendency to dip to one side or the other became apparent. I moved the stick in the opposite direction to which the craft was rolling, which seemed to work. At around fifty kilometres per hour the plane spent fractionally longer in the air with each bump.

Up to sixty, and a wing tip rolled heavily to one side brushing the grass. I overcompensated and the opposite wing tip dipped just as far the other way. The controls were having more effect as the speed increased, I noted, as I gradually reduced the side to side roll I had started with my heavy-handedness.

Back on a relatively even keel we passed seventy and the ride was getting smoother. I could feel the air taking over from the ground.

Eighty. Ninety. As the little plane passed a hundred kilometres an hour the wheels left the grass and the ride became smoother and quieter. The Jaguar's lights flashed by below.

I pushed the throttle back in to three quarters, which common sense dictated was probably a safe, economical load on the engine. I moved the flaps to zero and kept a little back pressure on the stick, which maintained a slow but steady climb rate. At a thousand feet I reckoned I could safely call us airborne.

The night was stunning from up here. The dark mass of the Cairngorm plateau to my left with slithers of silver as the moonlight reflected off high lochans. The world seemed brighter up here and threw the landscape in to a relief of blacks and greys. The stars clear overhead through the canopy.

We were soon cruising at two thousand feet and one hundred and eighty kilometres per hour. I fiddled with a notched wheel and discovered it was the trim, which I set and could then leave the plane to its own devices.

There was no GPS on the panel in front of me, no radar or other navigational aids other than the directional compass. I would have to navigate by sight. Looking down I located the A9 easily enough. I'd just follow it down to Kingussie, turn west into Glen Spean and follow Loch Laggan. As long as the night stayed clear, navigating was easy.

I turned the radio on, it only had a few channels, I guessed all it was used for was communicating between the ground, the tow plane and the glider it was towing. I flicked through the channels to see if I could pick up anything useful, like a weather forecast, but had no luck.

In the dim light from the instruments I fished out the thick folder between the seats and scanned through it, keeping half an eye on the landscape, the altimeter and the heading. It had all sorts of useful information in it. Like how to take-off properly. But now I was in the air, landing was my main concern. I memorised settings, stall speeds, approach angles and flap positions until I was as confident as a person who had never done it before could be of successfully landing a plane.

Loch Laggan was passing below like a vast plate of hammered steel with the huge bulk of Creag Meagaidh to the north. The dam at the eastern end of the loch was clearly visible as it flashed below in the night. The horizon behind me was already touched with the first watery brush strokes of dawn. The nights are short in the Highlands in midsummer. I could see the cloud cover was thick in the distance, it looked like it was just over the water, the land remained clear. The rising sun would hopefully clear the cloud. I needed good visibility to find *Sandpiper* before the four men ahead of me.

Roy Bridge and then Spean Bridge soon passed below, Fort William in the distance at the foot of Ben Nevis. The mountains looked spectacular in the dawn light, jutting ruggedly into the sky. I made a mental note to learn to fly properly when this was all over.

I gained height. Partly to give me a better view of the cloud cover ahead and partly to give me some altitude to practise. I climbed, dived, turned and banked as steeply as I dared, which was nowhere near the little plane's limits, according to the manual. But it was as far as my courage would let me go without an instructor sitting next to me. I carried on until I was not exactly competent, but at least vaguely capable.

From this height I could see a considerable distance. The sun was climbing behind me and the cloud around the coast ahead was breaking up as I'd hoped. By the time I was over Fort William the sun was over the horizon and the world full of colour again. The clouds were mere wisps, rising and dissipating before my eyes.

I flew straight down Loch Linnhe at around a thousand feet. I didn't think Harry would corner himself in this loch, but it was on the way to where I wanted to concentrate my search.

The narrows at Corran, where Harry had picked up Holly, flashed by below. No sign of them. I passed by the long thin island of Lismore, scanning the channel to each side and making several detours as I spotted possibilities which were swiftly discounted on closer inspection.

Castle Duart, on its rocky promontory, dominated the entrance to the Sound of Mull on the north-east corner of the island. Magnificent and ancient in the morning sun.

There weren't a lot of boats on the water at this time of the morning. Most of those that were out and about were working vessels that looked distinctly different from a yacht, even from a distance.

On the bus to Fort William, Holly and I'd discussed the best way to lay low on the yacht. We'd come to the conclusion that it was best to keep moving rather than drop anchor in a secluded bay, where you'd be a sitting duck. At least if you were in open water and moving you had a chance.

I was deliberating whether to head west down the Sound of Mull, keep going south or head east and take in the waters around Oban. I still reckoned they'd be around here somewhere, not too far away from what passed as major population centres in these parts, but in open water, moving. I took a sweeping turn east towards the waters off Oban but before I was close to passing over the island of Kerrera, that sheltered Oban, I noticed a bright white wake in the distance. It had to be something moving fast to make a wake visible from so far away. On a hunch I banked right, opened up the throttle and went to have a look.

It was a fast boat, but no match for a plane. I could soon see it was a large, powerful RIB. I guessed it was fifteen metres long with the bow high in the air and a rooster tail of white water rising from the stern as it cruised in a dead-straight line.

I hadn't found Harry and Holly.

But I'd found four men, dressed in black, going flat out in a RIB at dawn, on a very definite heading and in the area where I thought Holly and Harry might be. What were the odds?

Chapter 30

I flew in a circle with one hand on the stick and the other dragging the dry bag over in to the seat next to me. I opened it up and pulled out the two MP5s I'd taken off the men tied up in the holiday home. I sent Drake a small prayer of thanks that he equipped his men with weapons small enough to manoeuvre in a tiny plane's cockpit.

The bubble-like canopy of the plane slid back and forth on runners each side of the cockpit. There were bright red stickers on the securing latches warning not to open it in flight, which was good advice. As I closed in on the RIB from behind I reduced speed to a little above stalling and the altitude to a mere hundred feet and set the trim wheel to keep the aircraft flying level and then clamped the stick between my knees.

Opening the latches of the canopy I forced it forward against the wind resistance and as the plane closed in on the RIB I stuck both H&Ks out and opened fire.

A short-barrelled automatic weapon in each hand, shooting from a moving plane to a moving boat was not ideal for accurate shooting. I fired in short bursts, looking for splashes in the water and adjusting my aim before emptying the magazines. A split second before we were parallel to the boat and only fifty yards away I had the satisfaction of seeing little puffs emanating from the black tubes and splinters flying up from the box-like structure in front of the console that housed the inboard engine.

Three of the four men quickly retrieved H&Ks of their own and opened fire at me. The boat lurched under them as it suddenly lost speed, throwing their aim off, but a few bullets found their mark. One hit the gun in my left hand, the gun was smashed against the edge of the canopy and went flying, I snatched my hand in as pain shot through it.

Several other rounds hit the front end of the plane which dropped alarmingly.

I dropped the remaining weapon on the floor of the cockpit and grabbed the stick, hauling back on it. The plane was only a hundred feet above the sea to begin with, now we were skimming it. The engine was faltering and the whole airframe vibrating alarmingly.

My hands slipped on the stick from the blood emanating from a deep gash on the back of my left hand. I ignored it and we gained a little height. I glanced back and saw the RIB still moving forward, but with a greatly reduced bow wave. Slowed, but not stopped. Still, at least I knew I hadn't just shot up an innocent dolphin-spotting tour boat.

I hauled the canopy back in to place above me, it was riddled with small holes with spiderwebs of cracks radiating out from them.

Close, very close. Again, not one of my best ideas. As an afterthought I looked down and checked myself for holes. Finding none I cut a strip off my T-shirt and wrapped it around my left hand to stop the bleeding. Not so much for first-aid reasons, but because the blood was making everything slippery. I used another piece of T-shirt to wipe the stick clean.

The engine was missing the odd beat now and then, but still going, and the handling had become a bit sluggish. There was nothing I could do, so scanned the horizon through the cracked canopy.

Those men knew where *Sandpiper* was. No doubt about that. I flew on. The minutes passed like hours and the engine missed more and more beats. The increasing vibration was making the cracks in the canopy spread and a fine mist of oil was being sprayed from somewhere. I was reduced to looking through one clear section of the canopy, then another, in order to see the entire vista in front of me.

I swore to myself. I cursed the plane, then felt guilty, said sorry and praised it.

I was so close.

I was so caught up in the fact that I might crash before finding them that I nearly missed them. One of the cracks in the canopy was just off vertical and lined up almost perfectly with the mast in the distance.

I squinted through another clear section of the canopy and confirmed it was a yacht, altered course slightly and waited for tortuous seconds until I closed the gap enough to be sure it was *Sandpiper*.

There was no mistaking her now.

All I had to do was get on board, which was easier said than done when flying overhead in a plane without floats or a parachute.

As I closed in the engine note changed a little for the worse and a faint wisp of black smoke trailed from the engine. Burning oil. The dropping oil pressure gauge confirmed this.

The plane was going to crash soon. I didn't need to be an engineer to recognise the sound of an engine thrashing itself to death.

I'd once been a spectator at a Red Bull cliff diving competition in Spain. Those men and women were extraordinary, barking mad, but extraordinary. I'd learnt that they hit the water at speeds of up to sixty miles an hour, from a height of nearly thirty metres, and their bodies experienced up to three Gs in force when decelerating upon impact.

As a child, on hot summer days, I had sometimes played with the other kids in a local river where there was a deep pool below a bridge. A rite of passage for the boys was to jump off the bridge itself. It was said the bridge was ninety feet above the river. That's twenty-seven metres, give or take. It had taken me a while to pluck up the courage to jump from the stone ramparts of the bridge into the impossibly small-looking pool below, but I had eventually done it. We jumped feet first, not like the Red Bull divers, who scythed cleanly into the water headfirst. It had hurt, but we all survived, if more than a little winded.

I had read in the manual earlier that the official stall speed for this aircraft, with flaps down, was 45 knots, that's about fifty miles an hour.

My latest bad idea could work, in theory.

A water landing in a plane with fixed landing gear was not going to end well - as soon as the wheels hit the water they would dig in. Best case scenario was that it would flip on its back, probably killing me as the canopy, riddled with bullet holes, shattered under the force. The worst-case scenario was that the wheels dug it in and sent the plane in to a crazy, cartwheeling spin, breaking the plane, and me, into lots of little bits.

I had considered whether the landing gear would simply snap off on contact with the water, but I doubted it. The three legs and wheels were built to withstand heavy landings on rough fields, so they were going to be pretty sturdy.

I prepared for the landing. Flaps down, throttle in. The little plane settled in to a new, slightly nose up, attitude.

I shoved the MP5 back in the bag and sealed it, leaving it on the seat next to me. Closing in all the time on the yacht, I aimed for a point two hundred yards in front of it. The controls were becoming more and more sluggish and the whisp of smoke from the engine in front of me become a thick, noxious smelling stream.

Close now, and well to starboard of the yacht, I ran the canopy forward on its rails until it locked open. Most of the wind and smoke was deflected over and around the cockpit by the canopy. I could see Harry and Holly's figures clearly now, both staring, unsurprisingly.

The wings were dipping this way and that, my counteracting movements having little effect now as the controls were failing to respond due to whatever damage the bullets had done combined with the low airspeed. I pushed the throttle further in and pulled back more on the stick. The plane waggled alarmingly now as it lost height, speed and control.

Level with the yacht now and to starboard, I started a turn to port. It was messy, very messy. I fought the stick and had to increase the throttle to have any control at all, but we came around maybe thirty degrees, which would put me more than two hundred yards in front of the yacht. Given the circumstances, I considered that perfectly acceptable.

Lessening the backward pressure on the stick whilst slamming it from side to side in opposition to the dipping wings the plane dropped to fifty feet above the sea. Everything was vibrating too much to read the little dial of the altimeter and the black smoke from the engine was so thick now it made my eyes water. I couldn't read the air speed dial either, but we still seemed to be going pretty fast.

I admitted to myself I had no real control over the situation, undid the harness straps, and flipped the switch that killed the engine, so I'd at least be able to see. The world instantly quietened down to just the rush of air passing over the cockpit and around the open canopy. The stream of black smoke died away as the propeller abruptly stopped spinning, along with it went any last semblance of control I had over the dying plane. She nose-dived, I hauled back on the stick as hard as I could.

Keeping one hand on the stick and a death grip on the dry bag with the other, I brought my feet up under me to crouch on the seat. I gave up trying to gauge height, speed, angle. All I could really see was the water rushing towards us.

At the last moment before crashing I kicked the flaps lever to full-up with a foot, pulling the nose up and shedding the last bit of forward speed bringing her well below stalling speed. The plane lurched to the left, the wing tip dropping away as she transitioned from flying to falling. I took it as a hint and launched myself clear of the cockpit with the bag in tow.

I was very aware there was a tail behind me and could only hope I'd clear it, but that thought was rapidly displaced by the realisation that I'd jumped from higher than I'd thought.

I flailed my legs and arms in an effort to enter the water feet first. It didn't take long to realise I'd completely failed in this also, so I just wrapped myself around the bulky dry bag, like a Koala hugging a tree and waited for the impact.

It was a long time coming. Long enough that I had plenty of time to think about exactly how long it was taking. I tensed every muscle I had around the bag, tucked my head in, and waited.

Chapter 31

The bag took the brunt of the impact. After the initial pain, shock and chaos it went quiet, the pain in my ears started abating as the air trapped in the bag pulled me back to the surface. I felt, rather than heard, a thud through the water, followed by several smaller ones. The plane hitting and breaking up.

Surfacing, I couldn't help but grin, I was alive.

I was still chuckling when *Sandpiper* drew near.

"You're a lunatic!" called Holly, standing in the bow with her mane of blonde hair flowing in the breeze. A few days at sea had lightened her hair a shade whilst deepening her tan, she looked good. Beetle launched past her into the water to greet me.

Harry let out the main and jib sheets, the wind spilled from the sails and the yacht came to a halt beside me. They both helped me, my bag and Beetle back board.

"I didn't know you could fly," said Holly.

"Yep, I've had a lesson," I replied, dragging myself to my feet. "We don't have much time." I made my way back to the cockpit and found the binoculars above the chart table. I stood on the cabin roof and scanned the sea behind us, nothing yet.

I hopped down to the cockpit and handed Holly the binoculars telling her to keep an eye out behind us for the RIB.

Holly braced herself with the binoculars to her eyes.

"It's great to see you but, uh, why the dramatic entrance?" she asked.

"There are four armed men in a RIB coming to kill you."

Holly took her eyes away from the binoculars. "OK," she said slowly. "Remind me again how that came about?"

I opened the dry bag to discover the phone hadn't survived the impact. I handed Harry the remaining MP5 and a Glock.

Holly stared wide-eyed at the MP5. I indicated behind us with a finger, and she dragged her eyes back to the binoculars.

"What's the forecast?" I asked Harry.

"Steady as it is for the next six hours," he replied.

"We need to make landfall. We're sitting ducks out here." The wind from the south-east made a run to the mainland impractical. Too much tacking, too slow, too far.

I considered all the options. "Head that way as fast as possible," I said to Harry. "Please."

He pulled in the sheets and steered us around to our starboard. I started the engine to add another knot to our speed and we headed for the craggy coast of the south-east corner of Mull.

"Where's your phone?" I asked them.

"In the drawer with the charts."

I retrieved it and turned it on. Waiting for it to come to life I changed into dry clothes and put the kettle on. The phoned beeped madly with all the missed calls from Muzz. I started dialling and Holly called out. "I see them!"

I dropped the phone in a pocket and took the binoculars from Holly to have a look. The RIB was just visible on the horizon.

"Don't take your eyes off them," I told her, handing the binoculars back.

Pulling out the phone I finished dialling, there were two bars of signal. It rang once, twice, and was picked up.

"General? It's Ruraidh," I said.

I got a sideways look from both of them.

"I've found them," I said and reeled off the coordinates from the GPS unit above the chart table.

"Muzz?" I asked.

"Safe. The girls too. How'd you find them?" The general said.

"I stole a plane. They're in a RIB, I've slowed them down but they're still coming. Where's the cavalry?"

"Bank on at least two or three hours. Minimum," he said. "Best get that brain working again."

Great. They were over the horizon a minute ago, now we could see them, they were gaining, I reckoned we had an hour, tops."And Ruraidh?"

"Yes."

"They are government employees. Try not to kill them," he said dryly.

"I'll be gentle."

My tired brain ticked over and I ducked back into the cabin as the kettle whistled.

"Any one for coffee?" I asked.

"Seriously," Holly exclaimed, as she took a mug. "Talk to us, or I'm going to shoot you myself."

I grinned and kissed her on the cheek. "It's good to see you too."

I took a good slug of the coffee, up-ended the dry bag on the floor of the cockpit and sorted through the contents as I explained.

"General Mackay. I'm Ruraidh Maclean. We met in Ullapool," I'd said by way of greeting on the pavement in central London, just as he was about to duck into a Bentley.

He looked at me hard for a second. I was prepared to run, which was why I'd chosen to approach him on the pavement, not in a building.

"Indeed, we did. Get in," he said, indicating the Bentley.

I got in warily.

"Around in circles please, Sam," he said to the driver and slid up the privacy glass.

I ran through the events of the summer. He stopped me often, asking for more details and laughing regularly at the answers, which was disconcerting.

"You tied two embassy guards to a chest of drawers and dropped it out of a window?" he asked amusedly. "How'd you come up with that?"

"Dad was a game keeper, he taught me trapping and snaring as a kid. It was just a variation on a counterbalance trap we used for rabbits."

"Brilliant," he said, laughing, "carry on." I skipped through the events in the souks.

"Burning lamp oil?" he chortled. He seemed to be enjoying the story enormously.

He was serious only when I played him the recording of lunch with Drake.

"God, I hate spies. Always sneaking around double-crossing everyone." He buzzed down the privacy glass to the driver. "Sam, swing past the office, tell Barnes to come out to us and bring his toys."

To me he said, "Barnes is my assistant. Absolutely no sense of humour, but a first-class analytical mind, he keeps me on the straight and narrow."

A few minutes later the Bentley glided to a stop and a non-descript middle-aged man got in, pulling tablets and laptops out of his bag.

"Send me everything," he said to Muzz, once he'd been filled in, and via the miracle of the internet the information appeared almost instantly.

Scans of old paperwork. Pre-dating the digital era. Created on a typewriter and then sitting in boxes or filing cabinets gathering dust in storerooms until some low-level clerk had been tasked with scanning them all, where they then sat in some forgotten server until James's company looked into a particular property's history.

There were a lot of scans, a lot of documents which meant nothing to me, just page after page of legal speak. There were plenty of building schematics, plans and blueprints that made more sense to me.

In amongst all these documents were several that detailed the changes of property ownership to one Wotjek Banyaki in the mid-eighties. Not long after each of these properties had another change of ownership, each to a different name, presumably when he got smart and started covering his tracks more effectively, or maybe he met someone that knew how to keep him under the radar, give him advice, keep him out of trouble.

Back then it would not have been noticed, but nowadays powerful algorithms were an everyday tool, computers could cross-check millions of sales, amounts, names and locations within seconds. Once Muzz had entered Drake's name into the mix it all became clear as his computer presented him with a document containing both Banyaki and Drake's names. The document was a deed of sale from a Mr Edward Drake, a young MI5 officer in 1987. Decades later Drake's name appeared again, this time on a town house in SW1, acquired for a knockdown price in 2001, which is worth millions today. Acquired from a person with the same name a man called Banyaki had sold the property to back in the eighties.

It was just a thread, but pulling a thread could unravel a garment.

"You didn't trust him even before you knew all this. Why?" the general asked.

"At lunch, he specifically said 'no three-hundred-yard head shot' to kill Banyaki. That's a very specific distance to use. Most people would say a mile, half a mile, a kilometre. His men had been at my cottage, he knew I'd killed Banyaki's two men with head shots from that distance, that's why it was in his head."

"Show me what we have on Drake," he instructed Barnes. They both stared at the screen for a long while as Barnes scrolled. It seemed Drake's rise through the intelligence services was meteoric, almost impossibly so.

An international criminal in league with an up-and-coming intelligence officer? It explained both their successes. But why would Drake want Banyaki dead now?

The obvious answer would be to protect himself, he was where he wanted to be, Banyaki had outlived his usefulness and I had come along, an obvious answer to his dilemma.

"What's the chances of making a case?" The general asked Barnes.

"Nil." A curt reply.

"I hate spies," he said again. "We'll just have to catch him red-handed at something and bring him in ourselves, then those spooks can't spirit him away or let him off the hook." He chuckled again. "Any ideas?"

Chapter 32

"Holy shit!" For a reporter I thought she'd have something more eloquent to say.

"Yeah. Get rid of Banyaki and entrap Drake. The general's hiding Claire, Jessica and the girls till this is over, but I didn't count on Drake knowing about you two and Muzz though. Sorry."

"So, what now?"

"Stay alive till the general comes through."

"How?"

"When we hit the beach there," I said pointing to the slim, sandy coloured crescent at the back of a rocky bay we were approaching. "You two go up that gully and run, I'll slow them down."

"That's it? That's a terrible plan."

"Yes, but it's simple, so there's not much to go wrong." The sandy bay was the only place we could make landfall before the RIB caught up with us. If they got within range while we were at sea we wouldn't have a chance against four automatic weapons.

The bay was part of a rocky peninsula, roughly rectangular in shape and joined to the main island by a narrow strip of land. That narrow strip of land was a real bottle neck. If the men behind us were faster on foot than us, we wouldn't make it through. Hence, I had to slow them down to let Holly and

Harry get past the bottle neck and on to the island proper where'd they'd have more chance of evading the pursuers. Not a great plan, I agreed, but the best option that I could see as the rest of the coastline was sheer cliffs as far as the eye could see, the bay was our only realistic chance.

"I hate to ask, but how are you going to slow them down?" she asked.

"A few tricks I learnt as a kid."

Strangely, she still didn't look convinced.

"They won't even know I'm there."

As we neared the bay I ducked below and siphoned off fuel into glass jars from the galley. We dropped anchor in the bay fifty yards from the small beach and stripped off to our underwear. Holly and Harry put their clothes in plastic bin bags, tied tight. I stuffed mine in the dry bag along with everything else I'd been preparing over the last half hour whilst recounting the last two days to them both. Harry kept his eyes to himself, shook my hand as we swapped a meaningful look, slipped into the water and swam ashore. A man of few words, as usual.

"You jumped out of a plane for me," she said quietly. I refrained from mentioning it was also for Harry.

On tip toes, she gently placed her lips on mine.

I was waiting to feel the guilt, to see the dark-haired Rebecca in my arms, to hear the voice.

But nothing came.

It just felt... right, so I went to put a bit more effort into it.

"Whoa. Hold that thought," she said and was gone over the side.

"Go on then," I said to Beetle, who happily followed her in.

Holly emerged on to the beach, dried and dressed herself. I smiled as I saw her slip the Beretta into her waistband. With a wave they were off up the gully at the back of the bay. The nearest habitation was an hour or two away on foot.

The bay was maybe two hundred metres across and an almost perfect crescent shape. As with the rest of the coast around here it was sheer cliffs all the way around except at the back, where the angle eased a little off the vertical, and a deep gully cleaved into the land.

Holly and Harry had left an obvious trail in the sand leading from the water's edge to the gully. I jumped in the water with my bulky dry bag and swam to the very end of the beach. On land I dressed in the same trekking clothes I'd been wearing earlier, a bit damp still, but I wanted muted natural colours that would blend in. I made my way to the mouth of the gully, staying on hard ground so as not to leave tracks.

As I'd asked them to, Holly and Harry had moved through the ground as messily as possible. Obvious footprints in the damp ground and muddy prints left on rocks. I followed swiftly, but carefully, so as not to leave any trace of my own passing as I assessed the gully.

It was narrow, steep sided, dark and damp. The bottom of it was a boulder field with rotting tree trunks and branches criss-crossing everywhere. Almost everything was covered in moss and dangling lichen, giving it a fairy-tale look. Holly and Harry had taken the obvious path of least resistance through the damp, green, dripping obstacle course. Halfway along it narrowed to shoulder width for a couple of yards. I scanned the ground beyond it and where I'd naturally put my feet, I placed small devices from my bag, made up from water pipes cut from the yacht's galley, and carefully covered them up. I moved on through the remainder of the sloping gully.

At the top end the gully narrowed and steepened to the point you needed to use hands and feet to get out. I pulled out the reel of paracord I'd bought the other day and my dive knife and got to work. I set myself three minutes for this task before carrying on.

Once I was out of the top end of the gully, and on the flatter, thickly wooded ground above, I headed down the north side until I was above the shoulder-width narrowing in the gully below. I worked up a sweat shifting rotten wood and rocks around and wedging various things from the dry bag in amongst them. Whittling a stout stick into shape, and then a notch in a log, I wedged the stick in place to hold the log back then tied the end of the paracord to it and tossed the reel over to the other side of the gully which was only a few metres away at this point. The tree branches were so thick and entwined here the green paracord was invisible.

Back around the end of the gully I moved on down the south side to the cliff top above the beach. The RIB was just pulling up to *Sandpiper*. One man jumped aboard while the others lined up at the RIB's gunwales, weapons trained on the yacht. The man was back on the RIB in seconds before they carried on at a slow pace. I could see all the engine covers had been taken off and parts were scattered all over. My strafing run had worked to some extent. Shame it hadn't stopped them completely.

The RIB ran up on the beach and the men waded ashore in a well-practised looking formation with their weapons up. They were in black from head to foot with vests covered in pockets and bulges on their thighs.

One man seemed to be in charge, and assuming the other three men weren't dwarves, then he was huge. He moved well, unusually so for such a bulky man who are often lumbering and slow, he was very light on his feet.

He walked up the beach next to the tracks in the sand with the others behind and to the side. Stopping at the beginning of the gully He looked around, left, right and back to the gully. He made some hand gestures then himself and the one next to him dropped to a knee and raised their weapons to the gully. The other two headed for either side of it. Slinging their weapons on their backs they started scrambling up the steep slopes either side of the gully.

Which was not what I thought they'd do.

All my traps were in the gully.

I might have to resort to plan B, which consisted mainly of running.

Chapter 33

I didn't envy them scaling the loose rock and slippery moss. Both men were slipping and sliding constantly, often getting stuck and having to down climb to try another route. All the time they were covered by their team mates on the beach. It was a good plan. Annoyingly good.

They eventually made it to the top, not far from me. I moved off quietly, retrieved the reel of paracord I'd thrown over earlier, ran it around a sapling taking it ten yards further up the side of the gully, hiding it as best I could behind a fallen tree trunk, moss and grass. I took cover in thick undergrowth where I could overlook the gully below and waited.

I heard them coming before I could see them. The men in the bottom of the gully were moving swiftly. The man above on my side of the gully was ahead of the men below, staying at the edge of the gully where possible to keep the others in sight. It wasn't always possible for him to stay right at the lip of the gully due to the rough nature of the ground.

He detoured around the clump of undergrowth I was in as the men below moved into the narrow section. I had the paracord in one hand and a Glock in the other, the muzzle of it tracking the man as he moved past me close enough to reach out and touch.

I gave the cord a good yank which pulled the sturdy little stick from its position on the other side of the gorge, releasing the log that held back a pile of roundish boulders and more rotten logs. If you get the angle just right even a small stick can hold back a lot of weight. On the slope below this pile, where it dropped away to the vertical walls below, I'd carefully placed other boulders and hidden a jar of fuel from *Sandpiper*'s tank, with the lid loosened, along with a flare from the yacht's emergency kit. The flares were activated by pulling on a small length of string on one end, so it was no mean feat to tie the string to one rock and the flare to the bottle. As they fell and tumbled the flare should get a tug on the string and at some point, ignite the fuel, hopefully.

The men in the gully froze as the flaming boulders and logs fell. The man on my side rushed back past my hiding place and stood on the edge, not three metres in front of me, peering down. Way too good an opportunity to pass up. The man on the other side was also preoccupied with the scene in the bottom of the gully so I just crept forward and booted him over the edge, dropping flat behind a tree before the man on the other side saw me.

I crawled well away before looking over into the gully. One man was pulling himself out from under a burning log but seemed OK. The man I'd just pitched over was lying still. The big man was unscathed. The man on the far side had moved to the head of the gully and started making his way down. The big man noticed and bellowed an order for him to stay up there but was just too late.

He'd started slipping and sliding down the narrow entrance and his left foot took a long slide on slippery moss and caught the cord I'd carefully hidden under it by cutting through the carpet of moss. The cord pulled a small stone that was preventing a large round boulder, teetering just past its balancing point, from rolling down into the gully. It had taken a lot of effort, and a long branch as a lever, to get that rock just right.

The man arrested his slide and watched wide-eyed as the boulder gained momentum, bouncing off rocks with hollow booms as it went. The big man stood there without moving, following its changing trajectory as it bounced down. He placed a hand on the unharmed man next to him. On the boulder's last change of direction before it hit them, he threw the man to one side and calmly stepped to his right as the boulder sailed past him harmlessly and continued down the gully, narrowly missing the unconscious man on its way. Smaller rocks that had been dislodged clattered harmlessly down the gully.

Shame. Only one man down.

The unconscious man was checked and left in the recovery position. The big man started up the gully with the other one following. The man at the top stayed put, scanning the woods around him. I lay still with my head just peeking over the edge, hidden behind some undergrowth. I was watching their feet very carefully.

As they moved away from the narrow section I realised I'd miscalculated. I had placed three little devices where I'd naturally put my feet. But the big man had longer strides than me; I watched him miss all of them.

The man following him wasn't so lucky, he was more my size. He stood on the first and it didn't go off, to my dismay. He missed the second and then put his right foot directly on the third and with a bang and a spray of blood, a nine-millimetre round burst through the top of his boot. He looked down and then stood there, screaming.

I'd searched *Sandpiper* for a plastic pipe that a nine-millimetre cartridge would fit in tightly and cut it in to very short lengths. Supergluing the short lengths of pipe at right angles to squares of flat plastic cut from a Tupperware box lid, I'd screwed small wood screws through from underneath and jammed the rounds from the machine guns down on top of it. The sharp point of the wood screw was sitting against the primer, where a firing pin would normally hit, and the bullet was sticking out of the top of the pipe.

I'd placed them upright on suitably flat rocks and covered them up so that when someone stood on it they'd push the round down on to the sharp point of the wood screw, compressing the primer, and trigger the propellant. This sort of thing would work better with a shotgun cartridge, but the nine-millimetre round had done OK.

The big man moved very carefully back to his comrade, watching his feet, he bent down and picked up my little trap. He said something to the injured man before leaving him to tend to his wound and moving off up the gully, very slowly and carefully, putting his feet only on bare rock.

Two down.

I sighed. I'd slowed them down a bit, but not stopped them, was it enough? Could I justify leaving it at that, knowing that I'd given Holly and Harry a good head start? No, unfortunately I couldn't lie here, safe and sound, while they went after Holly and Harry, no matter how far ahead they were.

Back on the yacht we'd doled out the weapons I'd accumulated. Harry took the remaining H&K MP5 and a Glock. Holly had her Beretta which left me with a pair of Glocks.

The range was too much but I had spare magazines, so it was worth a try. I pulled out the Glocks, my right took careful aim at the big man, adjusting for the distance and the downward angle of the shot. My left hand was pointing in the general direction of the other man, who was far enough away that I had no realistic chance of hitting him. That big man was the problem, if I could put a hole in him the last man was unlikely to continue on his own.

I fired and knew I'd missed the big man. I emptied both guns to give them something to think about, and in the forlorn hope a ricochet or lucky shot might hit home, before taking to my feet and running south, away from the direction Holly, Harry and Beetle had gone.

I half-hoped they wouldn't give chase, but after the first couple of hundred metres I heard bullets thumping in to tree trunks, none very close, still disconcerting though. They were out of the effective range of the short-barrelled weapons, but that didn't mean they couldn't get lucky. I pulled out one of the Glock's I'd reloaded and threw some bullets back at them.

I put my head down and concentrated on the ground as I barrelled through the woods into another open section. They seemed to be following my trail exactly, obviously not worried about more booby traps, so I laid one. I rummaged in the bag as I ran, pulled out what I needed and paused at a good spot to run out some fishing line. Very thin, brown nylon with a breaking strain of just three pounds. The sort of thing I used when fishing for tiny trout in a hill loch. I used fifteen seconds to lay this simple trap, but I hoped it would buy me more seconds than it took to lay.

I ran on. A minute later I heard a shot behind me. Not a supressed *phut* from their H&Ks, but a single loud bang, followed seconds later by sustained *phutting*. I smiled as I ran.

I'd used another of the little plastic tube devices. This time I'd tied one end of the fishing line to a tree and strung it across their path. The other end of the fishing line was tied to a low branch in a fancy slipknot, it would drop a fist-sized rock on to one of my bullet-in-a-pipe devices, setting it off. It wouldn't hurt them, but it sounded like it fooled them in to taking cover and returning fire, which would waste time and ammunition.

I ran on, vaulting trees and rocks, dodging this way and that, but always heading south. I was acutely aware that this was a peninsula we were on so at some point soon, I was going to run out of land.

Coming over a rise I saw a rocky ridge ahead, running from the high ground on my right down to the coast to my left, where the land dropped away in sheer cliffs. Halfway up this ridge was another chunk of woodland. I changed direction and struck out for it across half a mile of open moor.

By the time I entered the woods my pursuers had appeared the half mile behind. They were closer than I hoped, but at least I knew how much time I had to play with. I ran on through the trees - a mix of pine, oak and beech, until I neared the rocky ridge. I passed under a beech tree with the biggest spread of branches I'd ever seen, easily thirty metres across. I moved under the vast canopy and scrambled up on the ridge to look over, which confirmed I was running out of peninsula. I had to go up or down. Looking down the ridge there was a big hump of rock in the way. I went to scramble around it.

As I passed below the great chunk of rock blocking my view down the top of the ridge I came across a cave at its base. Not a big one. A jagged black hole about a metre across. I ducked my head in. It was several metres deep, maybe a metre wide and two high and turned a corner at the back. The interior was green and dripping, the floor a mass of green rocks and rotting branches jammed in randomly. The rocky walls were deeply fissured and cracked.

It should buy me some time.

Entering through the metre-wide opening you had to drop a metre to the floor. I rearranged the rotten logs and used up the last contents of my bag. I reached behind me for the Glock I'd been using and with a sinking feeling realised it was alone in my waist band, the second Glock had fallen out somewhere during the running, jumping and scrambling. I pulled it out and checked the magazine. One round left.I'd been using this one to fire behind me randomly, secure in the knowledge I had a full magazine in the second Glock. No point in changing my plan now, not much I could do with one bullet against two men anyway.

I jammed the butt of the Glock between two rocks and it held fast. Glocks, I'd learnt, have complicated safety features. I used several lengths of paracord to overcome them and clove-hitched a length to the trigger itself. I sorted through the wood on the floor till I found a piece the right size and roughly hollowed out a bowl shape in one end with the dive knife. Balancing it on a rock and placing the hollowed bowl section under a drip from the moss on the roof I left it for ten seconds to check it would hold water and gauge how much it filled up in that time.

Emptying out the drips that collected I tied it to the cord from the trigger and positioned it carefully on the rock, adjusting the pivot point till I was a happy. I climbed very carefully back out of the cave, past the seemingly random branches below the opening.

In the open air I hurried back down the ridge, keeping an eye out for the second Glock in case it had fallen out somewhere near. My dry bag was now empty, save for a last length of paracord and the dive knife, which I stuffed in a pocket. I needed to draw them in, so I was planning to go back to the edge of the woods and let them see me, then drop the bag on the ground to help draw them towards the cave.

It turned out to be unnecessary, they were closer than I thought they'd be. I dropped the bag and ducked behind the trunk of the huge beech tree. I looked around and saw nothing useful, nowhere to run without being seen, and I would soon be within their weapons' effective range. I looked up. The ancient beech had a hundred branches in its vast canopy but even the lowest branches were well out of my reach.

The dive knife and the remains of the reel of cord, roughly twenty metres I guessed, were all I had left. The cord was only three millimetres thick, way too thin to climb up, it would cut into my hands like cheese wire. It also only had a two-hundred-pound breaking strain according to the label on the plastic reel it had come on. I weighed a little over that. I doubled it up. Six millimetres and four hundred pounds now. Strong enough, but still too thin to climb. I doubled it up again in a rough plait. Twelve millimetres thick with an eight-hundred-pound breaking strain, but only five metres long now. It would do.

I pulled out the dive knife but kept it in the tough plastic sheath and tied a barrel knot around the middle of it. I picked a likely looking V in the branches above and tossed the knife through. Or tried to. I missed the first time, recalculated and threw again. The knife sailed through the V and dropped down the other side. I pulled the cord until the knife was wedged firmly across the far side of the V and tested it with my weight. It held, so I climbed up it until I could grab a branch and pull myself up in to the tree.

I was just pulling the cord up behind me when the two men moved into the area below the tree and spotted the bag. They froze, stock-still, weapons up, and I could hear quiet words pass between them. I didn't even breathe.

I willed the water in the cave to drip faster. A few seconds later it heard me.

A hollow boom rolled out of the cave and the muzzle flash left them in no doubt as to where it came from. They both returned fire instantly, pouring short, controlled bursts into the cave.

They stopped firing and more quiet words passed between them. The big man moved forward with the smaller one covering him. The big man was leading from the front again and looked like he would go into the cave, he'd have to in order to see around the bend at the back to see if my body was there. With him taken care of, the last man, a normal sized one, wouldn't be a problem. Well, maybe with just a dive knife and a bit of cord it might be a challenge, but I was strangely unconcerned by the thought.

The big man approached the cave mouth. I knew you couldn't see into the darkness from outside. You had to go in. I was holding my breath and stifling the ridiculous urge to shout, "Go on, get in!"

He was at the entrance now.

I nearly fell out of the tree at the unexpected noise from uphill.

A deep boom and a barely perceptible *phut, phut, phut* came from my right, uphill. Both men below turned simultaneously and returned fire. I pulled the dive knife from the sheath and stood there, helpless. I had no move from here. Drop to the ground and I'd be riddled in seconds. Throw the knife? I couldn't throw knives, and I only had one, there were two of them.

It had to be Holly and Harry. The loud bark from Holly's Beretta and the *phutting* from Harry's supressed MP5.

They'd come back for me, or maybe they never left, just in case I needed help.

I cursed them. I'd told them to run. I really wished people would run when I told them to.

And I was up a tree, like a monkey.

Chapter 34

I expected the men below to take cover, but the big leader's body language was that of a stampeding bull. He was basically marching towards Holly and Harry's position, his weapon spitting fire constantly. He gave a bark and the second man joined him on his relentless march. As the big man's magazine emptied the other kept firing while he inserted a fresh magazine and resumed firing, while the other reloaded. As a result, they maintained a constant stream of lead, and there was no answering fire from the others. They were pinned down. Unable to come out from cover under the non-stop barrage.

I assumed they had enough ammunition to keep this up, in which case Holly, Harry and Beetle were doomed.

The two men just kept going.

The men hadn't come close enough to jump on and were about to pass out from under the enormous beech tree canopy.

I plotted angles and heights, soon gave up and slipped the knife back in the hard plastic sheath, that still had the cord tied to it, and tossed it through the farthest V of branches I could. The first throw failed. I threw it harder. It sailed through a different V in the branches than I'd aimed for. I tested it with a tug, wrapped it around my hands, and jumped.

The V with the dive knife jammed across was maybe seven metres above the ground. The cord was five metres long, so I covered ten metres of horizontal distance in the blink of an eye. The quadrupled cord took the strain without breaking, which was more than I could say for my hands, which were on fire as the full force came on to them at the lowest point of the swing. The pain eased on the upswing and I let go while I had plenty of momentum behind me which carried me the rest of the way.

For the second time today, I was falling through the air long enough to consider what a bad idea it was. Long enough to see Holly and Harry appear from behind the rocks, despite the continuing onslaught. Long enough to see the two men adjust their aim, one left, one right. Long enough to realise my new friends had seconds to live.

I straightened my legs in front of me and braced for impact.

And it was a hell of an impact.

The big man on the right had shoulders like a prize bull. My left foot contacted with the smaller man on the back of his head, I barely felt that impact. But my right foot contacted the big man between the shoulder blades, because he was that much taller, and stopped dead. Pain shot through my right foot, ankle, knee and up through my hip and then I sailed over him. Spinning, falling, the world exploded and went dark for a few seconds.

My entire right side was on fire. I opened my eyes and focused on the rock my head was lying on. Head pounding, I couldn't hear anything. I tried to move but my entire right side seemed paralysed with pain. Nothing worked. I levered myself up enough with my left arm to look around. I was slightly uphill from the two men. One was lying face down on the rocky ground, the smaller one. Not moving. Thank God.

But the huge black lump next to him stirred and I felt a momentary panic run through me. The enormous head rotated, almost in slow motion, and the furious eyes fixed on me.

I had nothing. My last weapon had been the dive knife. My right side was useless. The big man's right arm moved from my view and I knew what was coming. The handgun from the holster on his right thigh. He seemed to move in slow motion.

My left hand reached out and dug into the rocky ground as my left leg pushed against anything it got purchase on. I dragged myself towards him as he struggled to release the gun from its holster. He was also hurt. I couldn't tell how, but he was, or I'd be dead already. Another heave on my left arm and I was closer. I reached out again.

His arm started its return journey and the Glock appeared on the far side of him. He was lying head towards me, feet away, so from the holster his arm had to travel through a full one hundred and eighty degrees to point at me.

Another heave and I was nearly there. His arm passed the halfway point. Ninety degrees. I wasn't going to make it. I kept going. One more heave. My vision, my world, had reduced to these few inches between us. I grabbed a rock in my left hand and hauled it back in preparation for braining him with it.

The gun came around. I could see the muzzle.

His bullet was going to reach my brain before my rock made contact with his head. Somehow, I could see that so clearly.

That's OK, I thought. *I'd like to live, but they're all safe now. Claire and the girls, Holly and Harry, all safe, I hadn't failed this time, so it's OK.*

I knew I wasn't going to live through this, but if I started the swing with enough force, it might make contact after the bullet had destroyed my brain.

I put all I had behind the rock in my hand and started my final act in this life.

The man's eyes widened imperceptibly, and during the last degrees of the gun's travel to line up with my head, and the last few inches my rock had to travel, the muzzle rose upwards, but he was just too late.

A black shadow passed over me, knocking my arm out of the way, and powerful jaws locked on to the man's wrist.

A sickening crunch as Beetles teeth met through the man's wrist, crushing bones. The dog's momentum was so great that his body shot over the giant on the ground, taking the wrist with it. The huge man's arm was yanked around at such an angle the shoulder dislocated with a loud pop and the handgun went flying.

Then Beetle did what dogs do. Jaws clamped immovably on the wrist by the long canine teeth, he shook his head from side to side, using his entire body to generate force. The big man screamed as Beetle dragged him down the hill by his mangled arm in convulsive jerks.

I heard horrible wet tearing noises over Beetle's snarls and the man's screams. I was actually starting to feel sorry for the giant when Harry's long-legged form passed me by and delivered a crushing blow to the giant's head with the butt of his H&K.

I felt gentle hands roll me over and Holly's face filled my vision.

"Do you," I said breathing shallowly, "ever... do what," I took another shallow gasp, "you're told?"

She smiled through her tears. "No. Get used to it."

Beetle jumped on top of the huge, prostrate form and with a wet *schlep* noise ran his tongue around his jowls cleaning away the blood. A shake of his coat and the hackles flattened, the tail started wagging and he padded over and nuzzled my hand like a puppy.

"Good boy," I mumbled. "Really, really good boy."

There was a distant *whoomph, whoomph, whoomph* as an enormous, army-green helicopter appeared over the bay containing *Sandpiper* and the RIB.

"Just in time," said Holly.

We were miles away from the bay, they wouldn't see us up here.

"Toss a rock in that cave," I said to Harry. "And stand back," I added.

The pain in my ribs abated a little, but my vision was still threatening to close in, things kept greying out.

Harry gave me an odd look but did as I asked and threw a decent-sized rock in. A second later a belch of fire rolled out, followed by intense red light and billows of smoke. The whole thing looked medieval as my last trap, another jar of petrol and a flare, was triggered.

"OK. Maybe we should have just left you to it," said Harry.

If the giant had entered the cave, he'd have come out extra crispy.

I shrugged and felt the broken ends of bone grinding together. I gasped and stayed very still. The pitch of the helicopter's rotors changed as it saw the smoke signal and headed our way.

Holly was cradling my head and shoulders in her lap now. It was a nice place to be, so I stopped resisting the darkness and let it slip over me.

Chapter 35

For the second time in a year, I woke up in hospital.

I could remember my dreams. They were good dreams. Times past and things to come.

My cottage, possessions, memories, all gone, razed to the ground. But that was OK. It meant a fresh start. It meant I could build my own life, with only the memories I chose, and I would choose the good ones. Not dwell on the terrible ones.

Besides, James's little girls needed fun and laughter in their life, not a suicidal godfather.

Things had shifted somehow in my psyche. Guilt, anger, sadness. They were all still there, always would be, for if they weren't it meant I didn't care anymore. But it was as if all these had been thrown up in the air and settled in a different, more manageable order. I didn't look too deeply into it, just accepted that I had done my penance. I had a clean slate, and no baggage, except that which I chose.

I felt at peace. Looking forward to the future, not regretting the past.

I cracked open an eye and took in the hospital room.

A large room, typical hospital décor, with eight beds. Half of them occupied.

Holly was slouched in a chair by the bed, turned towards me. Her legs stretched out, crossed at the ankles and propped up on some part of the bed below me. Arms crossed loosely, head tilted to one side, asleep. That unruly blonde mane glowing in the last of the day's sun. I lay quietly, watching her, too pretty to wake. In my mind's eye I saw her at the helm of *Sandpiper* while we cruised the Hebrides. I'd be lying on the cockpit seats, recuperating, Holly at the wheel.

"I can feel you staring at me," she said without opening her eyes, a little smirk playing on her lips.

I said nothing.

She leant forward. Eyes wide open.

"The general called," she said.

I groaned.

"He says we're to lay low," Holly said. "While he sorts out the mess you made."

I looked down at the cast on my right leg, strapping around my ribs and the sling on my right arm.

"I know exactly how to do that," I said, picturing my daydream of sailing round the Hebrides "But you're going to have to do the hard work."

She looked at me for a long moment, raised an eyebrow, ever so slightly.

"I can do that," she said.

Printed in Great Britain
by Amazon

40279373R00165